WayFinder

by

Joseph Hullett

Answer Publications

San Juan Capistrano, California

Published by Answer Publications
27511 Vantage Circle
San Juan Capistrano, CA 92675, USA
www.answerpub.com

ISBN: 978-0-9844597-9-7

Produced in the United States

———————

Authors Note:

Some of the stories in *Wayfinder* appeared originally in a 2003 collection *Men with Women* (Aventine Press). Since that edition is out of print, I include them here to keep them on life support. A second collection of my stories *Another Time* is an integral composition that stands alone and still available. Hence, I decided against a *collected works* approach. Besides, I still have teeth in my head and may write more.

Although most of these stories had previously been edited and commercially published, the ever-tinkerer in me cast a sometimes decades-older eye over every jot and tittle as I prepared *Wayfinder* for publication. Plagued by a line from Rocky about the color of his trunks – 'it *doesn't really matter now, does it?'* – I, nevertheless, made changes here and there. And there. And *there*. Because ... well, because I couldn't do otherwise.

Contents

Man ♂

Woman ♀

Birth ✳

Death ✝

Infinity ∞

Man

A Simple Case of Sniffles

So drag your carcass out of bed, already, pal.
Do something.
Do *anything*.

Oh, wait … runny nose alert. Extra! Extra! Nose running, sniffles suspected. Post a new item to that ticker of aches and pains that crawls through your head. Stick sniffles right up there with rubbery backbone, weak knees, and crumbling feet. Can't get up now, can you? For a fossil like you, sniffles is nothing to sneeze at.

… Go ahead, ignore my little jokes. You used to listen back when you needed me, when you were writing. Now I'm just talking to myself. Although …?

Well, I'll be damned! Maybe not. Else why are you thinking that sniffles in an old man can lead to suffering; that an old man's sniffles can be a first sign of cancer or pneumonia or the beginning of that clammy dampness in the chest when the heart fails and the lungs rattle? Else why are you thinking you'd welcome a clean head-shot from death, but not some stray round that leaves you hurting, leaves you crawling off to some dark, desert place to wait for a bad end.

Oh, come off it! Tripe like that is precisely why you *did* need me and why you should have listened more. Death firing wild from a jouncing Land Rover? That's a conceit straight from one of your books, *all* of them, which is why you're not even back-listed anymore, why the only places you turn up now are fifty-cent, used book bins or on E-Bay. And, frankly, *welcome* is a stretch. Admit it! Death *torments* you. You squandered half your life writing over and under and around it like a magician trying to trap a demon in a chalked pentagram. Sure, you can face the bogeyman now, but less from grit than an old man's experience. You've talked yourself into believing death is merely a big sleep, which old men lack. And you don't fear dreams because old men don't dream. Not of lions, not of anything. Weary, they get clumsy rather than sleepy. They stoop to retrieve some worthless flotsam from a rushing stream of consciousness and fall in. They snatch at reality like they'd grab fistfuls of grass or an overhanging branch, but away they go, flailing in thoughts, choking on memories, bobbing and swirling through a long night, mostly awake, until finally, much too early, they wash back up on the bank, completely awake.

Waking is the rub, isn't it?

Particularly in winter. Especially the Goddamn, Palm Springs Desert winter. Winter you wake with the sniffles. Winter you wake in the dark before dawn. In daylight – even bad light – things are what they are. A chair is still a chair and the shadow of an empty chair merely a shadow. But in darkness, things pass away, or rather, passive things pass away. Active things rise again as gadfly phantoms of sound.

You're calling that hum a pregnant clock radio. That thunka-chee-chee-chee, a sprinkler watering the God-forsaken ice plants and prickly pears. That distant splat? A newspaper tossed onto a driveway. And as usual, without my help, you're *half*-right.

A dripping faucet? C'mon, pal. Is anything ever that simple? Night sounds are shades of what is, what was, what might be. That drip is also an intravenous line. That settling floor is the creak of departing footsteps.

Light a candle, old man, you've cursed enough and this night-music game is play for mortal stakes. If you won't listen to me and can't keep a constant woman beside you, a nightlight is your only edge.

Excellent! Another idea got through. Almost like old times, almost a conversation. You're remembering all the women you ever woke beside and the sound their breath made. Remembering how – when you were cheating or between wives – the sound was an echo that left you feeling so hollow, you wormed into whoever shared the darkness just to hear a catch in her breath. Remembering how waking to the full, familiar purr of a wife's breath felt altogether different. How hearing *that* sound was like finding the North Star. How you could close your eyes again and still see your way clear.

That's why you can't remember the sound of Jane's breath. What use was a pole star before you knew you were lost, when you were crashing through the thickets of those ferocious Trib years, when you were empty and hungry for everything at the same time, when you roared with the triumph of your first books, when you slept like a lion if you slept, and so rarely slept with Jane. Daytimes you saved for beating confessions from a typewriter, or napping, or touring and talking and signing, and fucking the paper-doll-chain women who lined up at bookstore tables. Nighttimes you spent carousing and singing and crying and shouting and laughing and brawling and sobering in precinct holding cells and apologizing emptily in night court. Your listening started only after Jane died so Goddamn suddenly, and nothing but the sound of Hoshiko's breath could finally fill you with sleep again. But you're also remembering those months when – swollen, pregnant, overbalanced – Hoshi slept on her back with a furtive, open-mouthed breathing that gnawed you with images of hot-prowlers creeping into your bedroom. You're remembering the sound of Erika's breathing, a low moan like a whistle

buoy, and how – even during that final, four-year
apocalypse with Tawny (how could you!) – waking and
hearing nothing, you coughed or tossed to make her stir so
you could count her breaths like sheep.

What's this now? Getting up? Was it something I said? …
No! No, not that. It's too early to call. You'll sound
toothless and besides … Dammit! That chair is *cold*. Show
some consideration for the feeling part of this coalition,
won't you?

Okay … six rings and no machine. He's talking to
someone. Hang up!

"Leo Kurtz."

Too late, pal. You just don't listen, do you?

"Hello, son."

"Dad?"

"That call waiting tone is a siren song, isn't it? Caller ID would let
you be more selective."

"I have caller ID, Dad. What's wrong? It's 4:30 there."

"It's Palm Springs, remember? It's *always* 4:30."

"Meaning what?"

"Nothing, nothing. I woke with the sniffles. I couldn't sleep."

"Ambien works for me."

"Sure, Ambien's good."

"Get some Ambien. So why are you calling?"

"It's my birthday."

As if he cares. Let it go.

"Your birthday already? … Yes, I suppose it is. Seventy-nine, right?"

"Eighty."

"Eight-oh. Throwing a party?"

"Who would I invite? I've outlived everyone I knew."

"Over the top, Dad. Your literary undoing."

"What was?"

"Your penchant for sentiment."

"Feeling isn't a crime."

"Sentiment is. To a *good* writer it's embezzlement. The spending of *unearned* emotion."

Ouch! The kid is still sharp. And you're too old for this game, too.

"My books put you through Columbia, son. Hoshi's lawyer saw to it."

"No, your books put me through grade school. Your television pap put me through Columbia."

"Money is money, though, isn't it? No one questioned the source. And you've done all right with it, Mr. Editor, back there in your *City* citadel fashioning dispassionately literary silk purses. This sow's ear might have taught you something, if only as object lesson."

"You made me what I am, Dad. Listen, I'm leaving for work and my secretary is still holding. I'll call you this evening. Happy—"

"You forgot last year. I'll wait."

"Oh … hold on."

He hasn't hung up. Why not break even this call? Just let it be.

"Okay, I'm back."

"I didn't leave *you*, you know?"

"Again with this?"

"I left your mother."

"The distinction was hard for me to draw in your absence."

"We talked, we visited, we—"

"We had a catch once, I think. Thanks."

Didn't I warn you?

"Hoshiko put the whole country between us, son. She didn't have to do that."

"New York was home. Remember?"

"The upper east side was not *home*. Trust me on this one. More kudos to her lawyer."

"Look, Dad, next time you need to talk to yourself, save the long distance charges. Or call one of the emergency, back-up wives."

"That's unfair. You know Jane died before I met your mother."

"Not so. She died before you *married* her. See why lies and good fiction are anchored in fact? The mitigation of a single truth makes for a more compelling story. Mom knew what you were. Just like wives three and four and auxiliaries unnamed. Call *them* when you can't sleep."

"The others call me. Stridently and far too often. My son, however, like his honorable mother, broadcasts hatred with words unsaid."

"Sentiment again, Dad. I only wish that I hated you ... You should call her, you know."

"Hoshi won't talk to me."

"She might. She's not sleeping either. Paul is on chemo again."

"Tough break. Paul was a helluva lawyer."

"Is. Paul *is*."

"Why do you call him that, anyway? He adopted you."

"Call him what? Paul? ... I don't."

"You just did. You do every time we talk about him."

Watch yourself, pal! That silence is a birthday present. Take it.

"Ohhhh ... I see. He's Paul when *we* talk. Should I say thanks?"

"Would I have to say you're welcome?"

"Wish your *Dad* good luck for me."

"I'll do that. I call him every day."

Kid goes straight for the throat. A Goddamn man-eater. *Someone* taught him something.

"I really have to run, Dad. *Publishing World* wants an interview this morning. I made senior editor last week."

"Really? You might have told me."

"I just did. Listen, I have to go."

"Wait! All night I was mulling over what's-her-name ... Casey or Carrie or whatever."

"Callie?"

"That girl who shares your bed now and then."

"Callie."

"What's up with that? On again? Off again?"

"I'm no good for her. Besides, the timing is wrong. You know how it is."

"Sure … you're young. A young lion."

"Talk to someone about those sniffles, okay?"

"I'll talk to someone."

"Good. I'll call you later."

"In other words, don't call me. Isn't that what editors say?"

"It depends on the story, Dad. I'll call you when I can."

Now *that* was Christmas with the Walton's, wasn't it? And, look, you've posted another item on the ticker, only it's heart*burn*, pal, not a heart attack. You're fine, see? Forehead is cool. No cough. Simply sniffles. So blow your nose and dry your eyes. Hobble to Starbuck's and sip your Venti decaf. Watch the sun rise again, watch the cactus grow. Sniffles or not, you have to face the day. No one ever died of a simple case of sniffles.

Okay … Okay, you poor son-of-a-bitch, I hear you.

That *is* the rub.

Tattoos

Otie had always felt a tide inside himself, a restless surging and slacking, an undertow drawing him away from his father's still, Kansas farm. He fancied that wayward tide as his blood's rebellion at bondage to beaten dirt, a rebellion stirred long ago when first he saw the serpent.

"See the flaming tongue, Otie. RRRRRRAWWW! It'll burn you up."

The fire-spitting sea-serpent tattooed on Uncle Luke's arm was a wonder to the five-year old boy.

"Ain't no giant snakes in Kansas," Otie had whispered, awed by the loud, laughing man and his tales of far places and strange things.

Swaying, Luke described how the deck had heaved when huge serpents slithered beneath his ship. Hand raised to God, he swore he had seen the monsters with his own eyes! … eyes as blue as the oceans in Otie's picture books.

Warily venturing a finger to touch the tattoo, Otie had flinched when Luke clenched his fist and the serpent shuddered.

"Did it hurt, Unc?"

"Yup. They scratched it in with a big, buzzy needle. *Lots* of blood."

"Gee! Can I get one?"

"You grow up, we'll sail to Yokohama where I got the serpent. Get you blued, tattooed and—"

"Otis!" Father had warned from the parlor. "Quit pestering your uncle. And stop filling the boy's head with notions, Luke."

Uncle Luke had stuck out his tongue. Since Father was out of sight listening to the radio, Otie did, too. Luke had chuckled and rubbed the boy's head.

The radio talked about war in a place called Ko-rea. Luke had told Otie all about war and soldiers and sailors. Otie imagined that Ko-rea was *very* far away, farther even than Yokohama.

"I'm gonna be a sailor like you, Uncle Luke. I'm gonna sail to Ko-rea!"

Luke had extended his beer bottle in salute. Hesitantly, eyes on the parlor, the boy took the bottle in both hands. The wet, brown glass felt icy against his palms. Tipping the bottle to his lips, Otie had sneaked a sip of what remained the worst and the *best* thing ever tasted.

* * * * *

"Hurry up, Otie!" Mother shouted from downstairs. "Folks are here already."

"OTIS, Momma! Jeez, give a guy peace in the bathroom, darn it."

He scrubbed his fingernails one more time with his sister's brush and rinsed off the lather in the sink bowl. His fingertips were puckered, the calluses on his palms dead white, but the faint crescents of Kansas dirt beneath his fingernails were his own tattoo. Tomorrow, however, he would be done of Kansas. High school was behind him, the Navy and the world before. The ocean would wash him clean, he thought. The ocean would bathe Kansas from him forever. The tide in his blood drew him to other places that would mark him, but not with dirt.

"OTIS!"

"I said I'm coming, Momma!"

Otie dried his hands and rearranged the guest towel. Standing straight, he snugged his church tie. The face in the medicine cabinet mirror had eager blue eyes and unruly blond hair. Otie flattened his cow lick and shrugged his shoulders to settle his blue jacket. A going away party was silly, but, to the good part, Uncle Luke was coming. It had been almost a year.

"There he is! There's the sailor man," Aunt Emma gushed as Otie started down the stairs. "My, how you've grown. Come hug your old aunt, boy," she said, fat-draped arms outstretched. Emma was mother's sister.

Otie embraced her loosely at the foot of the stairs and bowed his head so she could kiss his cheek.

"How's Nebraska, Aunt Emma?" he said, wiping away the lipstick mark he knew she had left.

"Jonathan, come see how this boy's grown."

Uncle Jonathan, holding a cup of red punch, shuffled in from the dining room and shook Otie's hand. He eased the boy away from Aunt Emma into the parlor.

"Congratulations, boy. Navy is a good choice for getting away. You aim to come back after or head for the city like the rest?"

"Can't keep 'em down on the farm after they've seen Paree," Otie cracked, but Jonathan was not a man of humor. Otie cleared his throat. "Guess I'll wait and see, you know? Got four years yet to make up my mind."

The grandfather clock filled a silence with a slow tick-tock.

"Well, uh ... best check on Emma," Uncle Jonathan said finally. "Come on by to see us, whenever, boy. Good luck to you."

"Thanks, Uncle Jonathan. I'll stop by first chance."

Jonathan ambled back through the archway into the dining room. Otie heard music and heels clicking across Mother's freshly waxed floor. Alone in the dim parlor, he sighed, spit on his palm, and patted down his hair.

"Four years is a long time," said a quiet voice.

Startled, Otie turned and noticed pipe smoke drifting above father's stuffed, high-back chair.

"Pa ... didn't see you," Otie said, moving around the chair.

"Won't be all carousing, you know?"

"I know how the Navy is."

"You know how Kennedy is taking us into a war?"

"Oh ... there won't be a war. Everybody'd just blow each other up. Anyway, if there *is* fighting, maybe I'll come home a hero like Uncle Luke."

"Someone has to grow what heroes eat."

"You know what I mean, Pa."

"Yeah, I know what you mean."

Awkwardly, the boy sank onto the arm of the quilt covered sofa. Through the open windows he saw the long shadow of his house stretched across the yard. Farther out, undulant in a summer breeze, wheat fields rolled eastward like a bright, orange-brown sea toward the purple, twilight sky.

"You could've waited 'til harvest at least. Your little brother isn't worth much yet."

Otie shook his head. "As soon as I graduated. I always said that. I never kept it a secret."

"No ... you never kept a secret."

"A hired man will do twice what I ever did around here."

"You're a hard worker, son. A little flighty sometimes is all. Young, yet. We all were once."

It was hard for Otie to picture Father as young. Only forty-one, he had always looked leathery and ancient despite coal black hair and clear, almost black eyes. Father's brother, Luke, although a year older, was a boyish contrast. Otie cast Luke as a Peter Pan who had escaped Kansas for some Neverland while Father had squandered his youth on his farm as surely as if he had irrigated the dirt with his blood. A 75-mile circle encompassed the passage of his entire life. Father's most exotic port of call had been Kansas City where Otie spent three days in hospital.

Otie touched the scar on his left arm. At six, Yokohama seemed impossibly far away, and one day – Luke gone to wherever Luke went –

Otie had used a rusty nail from the barn to scratch a snake into his forearm.

"Look!" he called, running to show Father. "Look, Pa! A tattoo like Uncle Luke!"

Father had scrubbed the bloody scratch as if he wanted to erase it. He burned it with iodine and then whipped the boy with his belt. Otie cried, not from fear or pain, but because he knew it was expected – mother had spanked him many times. Afterwards from his bedroom, he heard his parents talking.

"I've hardly hit anyone my whole life, Margaret," Father had groaned. "And here I go hit my own boy."

"You have to teach him, Peter."

"There are better ways."

When the blood poisoning showed – Otie's arm became dark and hard-swollen with red, spider-web streaks – Dr. Cooper in Ferris made father take Otie to the hospital in Kansas City where a surgeon drained the abscess. Otie remembered tossing on the hot seat of Father's pick-up truck, the hot sun through the window hot on his face. He recalled giggly dreams, his prayers that the scratched snake would stay, and the cool, wet handkerchief in Father's hand soothing his forehead again and again.

Otie often wondered about Father's meager furlough. Had he smoked his pipe and listened to radio news in the hotel lobby just as he did at home? Or had life been different? Occasionally Otie conjured scenes from paperback novels in which dangerous women in foreign cities enticed men to stray. He could never quite imagine his father in such scenes, however, because Father had been sitting at the hospital bed each time Otie opened his eyes.

"C'mon, Pa, company's here."

"I'll finish my pipe. Go on, no need to sit."

The front screen door screeched open and banged shut.

"What the hell is all the commotion here! You'd think somebody was going away to war like I did."

"Uncle Luke!" Otie shouted, darting to the vestibule.

Luke crouched and feinted toward Otie's chin with a couple of snake-like jabs. "Damn, you're too big for the Navy, boy. Bang your head on the hatchways. Bet you've grown a foot."

"Naw. Still just got two. See?" Otie chuckled, shuffling his feet.

"Well, counting me, you got three *ankles*," Luke guffawed. "Told you the boy was a crack up," he said to the red-haired woman beside him. "Otie, this here is your new aunt. Billie."

Luke always brought 'new aunts.' A few had visited twice.

"Pleased to meet you, Aunt Billie."

Brass bracelets clinked on her wrist as they shook hands. Otie guessed her age about the same as his, although she looked older in the eyes.

"Just call me Billie, honey."

"Where's the beer, boy? Cooler ran dry on the drive up."

"I'll fetch you one, Unc. How about you, Billie?"

"Sure thing, Opie."

"Otie ... Otis, really. I prefer Otis."

"Right."

Otie dashed to the kitchen. "Uncle Luke is here, Momma."

"I heard," she said.

Luke's voice boomed from the dining room. "Jonathan! Ain't you dead yet? And Emma! Look at you, girl. Run away with me to St. Louis. Get you a job dancing, make two hundred a week. We'll live high on the hog."

"Oh, Luke, you rascal."

Otie pulled two brown bottles from an ice-filled, tin washtub, pried off the caps, and scurried back. Swirling Aunt Emma across the floor, Luke bore toward Otie and hooked a bottle neck between his thumb and forefinger as deftly as a hawk snatching up a mouse.

"Dance with Aunt Billie, Otie," Luke said over the music. "*She'll teach you a few tricks.*"

Billie snickered when Otie took her in his arms. She pushed him away.

"Like this," she said.

The record was a slow dance, but Billie heard her own music. Eyes half-closed, she gyrated in some new Bandstand dance. Her bracelets tinkled like thumb cymbals. Otie copied awkwardly.

"Put some oomph in it," Billie urged with a thrust of her hips. She arched her back, leaned far forward, and shook her shoulders. Otie stared down into her lacy, red brassiere, but looked away guiltily at the sound of Uncle Luke's laughter.

When the song ended, Otie sat with his girlfriend, Penny, while Billie pawed through a stack of records.

"Your uncle is a great dancer," Penny said, watching Luke twirl Mrs. Farrel.

"Momma always said he was the best in the county."

"Your Dad isn't dancing at all."

"Never would. Calls it foolish. Momma says biggest fight they ever had, Pa wouldn't take her to the senior prom. Uncle Luke had to."

A flash bulb popped. Mother was making Polaroid's. Otie snatched away the camera.

"Here, Momma. Let me get you, Pa, and Uncle Luke together to take with me."

Herding them into a corner, Otie peered through the viewfinder and jockeyed to fit all three into the picture. He snapped the shutter and tugged the film from the camera. Guests gathered like moths around a porch light, eager to see the magic of a photograph in 60 seconds. Silently counting one minute, Otie peeled the snapshot from the foggy negative on the developing paper.

The picture was a good one – Mother squeezed between Father and Uncle Luke; Luke slouched, his tattooed arm thrown casually over

Mother's shoulders; Father standing as stiff and straight as a post-hole digger. Otie held the picture out for people to ooh and aah. Wiping the acrid fixer sponge across the photo, he marveled again at how different brothers could be. Luke – a lanky, tousled, towhead – restless, perpetually in motion – always a little blurred in snapshots. Father – short, dark, and solid – hard, resolute, immovable. Otie blew on the picture to dry it and slipped it into the jacket pocket over his heart.

After dinner, Billie switched on the radio and tuned in a loud-mouthed Chicago disk jockey who played rock and roll. Luke jitterbugged across the dining room with Mr. Farrel's wife, twirled her in front of Penny, and let go.

"Got to give 'em all a taste, Lucy," he snickered, reaching for Penny.

Penny glanced at Otie, but Luke merely grabbed her by the waist, lifted her in a spin, and guided her away with the pressure of his body. Her hair fanned out, her lips parted in a smile.

And Otie saw her blush.

"Mind if I cut in, Uncle Luke?"

"Hold your horses," Luke said, twirling Penny at arm's length. Her skirt flared, exposing the tops of her nylons.

"C'mon Unc."

Luke clutched Penny to his chest. The pupils of his blood-shot eyes swelled, revealing a blackness beneath the blue, a shivery, dark, deep Otie had never seen.

"Whoa!" Luke drawled suddenly, breaking into a grin. "Sorry, kiddo. *Your* turn."

Otie felt oafish two-stepping Penny away.

"What moves!" Penny whispered. "I felt like a movie star."

"Marilyn Monroe," Otie grumbled. "Your skirt was flying up around your neck."

"Why, Otie, you're *jealous*!"

"No I'm not, darn it. Let's sit down."

Otie dropped sullenly into a folding chair. Penny sat beside him and brushed at his cowlick. Otie flicked at her hand as if shooing a fly.

"For goodness sakes, Otie! He's your uncle."

"... Yeah ... I guess..."

Mr. and Mrs. Farrel stopped to say good night.

"When's your bus, Otie?" asked Mr. Farrel.

"Around seven. Catch a cab in Kansas City to the induction station and then fly to San Diego. Be swimming in the ocean by sunset."

Luke lurched up, eying Mrs. Farrel. "You're a darn good dancer, Lucy. Run away with me to St. Louis. We'll get you a job in a beer garden."

Mr. Farrel edged his wife away. "Take care of yourself, Otie. See *you* in another couple years, Luke."

Luke plopped down next to Penny. "Wouldn't count on that swimming part," he said to Otie. "They'll lock you in boot camp for a month or two. No swimmin', no women."

"I want to get a ship, Unc. Like you."

"Sea duty can be sweet, all right, if you play the angles."

"He won a medal, Penny. The Navy Cross. His ship was sunk by a sub."

"Were you hurt?" she gasped.

Luke snaked an arm across the back of Penny's chair.

"Broken-hearted! I banked the crap game aboard. Had three, maybe four thousand cash stashed in a footlocker I couldn't save. Broke my God-damned heart."

"Uh ... you were a gunner, weren't you, Unc?"

"Yeah, a gunner."

Billie sashayed over, her hips swaying with the music.

"Toss me a smoke, Billie," said Luke.

"All out."

"Otie, run to the store for smokes."

"Sure, Penny and me."

"Naw, you go on," Luke drawled. "Your little girlie here wants to teach me how to dance."

Penny smiled.

"Well, uh ... sure, I guess."

"Kools, honey," Billie said.

Luke tossed Otie a key chain. "Use mine."

Otie stepped onto the porch. The screen door banged shut. He paused for a moment to gaze at stars strewn across the moonless sky. Beyond the glow cast by his house, all was dark and uniform save for scattered lights of distant neighbors. The air was hot and completely still.

Turning at the squeak of the door spring, Otie watched Billie saunter onto the porch, raise her arms, and stretch like a bored cat.

"I'll go, too, honey. Need to get a few things."

Gallantly Otie opened the passenger door of Luke's white Olds and tried not to peek up Billie's skirt as she scooted inside. Bounding to the driver's side, he fired the engine and slung the big car toward the highway, kicking up clouds of dust on the rutted, dirt drive.

The road to Ferris was empty. Otie goosed the accelerator and grinned when the feverish Olds – unlike Father's weary pick-up truck – leaped at the touch of his toe. Wind through open windows groaned in his ears. Billie leaned back and combed her fingers through streaming red hair.

"Nice night isn't it?" she sang over a chorus of tires. "Chilly by the window, though. I'm all sweaty from dancing. Here, feel."

Sliding across the seat, she grabbed Otie's left hand from the wheel and stroked it across her chest just above the scoop neck of her blouse.

"I'll close mine," he said, pulling his hand away to grope for a crank.

"Electric," she said, pressing into him to reach a button on the door.

Otie wriggled to give her room, but she hitched even closer. Her leg rested against Otie's leg. Her skirt had hiked above her knees.

"Let's make it a party," she said, switching on the radio.

Rock and roll blared. Billie flung back her head and squirmed with the music. Her skirt rode higher – above the dark tops of her stockings. The green instrument-light glow cut a deep black shadow between her breasts. Reflections in her eyes were green flames.

Otie wheeled sharply into the dirt lot of the Ferris open-air market. A little out of control, he stomped the brake and slewed sideways.

"Well, here we are, I guess," he mumbled.

"Leave the radio on, honey?"

"You're not coming in?"

"You go."

"What else did you need?"

"Just Kools."

"I'll buy 'em for you."

"I know."

When Otie returned, Billie was smoking a cigarette. She took two pack of Kools from his hand, dropped them in her purse, and withdrew a can of beer.

"Got a church key? ... Oh, never mind, I do somewhere."

The car crunched gravel backing up and then shot forward onto the pavement. Billie rummaged through her purse, found an opener and spewed foam over her blouse when she poked open the beer can. Giggling, she gulped from the can and shoved it at Otie.

"Uh ... sure, thanks," Otie said, tasting lipstick when he tipped the can and swallowed.

Whining tires and rock and roll drowned words. Wiping at wet spots on her clothes, Billie placed her lips against Otie's ear and breathed, "Pull over a sec, honey."

"How come?"

Otie felt her warm breath in his ear again. "Gotta pee."

"We're just about home."

"Can't hold it. How about those trees up ahead?"

Otie coasted into a cutout.

"Finish it," she said, handing him the beer can. "And douse the lights ... unless you want to watch?"

She laughed as Otie fumbled for the headlight knob and laughed again when she opened the door and the dome light flared.

"*Sure* you don't want to watch?" she said. "I can leave the door open?"

Otie looked away until she closed the door. Turning back, he saw only her shadowed face framed in the open passenger window as she squatted beside the car. The streaming hiss he *heard,* however, etched a *mental* image.

"Any Kleenex?"

Otie started. "Uh ... no, I don't ..." He opened the glove box and slammed it when a bulb blazed on. "None there, no ... I, uh ... don't see any."

Still squatting, Billie wriggled as if freeing a restraint.

"Air dry," she giggled, opening the door and scooting across the seat. "Here, hold these. Keep 'em if you want."

Billie dropped her panties onto Otie's lap and turned the ignition key. The engine sputtered once and stalled.

"We have to get back."

"What's your rush?" she said, folding her left leg under her and inching closer.

Otie clutched her panties in his hand. "Uncle Luke will worry."

"He knows Aunt Billie will take care of you, sugar."

Hooking Otie's shin with her right leg, she turned him to face her. Trying to avoid her eyes, he looked down and saw, despite darkness, opaque stocking-tops and the hem of her skirt stretched above a vague whiteness of thighs and the black shadow between. Breathing too fast, he felt drunk.

Arm resting on the seat back, Billie stroked Otie's ear with a fingernail. Her other hand itsy-bitsy-spidered up his leg.

"Billie ... I..I – "

He jumped. The beer can spilled over his pants and rolled to the floor. He squirmed beneath her palm.

"Don't, Billie!"

"It's okay, honey. Just a little something before you go off to the Navy."

"But Uncle Luke? ... I can't!"

"Yes you can!" Billie snickered, squeezing her hand.

"Got ... got no protection."

"Luke never worries."

"I don't ... think ... we should," Otie gasped.

His left arm, however, rose from the steering wheel and swayed uncertainly like a charmed cobra. The hand opened wide and cupped her breast. Slinking over her waist and the swelling of her hip, it wormed between welcoming thighs and nestled in the lush crevice between her legs.

Billie's breath was a hot whisper in his ear – an unfamiliar song that mattered only for sighed esses and slow, breathed vowels. She molded his hand with her own hand and rocked slowly, swelling and retreating against his palm. Otie's restless blood surged. He felt himself surrendering to streaming darkness, liquid sound, fluid motion, and yet...

"What is it, baby? What do you want?"

"This isn't right!"

"Right as rain, honey," Billie cooed in his ear. "Don't feel shy. He said it might be your first time."

"He? ... Luke?!"

"Sure. A going away present."

"Luke?"

"Yeah, Luke. C'mon now, baby. We can't be gone all too long. Luke says your Daddy'd kill him if he knew."

Otie held out Billie's panties. The cool satin between his fingers felt strangely hot like dry ice.

"Oh, baby, it's okay. Here, let me–"

Nudging her away to clear his arm, he dropped the panties between her legs, turned the ignition key, and felt the car heave slightly as the engine caught. Yanking the light switch, he jerked the shifter into reverse and backed up to clear the trees. Exposed in the stark glow of the instrument panel lights, Billie shimmied into her panties. Otie pulled the lever into drive and floored the gas. The car roared from the dark grove onto the highway.

Entering the dining room, Otie halted beneath the archway. Billie strolled directly to the sideboard, helped herself to two squares of homemade fudge, and, smirking, licked her fingers.

Penny sat holding Luke's beer bottle. Heavy-lidded, she stared into his eyes while he conjured far places where hidden monsters dwelled. She extended her hand to touch the serpent.

"Uncle Luke, I want to talk to you outside."

"Oh, Otieeeee–" Penny began.

"Nothing to do with you, Penny. Unc?"

Luke glanced at Billie and followed Otie through the kitchen. Outside, away from the laughter and music, Otie wheeled.

"I can get my own women!"

"That's great news, Otie. Let's go back inside now."

"You were making fun of me."

"I figured you might want to get laid before you headed to boot camp. I did."

"But, Billie ... she's ..."

"It doesn't wear out, kid."

Otie shook his head. "Nothing *means* anything to you."

"Billie?"

"*Anything*. Like ... like that's my girl you're flirting with."

Luke laughed. "My girl you screwed in my Oldsmobile."

"I didn't!"

"Unlikely. I *know* Billie ... Oh, I get it. Couldn't wait?"

"No!"

"It happens."

Otie blushed. "No! I just ... *didn't*, because ... I don't know why, but I didn't."

"Dumb choice, you ask me. But you're old enough to make up your own mind. Penny, too."

"You really don't care, do you? I mean ... You just don't care."

"About what?"

"*Hurting* people."

"Do others before they do you," Luke said.

"*Family?*"

Luke sniggered.

"Then you're ..." Otie's voice broke. "... You're no kin of mine."

"Ask your mother about that," Luke said, walking away.

The screen door creaked and banged. Otie heard shouting from inside and the rasp and scratch of the phonograph needle bouncing at the end of a record. He dredged the saved Polaroid from his jacket pocket. Mother – back against the wall. Father – forced into a corner, hands clenched. Luke – arm draped impudently over Mother's shoulders.

Otie inched toward the house and up the back steps as if an incautious movement might topple something balanced precariously. The porch slats groaned under his weight. Through the dining room window he saw Luke – thrashing and blustering, an irresistible force – and Father – planted chest-to-chest, immoveable. Sobbing, mother tried to squeeze herself between the two men. Billie yanked at Luke's shirt.

"Luke, honey ..." she pleaded. "Luke, listen. No, c'mon ... Luke!"

"He's an ungrateful little–"

"Don't swear at my boy."

"Kiss my–"

"Don't swear in my house."

"What did you tell him, Luke?" Mother sobbed. "For God's sake, what did you tell him?"

"I told the little bastard to ask his mother."

With hands Otie had once fancied strong enough to uproot a stump, Father seized Luke, plowed him through the front door, and propelled him into the yard. Otie leaped from the back steps and fled into the blackness of the fields. His arms and legs beat against tall wheat. Tears streamed from his eyes. He heard the Oldsmobile engine catch and saw a swath of headlamps, like a lighthouse beam, sweep toward him, flash past, and disappear. His mother's cries – *Otie. Otieeeee* – came from far away. He staggered on until scorched lungs failed him and he fell. All around him, he felt wheat swaying in gusts of wind; thousands of acres surging in slow, great waves. He cried and the waves rocked him to sleep.

* * * * *

Waking stiff and achy, Otie stood and began to walk. In first light, his house looked small and abandoned. Black windows were breaches in white walls painted ember-red by the rising sun.

At the squeak of the screen door, Father – asleep in his stuffed chair – opened his eyes.

"You're home," he said. "No call to wake your momma yet. She cried herself to sleep. I'll make us some coffee."

Otie followed Father into the kitchen and sank at the table.

"You'll need to hurry," Father said, preparing the percolator.

"Don't know that I want to go now."

"Really?"

"Maybe I'll stay on and help you."

"So now you're a farmer again?"

Otie stared at the floor. "Is Luke my father?"

Standing with his back turned, the old man sighed. "The answer to that is a mouthful." He took some time to begin.

"Your momma and I, we loved each other since we were kids – long before we knew it – but no one disputes we're cut from different stock. I always held the world is right beneath our feet, while your momma liked to climb trees to peek over the horizon as if she'd see something better. Foolishness! She had a lot of foolishness in her. Like the dancing – she *lived* to dance." He took a deep breath. "You know about the Senior prom – the only real row we ever had. She told me she'd live her whole life in the prospect of this farm, but first let her have that one special thing."

The percolator began to gurgle.

"I was mule-headed, as usual, so Luke took her, and … well, he has a way with women. Not just the dancing and the flirty talk – something they see in his eyes, something that seems far away and special. It was once and Luke was it. When your momma knew, she told him, and Luke lit out for the Navy. Someone had to take care of her, so I kept the farm deferment and we were married. Best thing ever happened to me, and I guess your momma's happy, but … she never danced again."

"How could he just *leave?*"

"My brother is not a bad man, Otie, but never much for one person or place or thing. I think it scares him."

"Then he's a coward."

"Be better you didn't see it all one way. That medal they gave him wasn't for going in the water. It was for the things he did when the sharks came. The bravest man can have fears he can't weather."

Father removed two cups from the cupboard above the sink.

"Maybe we did wrong not telling you, son," he said, turning around to face the boy. "But what's done is done, and now you know. Decide for yourself who's your father."

* * * * *

The old pick-up truck rattled and clattered even on smooth black-top. The sun was an hour high and stooped men tended the fields that sped by. Otie sat with his elbow resting in the open window. His hair and shirt fluttered in the wind.

Father gripped the steering wheel firmly with both hands. They were wide, heavy, brown hands with large pores, stubby hairs around the knuckles, and thick tendons crisscrossed by purple veins. His ragged nails were dark crescents.

The truck bounced into the dirt drive of the open-air market, circled, and pulled up at the Greyhound sign fixed to the telephone pole. Penny sat waiting in her father's Chevy.

"I'll just get on back," Father said. "Give you two a little time."

Otie stepped out onto the running board, reached into the pick-up bed and shouldered a faded, green-canvas sea-bag Luke had given him years ago. He shuffled around to Father's side and dropped the bag.

"Your momma expects you'll write," Father said, wiping dust from his eyes.

Otie leaned in the open window.

"I love you, Pa," he said, throwing his arms around his father's neck.

"I love you, too, son."

Father clutched Otie's arms with his hands and released him. Otie stepped back. The old truck growled changing gears, groaned reluctantly onto the road, and rumbled away toward home.

Penny stepped up and wrapped an arm around Otie's waist. "What happened to you last night?"

The air was rich with the smells of wheat, fertilizer, soil. The warming sun striped distant highway pavement with water mirages. A single car hummed louder and louder as it approached, roared past, and retreated with a falling sigh. Otie looked at his hands and smiled at the dark crescents beneath his nails. Although the tide in his blood, surging and slacking, drew him away, he cherished all that he took with him.

Father's Day

Percolating since dawn with three words, John Henry closed his notebook when he heard father trudging downstairs. He loved breakfast with Father. He loved Father's morning smell of Ivory soap and Listerine; his morning cheeks, pink and razor-softened; his wet, black hair slicked perfectly into place. Late at night, when Father returned from work, he gave scratchy kisses. His hair drooped and his breath smelled of whiskey. He laughed more then, though; he told silly jokes, did card tricks, and sometimes sang songs or played games until he fell asleep in his TV chair. John Henry loved night times with Father, too.

Plodding to the kitchen table, Father sank into the window seat. Mother sat and bowed her head to whisper grace. Squirming in Father's shadow, John Henry also bowed, but peeked. Back-lighted by the November sun, Father's face seemed red and flat, almost barren. Mother crossed herself and said amen.

"No bacon?" said father, dragging his plate of toast and eggs closer.

"We're out."

"Get more next time."

"It's almost a dollar a pound, Sean."

"Try bitching at Eisenhower and the U.A.W. The auto strike is crippling the whole damn state!"

"I'm not complaining. I'm just saying—"

"Happy birthday, Dad!" John Henry boiled over at last.

Father mashed his eggs with a fork.

"Whacha want for a present?"

"Got a million bucks on you?"

"C'mon, Dad, for real!"

Father stretched to poke the boy's ribs with a finger. Squealing, John Henry twisted away, but not so far his father would miss.

"How about more time?" Father said.

"No! For real."

"White hyacinths to feed my soul."

"Don't tease him, Sean. Daddy wants some nice socks, I think."

"Nobody wants *socks*," John Henry scoffed. "What's a hi..a..sent?"

"Forget it, kiddo. Today's just one more Friday."

"You're late again, Sean," Mother said.

"The clock is broke."

"And yesterday?"

"The clock is broke *today*."

"Boy, I sure don't need no alarm come morning!"

"*An* alarm. You don't need *an* alarm," said Mother.

"I know! I can't wait to get up."

"That'll pass," said Father.

"Tell Daddy about the note from the principal."

"Aw Mom! Did you have to spoil his birthday?"

"What is it this time?"

"He's been expelled from homeroom every day this week," Mother sighed.

"Miss Ruskin makes us read the same stuff over and over real slow. And she makes me print just cause the other kids can't write yet!"

Father shrugged. "Do what you're told. It's easier."

"He was fighting again, too."

"Billy Wetzel drew a mean picture of Miss Ermine! I made him tear it up."

"Who's Miss Ermine?"

"His science teacher," said mother. "The one who suggested the telescope."

"Miss Ermine is smart! She knows all about space and clouds and electricity and flowers and rocks and even bugs and frogs. She knows I'm smart, too. She's my friend."

"You have to pick your battles, son. You can't fight them all."

"Billy was *wrong!*"

"That's a seven-year old talking," Father said wearily. "Do the right thing *all* the time, you'll end up fixing televisions at Grandpa's store like me."

"But Dad!" the boy exclaimed. "I *want* to be like you. *Just* like you."

Father fixed broken televisions at Grandpa's store. John Henry called it Grandpa's store because Father called it that, even though Grandpa was in heaven. John Henry remembered Grandpa only from pictures in Mother's picture books and from stories that Father told. As a boy, Father worked in Grandpa's store and learned about electricity. On Saturdays John Henry learned about electricity from *his* father at Grandpa's store. He loved the store. Father let him fetch coffee and doughnuts from the cafeteria next door where they called him "Mister" and "Sir." He paid proudly with a five-dollar bill and counted the change carefully. Father had taught him to count change so he could ring sales on the cash register. John Henry had never seen a boy his age ring a cash register *anywhere.* Saturday mornings, waiting for the first customer, John Henry would plop down at the messy desk and prop his feet up just like his dad. Together they ate doughnuts and drank coffee. The coffee was a secret.

Sometimes John Henry helped fix televisions by removing tubes and checking them with the tube-checker. He was cautious with the tubes since televisions held on to electricity and could shock a person even if unplugged. Father had shown him once by jumping a blue spark to a screwdriver. Tubes were good if the tube-checker needle moved to the green line, bad if the needle stayed in the red line. John Henry liked to check tubes, but there were never many tubes to check.

The boy swabbed a last bite of egg onto a brown triangle of toast, swallowed it down with milk, and nudged his notebook closer to Father.

"He wants you to look at his book, Sean."

The notebook was a bound composition book with stiff cardboard covers speckled black and white like the shell of a songbird's egg. John Henry had neatly inked out 'THEMES' on the label and printed 'ASTRONOMY' underneath. The notebook contained pencil drawings of the moon and stars. Father opened the notebook and flipped pages.

"More drawings?"

"So I never forget."

"The moon, huh?"

"Last night. It was almost full and tonight there's gonna be an eclipse. Miss Ermine said so in science. I could, uh … *show* you with my telescope?" the boy added timidly.

At the urging of the science teacher, Father had bought John Henry a telescope for Christmas. Unaware that support was the most important part of seeing far, Father had chosen a good telescope on a short, flimsy tripod. Disappointed at first, John Henry discovered that he could brace the telescope solidly through the back of his desk chair and lie beneath the chair to gaze at the sky. Each night with his telescope, the chair, colored pencils, a flashlight, a blanket, and his notebook, he built an observatory on the front sidewalk of his dead-end street. Lighted only by a single yellow lamp on the distant corner, the sidewalk was dark enough for viewing and open to the sky, except for the part blocked by his own house. It was a perfect spot, dark and cold and silent, like space itself. Conjuring distant worlds, his breath forming clouds in the night air, John Henry would lie with his back to the cold sidewalk and draw pictures of what he saw so he wouldn't forget. Sometimes his parents looked at his pictures, but they lacked his enthusiasm for astronomy. One night he saw Sputnik and woke Father in his TV chair to show him the drawing. Father said it was probably just an airplane.

Gulping his coffee, Father closed the notebook and pushed it back across the breakfast table.

"You have a good line," he said.

"You missed the eclipse picture, Dad. Lemme show you."

John Henry thumbed to a drawing.

"Miss Ermine taught us this yesterday. The sun is here, and sometimes the moon is way over here, so the big earth gets between the little moon and the sun and blocks the light – like this, see? Indians said the moon was bleeding cause it turns red. Betcha don't know why! Cause air bends some of the sunlight – just the red part – right around the earth, like these arrows, see? Sunlight is really lots of colors. True! Miss Ermine showed. So the moon gets red light from the sun anyway. Neato, huh?"

"And sometimes the moon blocks the sun, too," Father said. "Daylight turns dark."

John Henry studied his picture. "No way, Dad. The moon is too little."

Father stood. "Ask Miss Whosis. I'm late."

"What time will you be home, Sean?" Mother said.

"Usual time."

She nodded toward the boy. "Can't you make it earlier tonight?"

"The sign says open 'til eight. I have to be there."

"The sign is less compelling in the *morning*," she said.

John Henry squeezed between his parents. "We're gonna have cake and ice cream, Dad. Like a party!"

"Well ... I wouldn't miss a party now, would I?" He mussed the boy's hair and left.

"Daddy works too much," John Henry pouted. "Worser than school!"

"*Worse* than school," Mother said, clearing dishes. The pastel flowers of her old housecoat were faded almost gray. A tired lock of yellow hair drooped across one eye. "He wasn't *always* that way. He used to play more. You should have seen him roller skate."

"Dad? No way!"

"Frankly, he was *awful*. Always scraped and bruised, but he had fun and wouldn't give up."

"Get him skates, Mamma! That's a great present. We'll skate together."

"His old skates are in the basement somewhere, John Henry, but ... Daddy hasn't skated since high school. How about slippers?"

"Double-DOUBLE dumb!"

Downing his milk, John Henry bounded to his room – a cluttered sanctum splashed with color and frozen motion. Donald Duck bed covers lay rumpled and balled. Near the closet, miniature green soldiers assaulted a shoebox fortress. Propped like a pup tent next to the bed was a yellow *Child's Garden of Verses*. Lining a bookcase were a *World Book Encyclopedia*, a row of thin science books for children, and rainbow stacks of *Superman, Flash, and Green Lantern* comics. On one shelf sat his microscope and the red metal cabinet of his chemistry set. On another shelf, awaiting Spring, rested John Henry's brown, baseball glove, thick rubber bands compressing a grass stained hardball in its dark, oiled pocket. Over the bed hung a blue and orange Detroit Tigers pennant. On a blackboard a chalked rocket ship blasted through a field of stars and planets. In the cubbyholes and drawers of an open, roll-top desk were stuffed bottle caps, special pebbles, a knife, firecrackers, sea shells, a pen that wrote in red-green-black-and blue, homework papers, bubblegum cards, marbles, batteries, old coins, pencils, matches, and Tiger Stadium ticket stubs from the baseball game John Henry saw with his dad.

Atop the desk stood his telescope, a brass Little League trophy, a walnut framed commendation from Miss Ermine's science class, and a black-capped, wide-mouth jar labeled *Rana Pipens*. Inside the jar, black eyes staring, floated a half-dissected frog, its heart exposed and still.

Throwing on his red jacket, John Henry climbed on the bed and bounced until Mother shouted that he was cracking the ceiling plaster. Springing from the bed, he slid down the carpeted stairs on the seat of his pants, grabbed his notebook from the kitchen table, shouted goodbye as he whizzed through the door, and was almost to school before he slowed to a walk.

* * * * *

"Were you good today?" Mother asked John Henry after school.

"Yep!" he mumbled around a mouthful of peanut butter sandwich. "Dad wouldn't want no notes on his birthday."

"*Any* notes," Mother said. She placed a package on the table. "I bought his present."

John Henry took another bite from the center of the sandwich and pushed the circle of crust aside.

"Don't want the bones," he said. "What'd we get him?"

"Slippers."

"MOM?!"

"He'll like them. Here, sign the card."

The birthday card showed a puffing, cartoon man roller skating uphill. Inside the card, the cartoon man careened toward a cliff.

"At your age it's all downhill," John Henry read aloud. He pouted and pushed the card away unsigned. "I'll make Dad something."

"What?"

"Dunno yet. Have to look around."

Scampering to the basement, John Henry crawled onto a chair. Overhead silver heating ducts and sweaty pipes ran between wooden joists. He tugged a tinkly pull-chain on one of the naked bulbs dangling from black, braided cords and jumped down.

In the far corner droned the furnace. Against one brico-block wall stood a laundry sink separating the washing machine and dryer.

Father's dusty workbench occupied another wall, while the opposite wall bore sagging, box laden shelves.

Remembering the roller skates, the boy dragged over the chair and began pawing through battered boxes. Most were filled with folded clothes. A few boxes held old art supplies – pencil stubs, squished tubes of paint, stiff brushes, dirty erasers. One box was filled with new brushes, fresh paint, chalks, unopened bottles of yellow fluid, blank canvases. Rain had seeped onto the largest box through a cracked basement window. The box smelled spoiled. The stained cardboard crumpled at the boy's touch. Inside were sketch pads. John Henry pulled the pads from the decaying box and opened them one by one.

"Mamma! Mamma, come look!" he cried, but she did not hear.

The pads contained drawings – pencil, pen, chalk – *real* drawings, not like John Henry's. Sunlit scenes, faces and hands, old houses, dusty roads, a broken gate. And pictures of Mother, smiling, as the boy had never seen her. The drawings were signed by Father!

On the bottom shelf, buried behind a large box of baby clothes, sat scuffed, black roller skates. John Henry carried the skates and a sketch pad upstairs. He arranged the skates beside the hall closet for Father to see and took the pad to Mother in the living room.

"Look!" he said, holding up a drawing.

Mother glanced from her Bible and saw an image of herself as she had once appeared to a boy she loved. She put aside the Bible and propped the pad on her lap.

"Your father thought I was pretty, didn't he?"

"Daddy draws good!"

"He was going to be an artist once."

"Why did he stop?"

She shrugged and closed the pad. "He stopped doing a lot of things when he quit high school … a little before you were born."

Mother closed the pad and traced a stain on the cover with her fingers.

"He has lots in the basement," John Henry said. "They're getting wet."

"I know," Mother said finally. "Here, put this one in my closet, Pumpkin."

John Henry took the drawing pad upstairs, placed it in Mother's closet, and flopped onto his parents' bed. Mother's crochet basket sat next to the bed. Her rosary lay coiled around the clock on the nightstand. Her cologne bottles and silver-handled brush sparkled on her dresser. The boy smelled perfume, but no Listerine or Ivory soap, no cigar smoke or whiskey smells. The room was Father's, too, but ... where was he? Hidden in the chest of drawers and closet – no part of him visible except the clock.

The broken clock!

More *time*!

John Henry grabbed the clock and scurried back to the basement. He climbed the tall stool at Father's dusty workbench, switched on a goose-neck lamp, and examined the clock ... a round, six-inch, brass, wind-up clock with two bells on top. He twisted the winding keys in back. One key moved the hands, another the small alarm pointer. The largest key would not turn. He held the clock to his ear. It was silent.

"There's a wind-up spring or something, like my truck. I'll unstick the spring and it'll go."

Although he had never seen the insides of a clock, John Henry was seven years old and, consequently, had few doubts. He was smart. He could climb trees and hit a baseball and understand an eclipse. *Just keep the parts separate and remember where they go*, he said to himself. *Make a drawing so you won't forget*. He found a piece of paper and a pencil in the workbench drawer.

Star-slotted screws held the back cover in place. Confidently, he pulled a dusty star-pointed screwdriver from the pegboard holder behind the workbench, but it was too big. He chose a smaller one and placed the four screws in a pile to the side.

The cover, however, couldn't come off with the keys attached. *Think, stupid, think*! Tiny screws fastened the keys to stems. He selected the tiniest screwdriver, removed the keys, put the small screws and keys in a second pile, and added the parts to his drawing.

As he plopped the back cover onto his palm, John Henry glimpsed his smiling face in the glass of the clock face. Flipping the clock again, he saw its insides – gears and gears and gears, springs, levers, tiny mysterious things, and a big, spiral spring deep within. For a moment he pictured the complicated insides of the frog in the jar on his desk and hesitated. Although Father often told John Henry he could do anything he set his heart to, the boy knew that *no one* could make the frog go again. Shaking his head as if to scatter the thought, he began methodically to remove parts.

At first John Henry arranged things in separate piles. Later the piles ran together. *Remember where the pieces go, draw the picture so you don't forget,* he whispered, although he feared he *was* forgetting. He chased a small gear that rolled off the workbench, and when he crawled back onto the stool, the strewn parts looked unfamiliar despite his drawing. As he worked, an occasional shudder wrenched his shoulders, but it was at least an hour before he began to cry in earnest.

* * * * *

Father was late for the party.

"Where have you been? It's 9:30!" Mother demanded at the door. "John Henry has been crying all evening."

"Get off my back."

"For the love of God, Sean."

Father brushed past her, overlooking the skates positioned so carefully next to the hall closet. "John Henry!" he shouted, tugging off his necktie. "Daddy's home."

The boy crept down the stairs. Father lifted him into his arms, but stumbled a step backwards, off balance.

"Wha'samatter, kiddo?"

John Henry hid his red, swollen eyes against Father's chest. Father let him slip through his arms to the floor.

"C'mon, let's eat. It's a party, right?"

Father staggered into the kitchen. The boy disappeared down the basement stairway. On the table sat a chocolate cake atop a serving pedestal. Father dropped into a chair and scooped a finger through the icing.

"Tonight, Sean?"

"I'm celebrating, " he drawled, licking the icing from his finger.

"You talked to the bank man again, didn't you?"

"He talked to me."

"How long this time?"

"No more extensions," Father said.

"But ... but it's the strike. They have to—"

"Have to *nothing*, Catherine. It's *over*! I gave 'em the keys."

Father groped in his pocket, dangled his key chain, and dropped it among the thirty white, unlighted candles arranged across the cake in rows.

"Always hated the place anyway," he said.

"But ... What'll we do?"

"Eat cake."

John Henry returned clutching a cardboard box containing the half-dissected clock.

"Presents!" Father boomed. "Socks or slippers?"

"I w..w..wanted to fix it for you, Dad." The boy held out the box. "I ... I *couldn't*."

Father peered blearily into the box, picked at a few pieces, and allowed them to dribble through his fingers.

"Clock, huh? I tried this stunt, too, 'bout your age. Never did get the thing back together. Old man beat Hell outta me."

"Help me, Dad. Help me fix it."

Father looked away. "I can't fix it."

"P..please, Dad. S..show me."

Father squirmed in his chair. "It's broke. Forget it."

"I ... I couldn't d..do it," John Henry sobbed. "Show me how to make it go."

"Quit crying. It's just a cheap clock."

Tears distorted things. Objects seemed strange. Light through the basement doorway cast John Henry's shadow, tall and spindly, across a tilting floor. His father looked very far away.

"P..please, Daddy."

"Quit crying."

"Daddy?"

"Quit your fucking crying, you God-damned baby!" Father shouted, slapping the box from the boy's hands.

Clock pieces scattered across the linoleum. The glass of the clock face shattered. Father dropped to his knees in the boy's shadow.

"I..I didn't mean that, kiddo," he moaned, extending his arms. "Give Daddy a hug."

John Henry pressed balled fists into his closed eyes. His breaths came in raspy gasps until a pressure in his chest exploded.

"I *never* want to be like you. Never!" he cried, fleeing from the monstrous words he had unshackled.

In his room, the boy hunched over his desk and wept. When the tears stopped finally, he wiped his eyes and nose with the backs of his hands. Jostled, the half-dissected frog – its heart exposed and still – swayed in the liquid of its jar, but did not move.

John Henry zipped on his red jacket and gathered together a blanket, his notebook, colored pencils, a flashlight, the desk chair, and his telescope. He struggled down the stairs with his burdens.

Father sat slumped in the kitchen chair, head down, arms dangling limply. Standing behind him, Mother massaged his shoulders. Father looked up at the sound of the closing door.

"...Kiddo...?" he called.

"Let him be for now, Sean," Mother said.

Outside, the boy's breath billowed in the cold November air. Gusts of wind creaked and cracked the bare branches of trees. John Henry built his observatory on the sidewalk in front of his house and aimed his telescope at the blood red moon. He watched as the moon crept through the earth's shadow, watched the red darkness deepen, but finally fade. And in his notebook, he drew pictures ... lest he forget.

A Big House

Troubled by bearish forecasts for the Board of Directors' meeting, McDanald Information Systems executives saw little profit in a surprise cocktail party where three thinly-disguised *investors* might capitalize on a public offering of some private sentiment to bankrupt a career. Nevertheless, when Elliott Kreisler, McDanald's CEO, moved that the first day's session adjourn to his house, the motion passed unanimously. After all, MIS was an old-fashioned company, a private company, and the idea for the get-together was undoubtedly that of the firm's 85-year old owner and founder – Connolly McDanald.

"The crew is skittish, El," Connolly had drawled to his CEO over lunch. "Rumors are bad business. Throw a little soiree out to that big house of yours. Invite your investor cronies, too. Show folks the Lord's in his heaven and all's right with the world."

Elliott had objected to free-ranging threatened employees within earshot of meat-eating investors who Connolly needed to write a 10-digit check. The billionaire Connolly, however, had countered with a billion reasons to do things *his* way. Elliott engaged a caterer and phoned his wife to expect thirty dinner guests. Concluding the opening session, he, Connolly, and the three investors withdrew to Elliott's waiting limousine. The executives hastily organized a carpool.

"So far so good," said a regional vice-president to colleagues waiting for elevators.

"That's what the guy who jumped off Peachtree Plaza said on his way down."

"At least the ax hasn't fallen yet," offered another executive.

"Neither has the other shoe."

"Say, Tommy, you're in finance ... what's the real skinny on these three so-called *guests*."

"You mean our new bosses?"

Executives crowded into elevators.

"Man, we'll be lucky to *have* bosses. Did you see how the three of them hunkered off to the side smacking their lips?"

"Investors and jackals ..." mused a corporate compliance officer. "The meals of both demand the benediction of due diligence."

Outside, sagging clouds hoarded rain. Atlanta was sweltering through a heat wave unmatched since the siege. Waiting to pile into six recruited cars, the executives perspired. Muggy, motionless air pasted shirts to sweaty backs.

Relying on smart-phone maps – no one had been to Elliott's house – the cars caterpillared away from Peachtree Center. Exiting I-75 forty miles south, the caravan whizzed along a two-lane blacktop past monotonous miles of fallow fields. Lulled by a white noise of straining air-conditioners, groaning tires, and the yellow-blot pitter-pops of hapless bugs pocking windshields, many in the cars nodded.

Far ahead in the chilly limousine, Elliott was talkative. He enjoyed the camaraderie of the young investors. All three were fellow Ivy-Leaguers and members of socially responsible families. One investor even boasted a dotted-line Kennedy relationship – excellent bona fides notwithstanding a certain over-subscription in the Kennedy issue.

Sharing a joke about a German hunter and a French duck, Elliott volunteered Connolly a translation of the French punch line, a nuanced play on the word canard, which he explained meant 'duck.' The pun was impossible to render literally, of course, and the investors smirked at Elliott's patient attempt. Patience, however, was an art Elliott had mastered at both Wharton Business and Yale Law. Patiently he had endured a hand-crafted ladder of bosses, all specimens of a type Wharton professors casually dissected – entrepreneurs whose luck (mistaken for prescience) had landed them on the cover of Fortune. The last and final rung in Elliott's ladder was Connolly ... specimen *par excellence.*

Cracker-born of that greatest generation, Connolly, at seventeen, had earned hero medals in Naval actions at Iwo Jima and Okinawa. Recuperating at the Balboa Naval Hospital, he was briefly charged with updating the hospital library card-catalog and discovered, buried in the tedium of the task, his life's work – refining raw data into precious information. After the war, Connolly's GI Bill benefits unlocked the otherwise barred doors of Georgia State College. Quickly learning that college would teach him little about his life's work, he left school to found McDanald Information Systems. For fifteen years he plowed meager profit and copious obsession into what sophisticated business minds judged a folly – electronic data management systems made ridiculously expensive by unlimited capacity. Through luck or prescience, however, Connolly's infinitely scalable systems sat waiting when the Great Society and its evil twin, the Vietnam War, loosed a deluge of data. Drowning bureaucrats scrambled aboard MIS and survived. The firm, now perched on its Ararat, loomed as the largest, privately-held company of its kind. Nevertheless, as Wharton grads know well, every perch is also a precipice.

"All you have is good will," Elliott had admonished when Connolly hired him to take MIS public. "Intellectual property, but no tangibles. Where are your assets?"

"I have good folks."

"Human resources are ephemeral," Elliott had replied.

His words had been couched in that insolent but nevertheless awed tone professional managers exhibit with successful entrepreneurs – the insolence stemming from decisions often blind to conclusions so blatant in the managers' spreadsheets; the unbidden awe at how frequently those decisions proved correct.

"I don't hold to calling humans *resources*," Connolly had warned. "But I like that word *ephemeral*. Is that a Wharton word? I could come to relish a word like that. Regardless, El, if we are creatures of a day, it's been a good day and the sun is high yet."

The limousine slowed, turned, and began to joggle down a red-dirt, tree-arched lane.

"Bottom line, Mr. McDanald?" said one of the investors. "And we are close now, very close. Bottom line ... if we do come aboard, where does our minority interest take us?"

"Bottom line?" Connolly said. "Wherever my majority interest chooses."

The investor chuckled. "No one is mistaking you for a follower, Mr. McDanald. Even getting you in the car was a struggle."

Connolly drove his own Cadillac and detested back seats. He had acquiesced to the limousine only when assured he could ride curbside.

"I prefer to hold the wheel," he had drawled, patting the door handle. "But *not* going somewhere is steering, too."

Connolly realized that his stubborn self-reliance was hard for the young investors to fathom. Their generation – raised with a reverence for self-doubt – believed that Wisdom welled from a fountainhead of consensus. They worshipped surveys and work teams and focus groups and committees and boards, a faith that cast *them* as strange birds to Connolly who knew that all men *were* islands.

In no way religious, he believed nevertheless that each person possesses a unique and separate soul – a still, small voice that asks *true or false*? and demands a single answer – a free-agency that either chooses and acts on choice or necessarily descends into a neither A nor not-A limbo. Connolly chose and acted; sometimes rashly, sometimes tardily, sometimes mistakenly. He had learned painfully to encourage dissent, listen to others, and change his stubborn mind when he discovered that he was wrong. Ultimately, however, Connolly decided for himself. Independent reality, free choice, and autonomous action were the elements of Connolly's trinity.

"Actually, Mr. McDanald..." another investor began coolly. "We *could* hold out for control. Time is on *our* side."

Connolly smiled at the futility of the old *good-MBA, bad-MBA trick*. Although each of the investors had adopted some strategic persona, he struggled to tell them apart and called them all by a single name after their sacrosanct spreadsheets ... X.L. They enjoyed his gibes in the way laughing hyenas – with time firmly on *their* side –enjoyed the antics of a wounded beast.

"Look X.L. ... You boys know that success has stanched the flood MIS needs for steerageway. I've taken this private company about as far as she can go without a big infusion of capital. That's why I shanghaied Elliott here from that old pirate Friedman. To pilot me onto the exchange."

"Kudos for the grunt work on Friedman's public offering, Elliott," one investor said innocently, adding, "So why ain't you rich?"

The investors guffawed like schoolboys.

"I'm rich enough," Elliott burned.

"None of us is rich *enough*," retorted an investor. "Unless it's Mr. McDanald."

"That's the 64-dollar question, isn't it? I missed that IPO tide and ran us aground, so I'm needing a tow from boys like you. You can take a fat fee now, before someone beats you to it, or wait a spell to see how desperate I get. That's your dilemma. How rich is this old buzzard and how far will he go to keep MIS afloat?"

The limousine came to a stop.

"Wait, driver. Allow us to finish," ordered the bad, or perhaps it was the good, MBA. He turned back to Connolly and said matter-of-factly, "Even you won't write personal checks forever."

Connolly's syrupy drawl crystallized.

"Beached or not, boys, I'm still aboard, which means we're not salvage. Read your spreadsheets differently, and I'd say your sheepskins are foolscap." Connolly yanked the door handle and stepped from the car. "We're finished."

Surprised, the chauffeur scrambled to open the other passenger door. Elliott emerged followed by the investors. Connolly stood watching, eager to see the X.L.s' reaction to Elliott's house.

"Sure is a behemoth, isn't it?" he chuckled at their wide-eyed stares. "Befitting, though, mind you. A big house is very befitting, what with all a CEO does these days."

Back in the caravan, sudden lurches and the pings of stones against wheel-wells snapped the executives awake. Beyond the trees and split-rail fences on either side of the red dirt lane lay played-out, erstwhile plantation land.

"Long live King Cotton," quipped an executive, but no one in her car laughed, because – rounding a blind curve – the executives found themselves face to façade with their destination.

Brake lights flared. The cars bunched. Caution was a knee-jerk response to the enormity of the place, but something more – something in the edifice itself – triggered a kind of prickling-of-the-thumbs foreboding. Despite an efficient, near-scientific, form-following-function modernity, the house was slightly askew, almost crooked. It exploded up and out in unregulated lines that had probably seemed free and laissez-faire on the architect's elevations, but, in reality, had merged into an ominous redoubt of solid walls, slit windows, commanding heights, and a massive, oaken door.

"My Lord!" whispered an executive.

The cars halted before yawning iron gates. Hesitantly the point car proceeded across an exposed drive toward the parked limousine. Others followed, but several cars see-sawed through U-turns, opting for less encumbered spots on the well-worn berm outside the stone fence. Like a troop of wary soldiers seeking cover of a tank, the executives mustered behind the limousine. The massive door of the house opened and Connolly waved the group inside. His John Wayne stature eclipsed the master of the house who stood behind him, playing lady-in-waiting.

"Take a look," Connolly urged jovially, motioning the guests into a soaring, domed, rotunda ringed by a white marble staircase and balustrade. Eyes gaped upward at trompe l'oeil clouds. "Shrinks you, doesn't it? A house that imprisons the sky!"

Thoughts masked by his Wharton, or perhaps it was his Yale smile, Elliott slapped Connolly on the back. "I'll attend to our guests," he said, obviously meaning the investors since he wheeled and walked away.

"I think that lady yonder is the docent. You folks go ahead and take the nickel tour," Connolly said. He glanced through the open door. "I'll stay and play greeter in case we get some late birds."

The executives filed behind a maid in two straight lines. They veered into the smaller of two wings and tip-toed, open-mouthed, past various high chambers and great-rooms. Exiting through a looking-glass wall of tall, mirrored, French doors, they encountered tiered grass and stone terraces connected by wide risers. Tennis court lighting towers peeked from an upper terrace while the beamed roof of a stable was visible down a long, grass, tree-lined, middle terrace. A stone-tiled lower terrace overlooked a rolling, emerald slope bathed in the honeyed glow of a cloudy sunset. On that terrace stood a large, gold-roofed bar and rows of white-linen dressed tables. A swimming pool, dramatically cantilevered to extend past the brink of the slope, commanded the length of the terrace. At a poolside table sat Elliott and the investors.

The pool was Elliott's stamp on a house purchased two years earlier when he left Friedman and New York City to join Connolly. The seller of the house had been an eye-brow worrying, soon-to-be cashiered chief executive caught in a stock-price storm. Despite Elliott's gut-felt longing for the house, he had leveraged the seller's distress to wring fierce concessions, thus, convincing himself that his motives were economic.

"It's an investment," Elliott had argued when Connolly, who lived in a downtown condominium, ridiculed the purchase. "A big house is a tax shelter. Impregnable."

Argument became futile, however, when – never to recoup his costs – Elliott demolished the existing swimming pool to construct one of his own design.

The walls and bottom of his pool were gold leaf tiles. Illuminated by recessed lighting, the water glowed like molten gold. A Plexiglas infinity edge rendered invisible the lip of the pool's cantilevered far wall and created a stunning optical illusion. Jutting over the brink of the slope, the seemingly unconstrained liquid gold, in apparent violation of natural law, neither rushed nor trickled down.

Although Elliott could not swim, he spent much time alone in a poolside chair relishing his handiwork – the pool, the slope, and especially the sinuous depression of a dry streambed engraved as by an invisible hand along the bottom of the slope. And when, occasionally, the cost of the pool troubled him, he reminded himself that conspicuous consumption was the reward for noblesse oblige.

Elliott watched the executives spill onto the terrace and sweep toward the bar. He smiled when their advance was checked by the sight of the golden pool. They shuffled past, whispering and gesturing as at some heavenly sign. Last to appear was Connolly, flanked by two stragglers. Familiar with the pool, Connolly ignored it, while the excited stragglers peeled off to examine the fraudulent edge.

Approaching Elliott and the three investors – all dressed in business attire – Connolly slapped his bare forearm to swat a mosquito. Save for three weddings and an equal number of divorce court proceedings, he refused to be straight-jacketed in a suit or noosed with a tie. And since he had relaxed the board meeting dress code in deference to the heat wave, the executives, too, all wore slacks and summer shirts. Mosquitoes feasted upon exposed arms and necks.

"I guess that Armani uniform you boys favor has its pluses," Connolly said, greeting the group. He tapped a passing waiter, diligent to note the man's name tag. "S'cuse me, Tim. Round us up some bug repellent, would you?"

Urged beyond the insulation of his job description, the waiter short-circuited.

"C'mon now, Tim. We'll be eaten alive out here. Let me help you." Connolly relieved the man of his tray. "Bug repellent. Where do you keep it, Elliott?"

"It's a big house, Connolly. I'm sure I don't know."

"Poke around then, Tim. Thanks."

"What if I can't find any?"

"Ask someone inside."

"What if there isn't any?"

"Have the limo driver run you to the market."

"I don't know where he is."

"Oh, I expect you'll do a good job, Tim."

The man scurried away.

"Try these mushrooms, folks," Connolly boomed, extending the tray of hors d'oeuvres.

"Don't mind if I do, Mac," said an older executive, who, as did most, wore a *years-of-service pin* on his lapel.

"Is Mac hogging all the caviar?" bellowed a round VP from Portland, elbowing his way into a coalescing crowd.

"Stan loves fish eggs," Connolly chuckled, balancing the tray with one hand as he gulped a stuffed mushroom. "And he knows I wouldn't eat 'em with *his* mouth."

The executives laughed, most for the first time that day.

Elliott whispered to an investor, "And the wise shall be servant to the fool."

Working his way through the crowd to the bar, Connolly exchanged the pillaged tray for a tall club soda. Returning to Elliott, he said, "Rumor going round, says I'm half-deaf. Have you heard that one, El?"

"Have you?"

Connolly scraped a chair back from the table to accommodate his long legs. "See why I hired him, X.L.? Spunk! Can't trust a tight-lipped man."

The investors wore the expressionless faces of dinner guests embroiled in a domestic squabble.

"You ought not amend the Bible, though, El. The proverb says fools will serve the wise." Connolly slapped at another mosquito. "So … where's that pretty lady of yours?"

"She's punishing me. We had theatre tickets for tonight."

"That's a shame. I do love drama myself."

"She'll make her appearance."

"Business-widows," Connolly sighed. "The trials we put them through. Then the trials they put *us* through!"

Connolly laughed at his joke. Elliott and the investors sat silently.

"But soon you'll have all the time you can tolerate, won't you El?" Connolly said.

"How's that?" said an investor, eyeing Elliott.

"Friedman's IPO schooled him. El carved himself a hefty slice of any deal I make with you boys. Aims to be a man of leisure, although, truth be told, I've always smelled a little carpetbagger in him."

"The public sector can benefit from a dose of private sector savvy," said Elliott.

"Undoubtedly," replied Connolly. "On the other hand, *my* generation had to deal harshly with some public sectors that decided folks were human resources."

"Why, Mr. McDanald, isn't that, possibly, a somewhat regressive attitude?" blurted an investor, surprising himself with so categorical an opinion.

"Regressive..." Connolly repeated, mouthing the word as if tasting it. "That's one fine word. Say ... you X.L.s are all Wharton boys, aren't you? El found himself a slew of you young lions this last year, despite that ugliness."

The ugliness occurred when the stock market dam broke, making it impossible to float Connolly's IPO. Trying to salvage his lost percentage, Elliott devised a fallback scheme wherein an extreme makeover seduces MIS a blue-chip suitor. He began the transformation with an expenditure fast, then surgically restructured the bride's bloated budget, erased age lines with a Botox of selective divestiture, and dabbed creative accounting makeup over balance sheet blemishes. Looking once more the ingénue, MIS attracted suitable swains eager to merge. Unfortunately, the intimacy of an early due-diligence embrace revealed that what stood out as large, core assets were, in fact, recent acquisitions. In modern business society, the Journal's revelations hardly branded the bride a whore, but effectively dashed plans for a white gown. Eligible blue chips withdrew, forcing Elliott to buttonhole venture capitalists, a less fastidious class of gents lusty for a short-term sure thing; young sports to whom a checkered past meant nothing and an idyllic future even less. Elliott convinced the boys from One Knight Standard Funding that an experienced lady like MIS could be flexible, eager for whatever *they* were into, just the kind of fun gal they needed. All that remained was the placing of cash on the nightstand and the partnering.

"Ugliness is an ugly word, Mr. McDanald," said an investor who craned forward to squeeze Connolly's knee. "Listen, can we at least get past the Mr. McDanald?"

"Not too far past, X.L.," Connolly said, eying the hand on his leg.

"Connolly, my friend ... we have public faces, we have private faces. Going forward—"

"Easy to say, LaToya!" interrupted a slurred shout. "Young. Black. Female. Recruiters will fight over *you*."

A knot of anxious faces glanced toward Elliott. A cautionary hand shook the loudmouth's arm. The investors began to buzz.

"I would think you ran a tighter—"

"A tighter ship, Elliott! Especially since—"

"We need some of these people for now."

It tickled Connolly when the X.L.s finished each other's sentences like the witches in Macbeth. Elliott, however, was stern. His hot scowl evaporated the circle of guests surrounding the loudmouth. Left suddenly alone, the man shook his head to clear the fog, then resolutely crossed the canvas-colored terrace to face Connolly.

"Thirty-two years with the company, Mac."

"Next week, Freddie. I remember hiring you. Right after Labor Day."

"MIS has been my life. That goes for most of us!" The man flung his arm toward the others as if casting a net, but his colleagues, looking down or away, avoided capture. He swallowed hard and continued. "Okay, okay … we've got troubles now. But troubles are a drill we know. We pull together. All of us, Mac. Together. We save what we've built together. But this time it's—"

"Every man for himself? So I've heard," Connolly said. "How do I scotch a rumor like that, Freddie?"

"Look, Mac. MIS is yours and no one begrudges that. Cash out if you want, you've *earned* it. But … but what about sweat equity? Blood equity. Life's blood equity!" The man remembered his drink, raised the glass, and found it empty. "You don't suck the body dry! You can, but … but you just *don't*. Break us up and sell us piecemeal, you'll be leaving a lot of us with nothing but forced retirement."

The investors watched dispassionately, functionally blind to the impact of business decisions except as seen from high above through the telescopic bombsight of a spreadsheet where a trigger finger tapped on a mouse key razed values to increment a bottom line. Elliott, however, was no mere money man. Elliott was hands-on. A CEO.

"You're fired," he said.

Shrinking as his shoulders fell, the man sighed. Fear, anger, disappointment, guilt, regret, and finally, relief all ran together in his face.

"Hold your horses, El," Connolly said. "Freddie has struggled mightily with that Missouri operation. He's earned himself a few unfocused words."

"We can do without Missouri."

"He's been with me for ages."

"We can do without extinct species ... *Connolly*."

Returning to the table, Tim, the waiter, stumbled awkwardly into a tense silence. Noticing him holding three spray cans, Connolly rose.

"Good job, Tim! Just in time. I'll start one around while you circulate the other two."

Accepting a can, Connolly sprayed his ankles and arms. The investors covered their wine glasses with their palms.

"Here, Freddie," Connolly said, holding out his can. "Go help save what blood remains."

The man slinked back to the crowd.

"Your strengths are prodigious, El," Connolly said. "I mean that truly. Prodigious."

The heart-flutter of pride Elliott felt surprised him, since Connolly's praise should no longer have mattered.

"I fault myself for not minding more closely your weaknesses."

A wave of anger doused the pride. "I *rescued* MIS. You're making every cent possible."

"We've *always* made money."

"Connolly ... you're a brilliant man, but ultimately just *lucky*, because you never learned the basics. Less than maximum is a loss. It's called an opportunity cost. Add *that* word to your lexicon."

"Lexicon? You do like showing off for me, don't you, El?"

Elliott's face burned. "My job is to—"

"Maximize," said an X.L.

Connolly's gaze circled the table. "Gain the world and lose the soul, El. These boys are starting to finish your sentences."

The investors smiled.

"Explain something to me," Connelly said, turning to the nearest X.L. "Elliott signed on with me because, deep down, he's like a Tick bird needing a Rhinoceros. But I'm Adam's off ox to you boys. Why all this interest in me and the information management business?"

The investors looked amused.

"The business is irrelevant. Our interest is—"

"Maximum return. MIS presents an opportunity—"

"For maximum short-run yield."

"So you've said, so you've said … But what's still Greek to me, boys, is how you ignore the plain and simple truth that you can't make or build or grow anything in the short-run."

"You can harvest what's ripe," scoffed an investor. "It's there for the taking."

Connolly nodded slowly. "I guess I just had to hear it aloud. You boys aren't venture capitalists. You're venture *feudalists*."

Elliott rose and urged Connolly out of earshot toward the pool's infinite edge. Watching grimly from various huddles, the executives all sensed that their future teetered on the brink of the next few words. Confident that any *ultimate* balance sheet would reflect their loyalty to Connolly, they felt driven to consider *his* loyalty. Good Will was an intangible, ephemeral asset and, in fact, *every man for himself* described the times.

"Whatever you had in mind for tonight is finished," Elliott hissed. "I want your agreement."

"To what?"

"To an arrangement that leaves you as wealthy as you are now."

"What about my opportunity costs?"

"Don't be cute, Connolly. It's done. Follow my lead or you're ruined. Trust me."

"Ruined … trust. Those words sound so long-run, don't they?"

Connolly upended his club soda glass and shook a piece of ice into his mouth.

"This investment deal is a canard, Elliott," Connolly said, crunching the ice cube. He still had his teeth and liked the sensation. "I've known it for weeks now, but couldn't figure out what you boys aimed to steal. No tangibles, right?"

Unconsciously Elliott glanced toward the executives.

"Nothing but our folks. I found my answer buried in the financials this morning – the *real* point of that bond issue we floated a while back. Oh, don't look so surprised, Elliott. It's *insulting*. I may not fathom all the interlocking, paper-shell, wholly-owned subsidiaries of this-and-that you MBA's are partial to, but I know what I see when I see it. You've managed to bleed dry a multi-billion-dollar retirement fund and transfuse it with McDanald Bonds which soon will be just so much paper. You're seizing the future, El. *Their* future."

Elliott lowered his voice.

"We are, Connolly. *We!* … I make the Fortune ladder; the trio from One Knight Standard Funding climbs a rung or two; and *you* remain as rich as Crassus."

Connolly shook his head. "Ignore the classics at your peril, Elliott. Crassus was a Roman moneyman, an MBA type, and I guess he got his fill of gold. But the phrase is rich as Croesus. Croesus was a king and richer by far. Funny thing, though … for a while he lost almost everything."

"Spare me, Connolly. MIS is completely private and you're commingled. Collapse this house of cards I built before you divest, and you're left *personally* bankrolling that retirement fund. Croesus and Crassus together didn't have that much. It won't be *almost* everything."

"Maybe the tangibles."

Elliott sighed. "One final, thundering, head-down charge, Connolly?" His voice was tinged with wistfulness, a dissonant grace note of regret in his usual chord of awe mixed with insolence. "I almost wish you'd try. I'd like to see it, because you are a Rhino, Connolly. A magnificent Rhino. And you might be the last."

"*Après moi, le deluge*," Connolly intoned, indulging his melodramatic streak. "Forgive the gauche accent. German is kinder to the tongue. My French has always been *comme ci, comme ca*."

Elliott laughed despite himself, recalling his ridiculous struggle to translate the French pun.

"So. The old dog still knows some old tricks. Nevertheless—" He whirled. The two stragglers who had entered with Connolly had inched close enough to eavesdrop. "What do you think you're doing?" Elliott snapped. "And who are you anyway?"

"Don't lawyers recognize their kind?" said Connolly.

"They're not from the legal department."

"The *Justice Department*, El."

Elliott recoiled toward the edge of the terrace. The taller FBI agent lunged to catch his arm.

"Careful, Mr. Kreisler. That's quite a fall," he said. He spun Elliott to handcuff him while his partner – all quite business-like – read Miranda from a laminated card.

The X.L.'s converged from their table. The one with the dotted-line Kennedy relationship brandished it like Excalibur.

"Why don't you gentlemen ride along and file complaints," said the tall agent, jockeying Elliott away from the pool. "Answer some questions while you're at it."

The shorter agent re-drew the Miranda card from his shirt pocket, but halted. "Wait a sec, Mike ... do we have paper on these guys yet?"

"Not yet."

"Gotcha." He put away the Miranda card and said to the investors, "Just a ride-along. Friendly like. We'll let you work the siren. Buy you ice cream cones. Just guys together. Making complaints, answering friendly questions ... whatever."

The investors huddled, turned indignantly to exit, and realized they were stranded.

"Don't fret," Connolly said. "I'm sure Elliott's driver will drop you."

Producing cell phones, the investors punched speed-dial buttons and disappeared into the house.

"May I tell my wife?" asked Elliott.

"Sure," said the short agent. "Maybe she'd like to come with?"

"She had nothing to do with this!" Elliott blurted. Regaining his composure, he said, "Besides. It's early yet. She may still make the curtain." He tugged against the cuffs. "Would someone press the intercom for me, please? Master bedroom."

Connolly pressed a button on an intercom beside the pool chair.

"I said *later*, Elliott!"

"The FBI is here. I've been arrested."

Silence.

"Call Terry."

"Is that all?"

"Yes. That's all."

Preferring the illusion of choice over the agent's manhandling, Elliott stepped forward, but stopped. "You're a businessman," he said, his back to Connolly. "What sense does this make? You were in the clear. Why would you do it?"

"Why would I make good McDanald Bonds? C'mon, Elliott, that's a question for the X.L. generation. *You're* old enough to know the answer."

Elliott looked down as if to study the ancient bedrock pavers beneath his feet. The answer came to him in a voice he remembered, although, probably, his father had never spoken the exact words. "Because they have your name on them," he said.

"Take a coat, if you like, Mr. Kreisler," said the shorter agent.

"It's ninety degrees. Why would I need a coat?"

"Photographers," the agent said, gripping the handcuff chain to usher Elliott into the house. "You guys always like to cover your faces."

The terrace erupted in noisy anarchy. Connolly raised his hands.

"Alright, alright. My little show is over, but now there's work to do. If I'm to save us, we need to trust each other. I'll lay it all out at the meeting tomorrow. Plan on a *long* day."

"Then let's eat, Mac," bellowed the Portland executive. "We're starved."

"Are you fixing to treat, Stan? Elliott thinks I'm overdrawn."

"We'll all chip in," someone shouted as the executives trooped away, chattering.

Freddie, the loud-mouth, tried to blend into the crowd, but Connolly culled him by the collar.

"I ... I just had one too many, Mac. It was the—"

"A man who troubles his own house reaps the whirlwind, Freddie. Call the number on your insurance card. Call tonight, hear me?" He nudged Freddie forward. "Hey, wait up, folks! I gave away my ride. Me and Freddie need a lift!"

"Ride with me," said an executive.

"That's a deal!" said Connolly, striding quickly to the front of the pack. "Only ... say, how about you let *me* drive?"

* * * * *

In the fluid midnight beyond the glow of Elliott's pool, an autumn storm was rising. Wind moaned. Trees rustled. Branches creaked and cracked. Dry, copper-colored leaves whirled and skittered in whispers across the stone terrace and strewed the pool like pennies tossed on a glass table.

Alone on the terrace, reclining in his deck chair, Elliott watched the luminous, wind-troubled water stripe the big house with undulant reflections – incandescent ribbons that swayed, fluttered, and disappeared. Ephemeral, he thought, contemplating yet another martini as he nibbled a skewered olive.

A solitary shadow crossed and re-crossed the single lighted window of the big house, the master bedroom window. Elliott closed his eyes. The wind sang with the sound of garbled voices. Fingers of light and shadow played across his eyelids. He imagined the frigid caress of the pool, clear and autumn-icy, numbing like a Martini.

"Are you coming to bed?" blurted the intercom.

Reluctantly Elliott opened his eyes.

"Soon," he said, as if talking to himself.

"You're at the pool."

"I am."

"And you're drunk."

"Am I?"

"I won't have you shorting that thing out. I don't want the police fishing you from the pool, Elliott. Not again."

Elliott stared at the transponder fixed to his ankle. A tiny green light proclaimed that he was where he should be and all was right.

"I don't swim, dear."

"Come to bed," said the intercom.

"Everything in due time."

Across the pool accumulating leaves along the infinity edge spoiled Elliott's illusion. A single splash would push the dead leaves over the infinite edge into darkness. One large splash, Elliott thought, peering at the iridescent fingers beckoning deep in the crystal water.

Standing on wobbly legs, he teetered at the edge of the pool, but noticed the empty glass in his hand and considered his options. This was not the night for a swim, he decided, lurching toward the bar. Not with trials yet. And appeals yet. And motions and judgments and voir dires and demurs yet.

Not with years, yet. Years and years.

In the big house.

WebCrawler

After Smurfit-Stone shuttered the box mill, the Ontonagon Diner went from 24/7 to breakfast and lunch, weekdays only. Come midnights when I closed the bar, the closest hot meal was ten miles south – a crossroad, truck stop near Greenland that tapped both M26 traffic through the Keweenaw Peninsula and the east-west dribble from Marquette. The truck stop was where I first saw Clarence.

A pasty little fellow, still in his teens, he sat ensconced in a back booth with his laptop. He was short and oval, almost round, his heft hard to figure since he was a constant flurry of movement. Despite the confines of the booth, he seemed to go eight directions at once. His knees jounced, his toes tapped the floor, his butt slid over the bench seat like a shuffleboard puck. When his fingers weren't clickity-clicking the keyboard, one hand flicked at an ever-falling lock of stringy black hair while his other hand zigzagged a portable mouse as if goading it through a maze. And then suddenly, with a strange, noiseless, patient focus, he would freeze.

As if waiting.

After a few nights, I realized that he was a regular, too, but I kept quiet. His averted stare was like a *do not disturb* sign on a closed door, a plea for privacy. His wild hair, crude tee-shirts, grubby black Levis and worn-out, never run running-shoes struck me similarly. The grunge, intended or not, was like the distinctive colors and patterns of some creatures that warn *stay away* or *not good eating*. Naturally, he was always alone. And that made him interesting.

I've heard great men described as always alone and never lonely, or conversely as never alone and always lonely, but I see greatness as a compensation for its personal toll. Those who are never alone and never lonely are undoubtedly normal and as happy as the next guy. Which leaves those who are always alone and always lonely. I imagined Clarence in that lot – one of the sad ones. Often that sadness stems from some *sine qua non* lost or never attained; the lack of someone or something without which one is not. We in that group are unhappy in singular ways. Extruded into the abhorred vacuum of that missing piece, we are shaped in its mold – a unique casting, sometimes grotesque and sometimes beautiful. For Clarence that question was not yet answered.

Usually he was still there when I left, but one night he didn't show and Connie, the gossipy waitress, shared what she thought she knew about him. His name was Clarence Dodson. He had recently moved to town for an afternoon job as an internet service tech with Peninsula Phone. He came in most weeknights a little after midnight and often sat 3 or 4 hours. She volunteered his unvarying diet with the air of a haruspex divining some eternal truth from five well-fried eggs, a double portion of hash-browns, and four slices of untoasted, white bread with extra butter and strawberry jam.

"No meat," she said with a telling nod.

Obviously Clarence talked *sometimes*. And given the biography, it was hard to consider him a stranger. The following night I smiled across the space between our booths.

"A couple of regulars," I said. "Marlow's the name."

He continued to look down as if ignoring me, but after a moment, he muttered, "Clarence."

That was it.

Next afternoon, a phone company installer came to hook-up a new computer system a telemarketer had guaranteed would catapult my bar into the 21st Century although, frankly, the Upper Peninsula was quite content with another time. The installer turned out to be Clarence.

I greeted him by name. He seemed pleased by the recognition, but avoided my eyes and was flustered when I tried to shake hands.

"I … I, uh … it's hard for me to touch people. It's … it's not *you*, honest. It's me. Just me."

"Fewer hitchhiking germs is good for everybody," I said.

"I don't sweat germs," he said off-handedly. And then, freakishly, he locked on my eyes and intoned, "How is your family and your job?"

"Uh ... *fine?*" I said.

"Good. I'll do my work now."

I gathered that he preferred to work in silence, but it was Tuesday afternoon, the bar was empty, and I'm old enough that computers baffle me. I kept asking questions.

"What's your name again?" he said finally.

I repeated it.

"You're *really* stupid, Mr. Marlow."

"That about nails it."

He paused a moment, as if replaying the conversation.

"Stupid about *computers*. You don't know much about them is all I meant, but I use wrong words a lot. That's what they say anyway."

"Who's *they?*"

"Doctors. They say I'm Asperger's."

"That's like autism or something, isn't it? The genius' disease. What's his name, that billionaire computer guy, he had it."

"I'm no genius, Mr. Marlow. I'm just backward. They say my talk is weird; that I focus on weird stuff. No social skills, they say, whatever that means. I guess it means using wrong words with people. I don't mean to do that; I just don't *relate* to people." He shrugged. "Relate ... that's another doctor word."

"You don't *like* people?"

"*Like* people?" He frowned. "Communication is so hard. I *like* hash browns. Does *like people* mean they're the same as hash browns to me? ... I just don't *get* people. A computer is easy. Programs use simple words that mean one clear thing. If you read the program, you know exactly what a computer will do. Every time. Always the *right* thing. But people? ... No telling. It's less confusing to keep to myself."

"Sounds lonely though," I said.

"I don't ... *think* so, but maybe I don't know what that means either. I know I wish I wasn't alone all the time."

I regretted making him struggle, so I apologized and said I'd let him get back to his work.

"No, listen, it's okay. I'm paid by the job, not the hour, so I'm not stealing from the company. I know I need to talk more, work on my social skills, but not many people talk to me, or when they do, they stop pretty fast. I guess I can't blame them if I'm weird, but it sure makes it hard to learn what's what when people don't notice you or talk. You're different. Are you Asperger's?"

"I ... I don't *think* so."

"Really? Because I don't see people remembering my name much and the way you kept blabbing away was pretty weird, too." He pondered something. "Look. We're both dumb, but about different stuff. I could learn social skills talking to you, and you could learn computers from me, so how about we bargain. Nights at the diner, I'll teach you."

"Well, uh ... sure," I said, "I couldn't pay you much."

"Even trade," he said. "I don't sweat money."

"Okay, deal," I said. I started to shake his hand, but refrained.

"That's social skills, isn't it?" he said thoughtfully.

* * * * *

The following night when I entered the diner, Clarence sat typing and pretended not to see me.

"Hi, Clarence," I said, walking up to his booth. "Is school in session?"

He glanced at his watch and then looked out the window as if to confirm.

"It's nighttime. Schools are closed."

Clarence, I discovered, could be quite concrete.

"Our lessons? You teach me about computers? Our bargain, remember?"

"I have an excellent memory."

"So ... ?"

"What?"

"May I sit down?"

"Not on this side," he said.

I slid onto the opposite bench. Connie brought Clarence his eggs, bread and potatoes.

"Are you a vegetarian, Clarence?"

"Why?"

"Your plate. Just wondering if what I eat might bother you."

"Why would I care what you eat? And why would you care if I did?"

"Coffee, two scrambled and hash-browns, Connie. No toast," I said.

She ambled back to the counter, barked my order through the serving window, and returned to drop off a steaming, white mug of coffee and a stainless steel pitcher of cream.

"First lesson, Clarence. We don't *have* to care, but being considerate of others is one of those *social* skills."

"Considerate of what? I just don't eat meat."

"But I do. I wondered if someone eating a steak would make you angry or sad or sick to your stomach."

"I don't sweat it."

"So now I know. People don't *want* to hurt each other."

"That's not true."

"It was true just now."

"… Okay … Okay, I see," he said thoughtfully. "But not *all* people. Some people know they're hurting you and do it anyway."

"Those people are rare."

He looked skeptical.

"Do you play the lottery much, Clarence?"

"It's stupid. You lose."

"You lose even more betting that most people want to hurt you."

He considered that, too.

"This is exactly what I meant," he said. "So, okay, we'll talk for one hour. We began …" He looked at his watch. "12:42. We'll stop at 1:42 tonight and then you'll have to sit somewhere else. I have things to do. I'll start basic since you're really … uh, really *new* to this."

I smiled.

"Hardware first," he said. "Then warez."

"I don't know that word."

"You wouldn't. Mostly it means programs – instructions that tell the hardware what to do. Finally, we'll cover communication. That's the hardest part."

I liked the curriculum already. Brain, mind, and other minds was how it struck me, but I kept that to myself since I doubted Clarence was a fan of metaphor.

* * * * *

Over several nights, he taught me that a computer, like a brain, is a machine hardwired to take in, store, work on, and communicate information. It *senses* the information through a keyboard, a mouse, a camera, a scanner, or reads it from a disc or a drive. Communication ports allow an electronic back-and-forth between the computer and accessories like a printer, speakers, a monitor, and even other computers.

The brain cells of the computer are microscopic, electronic circuits on silicon chips. Okay ... Silicon Valley ... that made sense. Clarence launched into a disquisition about the properties of silicon.

"Do I need to know this part?"

"No," he said.

Apparently the chips contain billions of transistors. I had to take his word for that. As a kid I had a six transistor radio the size of a paperback book. I remember the stir when Sony came out with a 12-transistor radio twice as big.

I knew what transistors *looked* like – the ones in old radios, anyway – although what they *did* was a mystery. According to Clarence, they were electronic switches, but how six or twelve switches let me listen to a Tiger game was even more a mystery.

Some of the chips are hardwired with simple instructions that allow the main chip – the processor – to store, recall and work on information converted to binary numbers. I understood the math – base 2 numbers that use only digits 0 and 1 as opposed to decimal numbers with 0 to 9. And I got the connection with switches – 0, 1 ... off, on. I even saw how a binary decoder ring could store the *words* of *Les Miserables* as 10010101010101011 *ad infinitum*. But how could things we see and hear, a picture or a song, for instance, be numbers?

Clarence said that the computer translates 'infinitely continuous analog signals' such as sound and color into discrete, finite signals – very long numbers. A lot is lost in translation, but what's left is apparently good enough. I could have said the same about Clarence's explanation. His details were pretty much Greek, but I realized that the brain does the same thing. A child sees a man – so infinite in faculty – but can store only so much in some shorthand fashion. He digitizes the man, so to speak, abstracts him, stores him as a stick figure. Over time experience refines the abstraction. Stick figures become Vermeers, or in my case, more detailed stick figures, but either way the translation is good enough.

It's exciting to glimpse the mysterious in a better light. It's like peeking beneath a veil. I was eager for the next lesson and disappointed when Clarence wasn't there the following night. I hoped he wasn't sick, but I had no easy way to check. When I saw him again, I asked if he'd been okay.

"I told you I'm working on something."

"What?" I said.

"I don't have to tell you that."

"Okay. I can take a hint," I said.

"I'm not giving you a hint. I don't want you to know."

"I don't need to know, Clarence. What you do is *your* business. But friends can *reach* each other if they want to. I was worried you might be sick."

"Don't sweat it."

"Concern is hardwired in friends."

"Friends ..." he said, pondering it as if parsing the word. He took a phone company business card from a tee-shirt pocket and wrote a number and address on the back. "Does this make us friends?"

I chuckled.

"You're laughing at me."

"I'm not, Clarence. Honest, I'm not. It's just ironic how our lessons overlap."

"I don't understand."

"Digital and analog ... See, a phone number is a digital part of being a friend. Yes or no. You have it or you don't. It's a requirement. There are lots of those."

"Social skills," he said.

"Sure. Call them social skills. Digital checkboxes. Certain checks, a certain number of checks, are necessary for friendship, but not *sufficient.* Another part is analog – like hearing or seeing. How you *feel* about the other person? Do you *like* him?"

He grimaced. "I told you. *Like* is like hash browns to me."

"Fine. Take your hash browns then."

He looked at his plate. "Where?"

"*Consider* your hashbrowns. Would you trade your hashbrowns for a steak."

"No."

"Because, know it or not, you give things a score. You prefer, you choose … you *like* things with a higher score over a lower score. Single things or groups of things. Hashbrowns over steak. Vegetables over meat. Same for people. Would you trade seeing me for a plate of hashbrowns? I don't mean if you were starving or for all the hashbrowns in the world. I mean right now. One plate of hashbrowns. Me or the hashbrowns?"

He stared at his plate for a second. "I wouldn't sweat the hashbrowns."

"That's *liking* me. I get a higher score than some things, lower than others."

"Okay … okay, I understand," he said, nodding slowly. "But these scores. Where do they come from?"

"It's like a program, I guess, mostly automatic. The easy part is digital. Those checkboxes. A person smiles at you … check! Knows your name … check!"

"Asks about your family and your job," he said excitedly. "The doctors said that was important. Always ask about family and job so people will like you."

"You got it! That's a check, too. The program sums the checks, but *between* the checkboxes are an infinity of analog points that also add up. Personal points. Things important to you and no one else. Things you don't even know you know."

"So … I might not know exactly *why* I'd pick someone over hashbrowns, but I know I *would.*"

"And *some* people you'd pick over a whole lot of things. Those are friends. If you're lucky, you find a few people you wouldn't trade for anything. *Best* friends."

"Do *you* have a best friend?"

"I used to. A long time ago. He died. I don't talk about it much."

"You *can.* I won't sweat it."

"Thanks, Clarence. Another time."

"Well … do you have *any* friends?"

"At least one, I think."

"Do you wish you weren't alone so much?"

"All the time."

"Are you *sure* you're not Asperger's?"

"I'm just backward," I said with a smile.

He sat silently for a long time. I pictured the little spinning clock on a computer screen.

"Okay, I think I get it. And something else, too. No matter the list, the rules, the social skills, if someone trades you for something unimportant like a single plate of hashbrowns, you know he's only *pretending* to like you. You know he's not really a friend at all."

"You *do* get it. That's true."

"It's a Turing Test!" he beamed.

"I don't know what that is."

"Another time, Mr. ... what do friends call you?"

"Just Marlow, I guess."

"Another time, Marlow."

* * * * *

Over the next few weeks my teacher was a frequent no-show. I asked Clarence jokingly if things were okay with the job and family, but he seemed upset and told me not to sweat it. Slower going, I nevertheless learned that a computer is really two parts: hardware and software; the machine itself and programs. The hardware is just a counting engine that crunches binary numbers with a few simple operations such as *plus, minus, divide, times, AND, OR, NOT*. But if everything you need know – truth and beauty and a slew of instructions for handling binary numbers – is translated *into* binary numbers, a computer can do almost anything just by performing the right sequence of simple operations incredibly fast. The hardware is an amazing brain. It can balance a checkbook or guide a spaceship to the moon and back. But, actually, the brain is pretty stupid because it doesn't *know* to do either. Programs are the brain's *mind.*

Programs are instructions that tell the hardware to combine those few, simple operations in ever more complex routines that accomplish specific tasks. And programs need not be hardwired – they can be read from software if and when needed. Consequently, computers aren't limited to their birthright. They're all the same, but each one is different because they *learn*.

The night after Clarence's third no-show, he sat silently. I tried to make conversation to keep up my end of our barter.

"How'd you get interested in computers, Clarence?"

"Why?"

"Just being social."

"My father," he said, nudging the mouse for his laptop and tapping a key. "He was a fourth grade teacher in Toledo. He owned a computer, mainly for the internet, but he had games that gave us something to do together. We were alone. My mother was dead."

"Oh, I'm sorry."

"You didn't do anything."

"Yes … that's true."

"He taught me what he knew, but he didn't know much, and he always said teaching was a bother. I got excited about computers, though, so I talked to a smart neighbor. He gave me lessons like these."

"How old were you?"

"Nine."

"Not bad for nine. Is your Dad still around?"

"Around where?"

"Is he still alive?"

"Yes."

I waited for more but he just stared at me.

"Okay," I said, to break the silence. "We were going to tackle communication, right? The hardest part?"

Nodding agreement, he retrieved a second laptop from his bench seat.

"This is for you. I don't use it anymore."

"Gee. I, uh … don't know. How much do you want for it?"

"Nothing."

"I couldn't accept that, Clarence."

"I don't sweat money."

"So you've said … Genius disease or not, you didn't get the billionaire strain."

"You're making a joke, aren't you?"

I nodded. He laughed robotically.

Social skills.

"Okay," he said, swiveling his own computer so we could both see the screen. "If paying is important to you, let's see what it's worth. I'll make it part of the lesson. Mostly computers communicate through wires, but some can transmit and receive information by radio."

"Like a cellphone?"

"That's extra," he said as he typed. "Regular wireless is short range, about 50 yards. The computer communicates with a nearby hub, a router, that's linked by cable or a phone line to an internet service provider like Peninsula Phone. The diner has a free wireless hub."

"Is that why you spend so much time here?"

"I buy a meal."

"It wasn't a criticism, Clarence. I just meant, people get internet at home, right?"

He looked around, leaned closer and lowered his voice. "Everything that connects to the internet has an address that's visible to every site it visits. The address doesn't reveal *much* about you, but it does tell your whereabouts." He pointed to his screen, a sidebar ad for Peninsula phone. "E-Bay isn't posting that ad to people in Toledo."

"Get out!"

"Exactly. E-Bay knows where I am. Guy in Toledo gets a Toledo ad."

"That's scary."

"And sites put bugs on your computer. Tracking cookies. Your address is followed wherever it goes, linked to everything you look at. Say I Googled tire prices last night. Today this ad might be a coupon for Ontonagon Firestone."

"Like Big Brother."

"I never had a brother. Do they follow you around?"

"It's just a figure of speech."

"I don't get it ... Anyway, if you use computers at all, it's hard to hide unless you're really smart. Me, I block all the tracking cookies. And as far an address, all E-bay knows is the diner's address because it's the diner's router connecting to the web."

"So you're *invisible* here."

"It's not foolproof, but I have other tricks, too."

"Do *I* need to be invisible?"

"It depends on what you're—" He paused. "It depends on your *brother*," he said finally.

"Good one!" I said.

He almost blushed.

"Okay, so here's the same laptop on e-Bay."

I scanned the screen. "Looks like they go for around $100. That's not too bad."

"I'll let you have this one for $145."

"Really?! ... How come?"

"You know it works. I've put programs on it for you. No shipping. No waiting. Up to you."

"You might be a billionaire yet, Clarence."

"Or I'll still just give it to you. Either way."

"Then maybe not," I said. "Okay, deal."

He turned on my new computer and positioned it so we could see both screens.

"If you sell or give away or even trash a computer, you should always wipe the drive clean."

"Delete your personal stuff."

"More than that. See, a computer needs to retrace its steps sometimes, so everything it does – every file, picture, website, keystroke – is stored in hidden files you don't know to delete. They're simple to find, though. A kid could do it."

"So?"

"So people have secrets."

"Like social security numbers."

"Sure. Social security numbers," he said flatly. "I wiped this one clean and installed a new Linux operating system and a Firefox browser. Those are freeware – software you don't have to pay for, but some is good enough for most things. I also loaded calendar, wireless, text and image programs and set up a free email account for you." He slid a paper printout across the booth. "Here's the details."

I scanned the page.

"Wow," I said. "I'm a netizen."

"You ought not to say that, Marlow."

"Why?"

"You sound stupid."

"A word for the unwise," I laughed.

"You can get other programs for special purposes. Taxes, accounting. Almost anything. It's probably best to buy them unless you're sure about a freeware package, but some people download pirated stuff."

"Pirated? ... Like pirated music and movies? That's stealing, Clarence. It's wrong."

He nodded. "Something else I don't get about people. How can they do wrong things?"

"Socrates said you can't know wrong and do it, but people sure seem to, don't they?"

"But *how*?" he said.

"*Anti*-social skills, I guess."

He frowned as if he were trying to force his mind around the words.

"That's a ... what did you call it? ... a figure of speech? Yeah! Okay, I think I get this one."

He spent the rest of the hour talking about the web, browsers, and search engines. He said browsers are programs that convert the language of the web into pictures and pictures of words.

"But watch out. Browsers can fool you," he said. "The pictures and pictures of words don't look or act exactly the same on different systems. Plus, your computer stores a copy of each page you look at. Unless you've told the browser to refresh the page each time you go back or do it manually, the browser doesn't even look on the web. It just displays the copy on your computer. The real page might have changed or even disappeared and you'd never know."

"Wow. Lessons in both our curricula," I said. "People experience things differently, too."

"I always thought so. Some things freak me out when they're fine for other people. Like ... like velvet! The feel of velvet is like hot grease splashed on my skin. No one understands."

"For me it's fingernails on a blackboard."

"Really? I don't sweat that."

"Different strokes," I said.

"No matter how I stroke it."

"You're lucky then, Clarence. It's a horrible feeling. And that refresh thing is part of the human condition. Memories are hard to let go. We get stuck in the past."

"F5," Clarence said.

"What's that?"

"The refresh key. The browser starts fresh."

At the end of the hour – when he always shooed me away to "work on his project" – he squeezed in what turned out to be his last lesson.

"Somewhere on the web is something you're looking for. How do you find it?"

"Google," I said.

"But how does Google find it? How do they catalog a billion pages they don't know exist?"

"Search me," I said, surprised when he smiled.

"Robot programs are sent swarming over the web to digest the pages they find. They go to the links on those pages and the links of the links, on and on. They're out there right now, Marlow. Relentless. Ever searching. Perfectly focused. Prowling like hungry spiders. Webcrawlers, they're called."

The following night he no-showed again, so I spent the time diddling with my new laptop. I Googled myself and found about a million links. I'm not that well documented, of course, so I Googled *how to search on Google* and learned some tricks. When I put quotes around my name to search for the exact phrase, I still had too many results, but adding Saginaw, where I grew up, winnowed it to a page and a half. One link even referred to me – a squib about my medivac stateside from 'Nam. I didn't relish resurrecting those years, so I skipped it. Typing Ontonagon in place of Saginaw fetched a single link that I did click: a front page story the Gazette ran when I bought the bar. Even a *picture*. I felt like a Kardashian!

I studied my picture, as people do. More hair back then and it wasn't gray, although the eyes were the same, or rather something *about* the eyes was the same. The internet isn't true, but I guess it's something *like* the truth and what you make of it is up to you.

Not ready to head home, I Googled Clarence Dodson in quotes and, remembering that he'd said his father was a grade school teacher in Toledo, I added Toledo. I thought I might have fun with an old yearbook picture of him or maybe some blurb about a science fair project. I found a half-dozen links: an old, front page Toledo *Blade* headline and follow-up stories farther and farther apart, deeper and deeper in the paper.

District Teacher Sought in Rape of Son, 9

* * * * *

Closing up the bar the next night, I weighed going straight home. How do you tell someone you uncovered an intimate secret? How do you face them if you keep that secret secret? Or can you even do that? Wouldn't it show? I doubted that Emily Post had an answer. Such manners were unneeded until privacy was trapped in the web and devoured. I kicked myself for hesitating, climbed in my car, and made the long trip to the diner.

Clarence was settled in his booth. He smiled when he saw me – a social skill he'd been perfecting – although for once he actually looked *happy*. I worried my own expression would betray me, but knew that reading faces wasn't Clarence's forte.

"Something wrong?" he said, as I sat down.

"Why do you say that?"

"I dunno. It's weird … All these nights sitting, talking, studying you, it's like sometimes I can see what you're … not *thinking*, not like words or anything. Something else."

"What I'm feeling."

"… Feelings … I know that means something to *you*, Marlow, you say it all the time. But to me …?"

The waitress brought two plates.

"I ordered for you," Clarence said. "You always eat the same thing."

"You do, too."

"Peas in a pox," he said. "Isn't that what they say? Peas in a pox? I never got it, though."

"Peas in a *pod*. It means similar. Peas grow together inside a shell, a pod, and they all look the same."

"Well, I don't get that at all," he scoffed. "It's just not *true*. Every pea is different. You never noticed that?"

"I guess I missed it."

"You should pay more attention."

We ate for a while in silence. The waitress brought milk for Clarence and coffee for me.

"Okay, Marlow ... These *feelings*. They're *inside*, right? In your brain, in your mind. So how am I supposed to see *that*? X-ray vision?"

I seized on the distraction hoping to run out the clock.

"Sure. Feelings have a part you *can't* see, but also one you *can*. Like an iceberg."

"I've never seen an iceberg."

I sighed. "Okay, well, uh ... take houses then. *Consider* houses," I added quickly. "Those small windows just above the ground. What are they?"

"Basement windows."

"Now pretend that—"

"I don't get *pretend*. Never did."

"How about *what if*? Can you do what if?"

"I dunno. What if what?"

"What if you peeked inside one of those windows? What would you see?"

"I don't peek in windows. It's wrong."

"*What if*, Clarence. What if you did? What would you see?"

"A basement."

"Voila!"

"Is that a word? I don't know that word."

"It's French."

"Why would you say it then?"

"Stupid on my part," I said.

He nodded.

"My point is, you can't see the basement from the street, just the windows. But you know the basement is there. How?"

"*My* house had those windows."

"Exactly. You've been in basements. You know what those windows *mean*."

"So?"

"So you've also had every feeling anyone else ever had."

He took two bites from a triangle of white bread and chewed silently. "You're saying I can see something on the outside of people that tells me there's something inside I know about. So what do I see? *Please* don't say windows."

"Touch your milk," I said.

"More windows," he grumbled.

"We're both struggling here, Clarence. Do it."

He touched the glass.

"What do you feel?"

"The glass."

"What does it feel like."

"A glass."

"What else?"

"Cold."

"Now what if you looked away for a second and I filled your glass with boiling water?"

"You wouldn't do that."

"*What if*, Clarence? What if I did and you touched the glass again?"

"It would burn me."

"*Pain.* A feeling on the inside. Just you. *I* couldn't feel it. But you would wince. Maybe drop the glass. Maybe yelp or swear."

"I don't swear. It's wrong."

"But you'd do *something*, right? Something I could see and hear. Something I'd remember doing when *I* was burned."

"I know when people are burned, Marlow. I'm not stupid about *that*."

"Great. But sometimes the cause of feelings is less obvious. Not just physical pain like a burn, but something that causes a pain in your mind that's just as real as a burn – maybe worse because it's harder to refresh." I realized suddenly how close I was to what I had hoped to avoid. "Or something *good* happens," I said quickly. "Your face changes. Your voice changes. You smile, you're energetic. People see that and recognize those signs as *happy* because they know happy in themselves. They respond in the way they hope people respond to them. Social skills."

"I'll have to think some on it," he said.

We sat silently for a moment. Leery of his new spidey senses, I found myself avoiding his eyes and decided to confess because ... well, because *not* confessing was wrong.

"So, uh ... listen, Clarence. I missed you again last night," I began. I didn't expect an explanation. He hadn't offered much of one yet.

"I finished my project."

"Oh!" I said. "You never told me what that was."

"I've been searching for someone," he said matter-of-factly. "On the internet. For nine years. I finally narrowed down his location to the Keweenaw Peninsula, but that was as close as I could get. I took my job with the phone company to see records and finally found him. Last night. He was living in Copper Harbor. A fisherman of all things. He *hated* fish."

"Your ... your father?"

"He's gone now," he said indifferently, but he halted, puzzled. "How did you know?"

"I was practicing with my laptop last night. I Googled your name and Toledo. I wasn't snooping. *Honest.*"

"You saw those stories?"

I nodded.

"You probably want to sit in another booth now. I'm sorry about that. I wouldn't trade our time together for several tons of hash browns."

"Back up, Clarence."

He glanced at the wall behind him.

"I mean hold on, wait a minute ... You think I'll dislike *you*? For something horrible *he* did? That's ludicrous. No. No, of course not. It wasn't *your* fault."

"People always said that. The Police. Doctors. Social Service. But it's hard for me to know for sure. See, when he did that thing to me, he kept calling me a bad name."

He turned and waved to the waitress. "Another glass of milk, please. And you want coffee, don't you?" he said to me. "You usually have *two* cups."

"Uh ... sure. Coffee," I mumbled.

"And coffee for my friend, Marlow," he said cheerfully.

"Listen, Clarence, you don't have to talk about this, you know?"

"You'd sweat it?"

"No, no. I'll listen. But ... if you're uncomfortable or anything ... I mean, you don't know me that well."

"I know you better than anyone, Marlow."

The waitress brought the beverages.

"You didn't put boiling water in my glass, did you?" Clarence said to her.

"Do you want some?"

"Of course, not. I'm making a joke."

"Oh," she said, walking away.

Clarence looked perplexed.

"Some people have no sense of humor," I said.

He nodded, took a long drink, and began.

"My father knew I was stupid, he told me often enough. I didn't get why it bothered him, though, since it was *my* problem, not his. One thing he complained about was having to talk to my teachers all the time. He said it was hard because *he* was a teacher. I thought it should be easier, but he punished me if I said that.

"My mother died ... I don't know when. I never met her that I remember. I didn't blame her for dying, but I think she ran away before that, and the running away part was wrong. My father and I were quite close, though. Isn't that what people say? Close?" He shrugged. "We didn't sit together much; we didn't touch a lot. Still ...he let me live in his house. That was *very* close. He bought me food, too. I don't know what I would have done without food. I was hungry all the time. He never bought meat though. He used to make a spitting sound and say, 'eating meat is like eating pussy.' He was always saying weird things I didn't get. I mean ... *no* one eats cats, right? Nevertheless, it grossed me out.

"As I got older, my stupidity bothered him more and more. He shouted at silly things. *Put on your robe. Pull up your pants. Zip your zipper. Close the bathroom door.* The only good times were times he was teaching me about his computer or when we were playing games on it. I think those were good times because I wasn't stupid about the computer. I seemed to understand it, right from the first.

"Sundays he always slept late while I dressed for church, fixed my breakfast, and played games on his computer. This one time, however, I was interested in the computer itself. That smart neighbor had showed me how to use Windows Explorer to find things like the web history file. The site names I saw were confusing. Some were even swear words! I could have clicked on the sites, but wasn't allowed to use the internet by myself.

"A simple trick hides things on the computer, but the neighbor had taught me the trick and I found some hidden folders. I wondered why my father would hide things on his own computer? We were the only ones who used it."

Clarence shook his head. "See, Marlow? I was smart about computers, but not people. I didn't understand secrets, so I looked."

"Pictures," I said.

"You know about hidden folders?"

"Just secrets," I said.

"The pictures were boys like me. All my age. I didn't recognize anyone and wondered why my father would have pictures of people he didn't know. The boys were naked, too, which was also strange. I had never seen pictures of naked people. They were in weird positions. Some were doing things to themselves I didn't understand at all … with their *thingy* or their butt. Some pictures showed two or three or four naked boys hugging or *touching* each other. It looked quite horrible to me. And then I saw pictures of old men doing things with the boys."

"Your father?"

"No. I didn't see him in the pictures and doubted he would join in. After all, he touched *me* only when he had to – nothing like a hug or even a handshake. And if he saw me in my underwear or naked in the shower, it just made him mad. I remember thinking, however, that maybe the boys in the pictures were more attractive in some way, in whatever way made men want to touch boys like the men in the pictures did. After all, I was pretty fat and probably looked stupid."

"Did you tell anyone? That neighbor? A teacher?"

"I don't think I would have. My father must've hidden the pictures so no one would know he looked at them. And why should I sweat what he looked at? Some people like pictures of flowers or sunsets or even cats. I don't sweat pictures. He found me looking at them, though, so it didn't matter."

"What … what did you say?"

"I said, 'Look, Dad. I found your hidden pictures!' I wanted him to know I was smart about computers."

His voice cracked at the end. He swallowed a gulp of milk.

"My father said, 'Funny!' Actually he yelled. It made me jump. He wasn't laughing either, which seemed odd if something was funny. 'Do you like these pictures?' he said. 'How long have you been sneaking in here to look at them? You like them, don't you? You touch yourself when you look at them. You *do*. I know you do.'"

"He meant me, I suppose ... it was just the two of us. But he wasn't looking at me. No *eye-contact* ... That's what the doctors would have said. You lose points for no eye contact. It's an important social skill."

"'Look at the screen. LOOK AT IT!' he shouted. 'Do you do this with your friends? Do you all get together and wallow around like pigs?' What an odd thing to say. He *knew* I had no friends. 'Scroll through the pictures. LOOK at them!' I did, of course, because he was so loud, but what was the point? I mean, I'd seen them already."

"He was shaking his fists and stamping back and forth between the desk and the doorway. I kept thinking he would leave and dress for church, especially when his robe fell open. I had seen his *thingy* before, but I was surprised by how big and straight it was. The same happened to me some mornings, though, so I didn't sweat it much. I thought he had to pee."

"'Why are you in your underwear?' he said suddenly, shaking his fist. 'I've warned you about prancing around half naked, but you don't listen, do you? You'd rather show off.'"

"Were you scared?" I said.

"Like at thunder? ... No. No, I don't think so. He was loud, but he *was* my father. I just thought I was stupid for not understanding. That maybe we would play a game now. On the computer. I would sit on his lap and we would play a game."

"'This one!' he said, ripping the mouse from my hand. The picture on the screen was a naked old man lying on the back of a little naked boy. 'This is your favorite, isn't it?' My father's face was all sweaty. He couldn't take his eyes off the monitor. 'You *like* this, don't you?'"

"'No, it's wrong,' I said. 'The boy is crying. The man is way too heavy; he's hurting him. The boy should be on top.'"

"That must've been a really, *really* stupid thing to say because he hit me like he never had before – right in the face with his fist like bad men do on T.V. I saw a big flash and then I was looking up from the floor at the ceiling. I felt all floppy and woozy, almost as if I wasn't there, but watching from somewhere else. That sounds goofy, I guess. You probably don't understand."

"I do. I know *exactly* what you're talking about. I've been hit like that, too."

"That's good!" he said, but added hastily, "Not good you were *hit*. Good that you *know*." He paused a moment. "You read those stories, but … do you know what he did? I don't know what other people know about such things. The police, the doctors, social services, they all wanted me to talk about it, and I told them, but … it was so *weird*. I never thought they knew. Not really. How could they? I never thought anyone knew."

"So why don't you tell *me* until you *know* someone knows."

"Well … like I said, I was woozy, but I *do* remember. I have an excellent memory. He knelt down and yanked at my underwear. I tried to help him, but I was all floppy. He got mad and ripped them off. He rolled me onto my back and pinched my thingy between his fingers. He squeezed it and tugged it and started to swear, so I knew I wasn't doing something right. Then he put his mouth over it. Do you do that, Marlow?"

"No, uh … not that *particular* thing."

"I don't sweat it if you do. I mean, as long as you don't hit the other person; as long as you ask and it's okay. I just wondered if you knew *why* a person would do that, cause I don't get it."

It was an awkward place to have a talk about the birds and the *beasts*, but the diner was empty and Connie was in the kitchen.

"Okay, okay … first of all, no one should do anything like that to a child. Asking is irrelevant. You don't touch a child like that. At all. Ever. No reasons, no excuses. It's wrong. Just plain wrong."

"Yeah … I always thought so."

"But grown-ups together are a different story. Asking matters. They can say yes or no. Grownups do all sorts of stuff like that with each other because they want to and, when they want to, it feels good."

"Sex stuff."

"Sex stuff … things people do with their bodies because it feels good. To *them*. Different people, different things. No telling what it might be, because … Well, look at it this way. The *feeling* part isn't zero or one, but the infinity in between. Sex is like an analog game adults make up as they go along. When people are playing the same game, it's fun for them, and, like I said, it feels good."

He thought about it. "Okay … Sure. I've heard boys talk and I've seen movies, so I think I understand it *some*. But it makes it even weirder, Marlow, because it wasn't fun or good for my father at all. He just got madder and madder. He tried to put *his* thingy in *my* mouth and I..I just *couldn't*. He slapped my face over and over. I started to cry, but he slapped me harder, shouting, 'Shut up! Shut up!' as if hurting me would make me stop crying when I was crying because it *hurt*. Why would he think that? It seemed so stupid, which surprised me. I knew he wasn't smart about computers, but I hadn't known how stupid he really was.

"All of this was dragging on and on, Marlow. I knew we'd be late for church unless we hurried. He stopped slapping me and I thought we would dress and go. Instead he rolled me over like a stuffed animal and scooched me onto my knees … like some people pray, you know? He got behind me and squashed my face into the floor with one hand. I couldn't move my head to see and had no idea what to expect since all of it was so strange. I know he put something in my butt. I think it was his thingy, which made no sense at all! He *hurt* me, Marlow. I screamed, "No more. It's good now. That's enough. Please, no more," but he wouldn't *stop*."

Clarence fell silent and suddenly he was staring – not at me, but a thousand yards beyond me. His nostrils flared and he spluttered, "M..my toast is burning!"

"It was, Clarence. Back then when it happened, it *was*. Back then."

"Fire! Fire!"

"F5 Clarence. Refresh, remember. F5."

After a moment, he shook his head sharply and seemed to see *me* again.

"He ground my face into the rug," he said with effort. "That hurt, too, but not as much as the other. He kept hunching into me, growling in my ear, 'You little whore. You little whore. You little whore.' I could tell that a little whore was a *very* bad thing to be. I wasn't sure, however, whether it was bad to be a whore, or just bad to be a *little* one.

"All at once, he oinked like a pig and fell on top of me. I could hardly breathe! I was glad he wasn't hunching anymore, because it hurt less, but it scared me, too. Sometimes on TV people stopped moving like that and they were dead. When I tried to wiggle out from underneath, though, he grabbed my throat with both hands and choked me. The room got dark, but suddenly he let go and jumped to his feet.

"I crawled under the desk and sat up. I was hurting and touched myself behind. I saw blood on my fingers and it scared me. "I'm bleeding, Daddy," I said holding out my hand.

"He slapped the hand away and started to pace again, saying, 'What am I going to do? What do I do?'"

"I didn't know, so I kept quiet. He kept coming back to stand over me. Sometimes he squeezed his fists together. Another time he grabbed a lamp from the desk and raised it over his head, jerking the plug from the socket. That's not safe. It can start a fire. He seemed to freeze for a moment, but something about the lamp made him mad, I guess, because he threw it against the wall and dragged me out from under the desk by my feet. He tied my wrists behind me with the velvet belt from his robe, and then tied the belt to the desk. He hurried out of the room, banged closets and drawers, and came back dressed, carrying a backpack. He seemed rushed, although we'd already missed church. When he bent down, I thought he would untie me, but he merely tugged the belt tighter and ran out the front door.

"'When are you coming back?' I shouted because it was almost lunchtime. I didn't hear an answer."

Clarence was silent again. I waited, but when he said nothing, I asked, "How did you get loose?"

"I was stupid about that. I couldn't see the knots to figure out a way. I squirmed and squirmed, but my fingers fell asleep. After a while the velvet was all wet and sticky and it hurt too much to move my hands. I yelled, but no one came. Crying doesn't help anything, I know, but I couldn't stop. I was so hungry. And *cold*, too. I wasn't used to being naked. All night I wished and wished for a blanket, but wishing is as stupid as crying.

"I was lucky, though. By the next day my voice was just a scratchy peep from yelling, but the postman heard me anyway. And my father had forgotten to lock the front door. How lucky was that?

"The postman untied me and called police, telling me to sit still until they came. For *evidence*, he said. I did at first, but being naked seemed unsafe. Maybe *he* had hidden pictures, too. He followed me when I put on clothes and kept saying *evidence, evidence*, especially when I used the bathroom. I thought he was going to tie me up again!

The stink of burnt toast in the kitchen made me sick, but I was starving. I stood at the counter and ate almost a whole loaf of bread with butter and jam. It helped. A *lot*. The postman stared at me the whole time, but running away was a stupid idea. My father's house was all I knew.

"When policemen came, I knew I was safe because policemen help people. One policeman even gave me gum. They said I would be okay when they left me at the hospital, but those doctors and social workers seemed as weird as the postman. For a while I had to stay in a place with other boys. I think it was jail, because most of them were *very* mean. I never understood why I had to go to jail, but maybe it was because of what my father called me. Finally I lived in foster homes. Some were okay. Sometimes."

"Your father disappeared?"

"What? Like a ghost? No, I don't think he could do *that*. He just ran away so the policemen wouldn't find him."

"But *you* did."

"I'm very smart with computers. And *very* focused."

Clarence pressed the off-switch of his laptop and closed the screen. "I'll miss our lessons, Marlow. I learned a lot. I'm finished here, though. My car is packed. I'm going back to Toledo tonight."

Whatever had happened, I'd hear soon enough, but I thought I owed it to Clarence to hear it from him.

"Listen, Clarence, whatever you did, your father deserved worse, so I don't care *what* it was and I won't say anything. It might be better for *you*, though, if you tell *someone* and I'm probably your best bet."

"Don't sweat my father. He's gone."

"You ... *killed* him?"

"No! I told him he hurt me. That it was wrong for him to hurt me. Wrong for him to run away. I wanted him to know because I never thought he did."

"You told him to his face?"

He nodded. "I made eye contact. That's still hard for me to do, but I'm getting better with social skills."

"You were right there with him? In his house?"

"1622 Superior, Apt B. Copper Harbor. 213-555-1621. Our house in Toledo was much nicer. It had a basement. Even the foster homes were nicer."

"Clarence! He could have *hurt* you."

"Of course. That's why I took police with me. Policemen help people."

"Oh ... I see!" I said. "He's gone with *them*."

"For now. He has to go back to Ohio for a trial and live in prison forever. I asked the policemen if he would be spanked or punished, too. Every day apparently. That's what they said anyway."

"You waited a long time to tell him. Do you think he understood?"

"You know, without realizing it, I think I did what you said earlier ... that thing about watching the outside to see inside? And honestly? ... I don't think a word I said was real to him. I might have been a TV talking in another room – empty sound. The only *feeling* I saw was about the handcuffs. *They* were real enough, probably because they were on *his* wrists. He sweated the handcuffs."

Clarence read my face again.

"Look, it's okay," he said. "Really. I only wanted to tell him because I never had a chance. I didn't expect much from it although not because of what the doctors said."

"What was that?"

"Well ... they talked about him a lot. More than *I* wanted to hear. They said that if I understood him, it would be easier on me somehow. They said he lacked *empathy*. Do you know that word?"

"Feeling what other people feel. Caring about them because they're like you."

"Something like that. The doctors used lots of words no one knew. I wondered why, if communication was the point. Anyway, they went on about Asperger's and how it can run in families. They said I would sleep better if I thought what he did was nothing personal, that he was sick. I think they meant sick like me." He shook his head and snorted. "Talk about lacking empathy! Stuff like that let *them* sleep better. But, hey! ... I don't sweat doctors."

"You think they were wrong?"

"I *know* they were."

He called over the waitress and handed her a hundred dollar bill. "For both of us. The rest is yours."

Clarence's billions were looking more and more a longshot. Connie thanked him and left. I thanked him, too.

"See, Marlow, my father and I were as different as two peas in a pod. I lack social skills. I don't get when people are happy or sad or mad or hurt or scared. But I know they are sometimes. It's like … like, uh … well, take babies."

"Where?" I said.

"Good one," he chuckled. "*Consider* babies. I don't know what they're thinking or feeling or trying to say. I mean, they're pretty stupid, right? But, stupid or not, I know there's *something* inside them, something really special. A *person* inside. Just like me. So even if I can't make sense of them, I wouldn't hurt a baby *ever*. It'd be *wrong*. Because what happens to them *matters* to them. Even stupid people are pretty smart about that part."

He paused for a moment. "Remember asking me about choosing between you and a plate of hashbrowns?"

"Sure. You called it a Turing Test, but you never said what that was."

"It's about telling the difference between a real person and a phony person like a computer program. My father wasn't a real person at all … just a program with anti-social skills. How do I know? He couldn't tell the difference between me and a plate a hashbrowns. But, see, I'm *not* like that. I'm just backward."

He threw a pack over his shoulder and stood.

"I sent you an email," he said. "So you can reach me if you want to."

"Great. Friends can do that."

He stuck out his hand. We shook.

"You're a good person, Clarence."

"You are too, Marlow."

Woman

Outside Mombasa

I stand in a black dress beside the orchid draped coffin of my father. Although the hilltop cemetery overlooks teeming Djakarta, my thoughts escape to Kenya, and I am puzzled. World and time remove this canopied breach in the Djakarta soil from the cobbled pavement of London where my father and I began our journey, a journey upon which Kenya had been but a lay-by. Why, then, would I summon images of roads diverging outside Mombasa? Kenyan Federal Road One, 400 kilometres of gently sloping grassland to Nairobi, a day-traveler's play at safari. And Highway Two – lesser traveled.

Thunder rumbles overhead. Undeterred, the vicar drones mawkishly. Raindrops patter and stream from the scalloped edges of upraised umbrellas gathered beyond the tiny sheltering canopy. The umbrellas – beneath which peek faces of various colours – form a half-circle at my back. The half-circle creates an empty, no-man's land separating me from my father's friends as if the force of my grief repels them to some precise distance determined by physical law. Alone in the no-man's land, I stand head bowed, empty hands folded at my waist. Idle thumbs worry the wedding ring I still wear which, of late, slips from my finger if I am careless. John did not come, of course. Half a world and a year away, his absence meant nothing, however, nothing at all.

I look toward Djakarta's vast harbour which my father called *his* harbour. A path of bent, wet, grass leads from the grave to waiting cars and a tiny dirt road that winds between tombstones down the hill toward the harbour and the airport from which I will soon leave. Once more, Kenya returns in memories culled from that helter-skelter Hegira my father and I made from London after the War, that year-long odyssey during which we crisscrossed three continents, our giddy course like the paths of wind-driven embers I watched zigzag skyward after the air raid which killed my mother.

In the main, I recall Highway Two – the road that winds south from Mombasa toward Tanzania then veers inland up the disputed Kundi range to Tsavo National Park. Of course, the mud-choked, cinder track I knew as a six-year-old girl no longer exists. Today – as John and I discovered that last infelicitous trip to Kenya – the road is well-kept tarmac. Air-conditioned coaches deposit dry-bloused tourists at Tsavo and trundle them back to the Colonial Bar in Mombasa before nightfall the following day.

Beyond the Tsavo Reserve, however, in the wilderness past Namanga, the road remains every whit the bone-jarring trek I remember from childhood. Beyond the Reserve, Highway Two reverts to a furrow gouged across the breach between the mountains. It falters through the rift valley, then ascends in knotted switchbacks the Siria Escarpment to Kisumu. The road circles Victoria warily, then careens downward across Uganda into the wet jungles of Zaire where, by and large, it exists only on a map – as a thin, red, wormlike line inching toward the continent's heart. John and I did not go that far, of course, since the road to the heart is an impossible road at times, even for a Land Rover, a road, sometimes yet, utterly unforgiving, a road –

The vicar's hands distract me. He sprinkles water, a freakish action amid the dripping umbrellas and wind-whipped rain. Instantly, sun-drenched memories resurge like the relentless Indian Ocean waves that batter crumbling Fort Jesus in Old Mombasa.

Strange, such whims of memory – the perverse logic by which the heart plucks an instant out of time and imbues it with a world of importance. When I was six, Kenya had seemed but a respite on a journey whose terminus was unknown until my father and I lighted in Djakarta. Djakarta rekindled my father's heart at last and became the place from which he never again departed. Establishing his business on Jalan Thamrin near Merdeka Square, he conscientiously tended accounts well into his eighty-seventh year – until the stroke last summer.

Djakarta is, thus, to me that Eden, that Hesperides left behind in childhood. The ching-ching bells of the *betjaks* – the sweet, orchid smell and sing-song chatter of the Cikini Market – the fertile essence of that gentle place nurtures me, supports me. Djakarta, not Kenya, is the rich topsoil of my life, that layer of childhood and adolescence within which is rooted the rest. And yet – perversity of memory! – beneath the topsoil lies Highway Two like bedrock, such that – looking back as now – the moments that rise from the plain of my past like mountains, like monuments, are moments spent with my father or with John on Highway Two.

So rich in distractions was that road for a six-year-old London girl whose thoughts – undistracted – exploded with images of cinderblock shelters and the wail of sirens. I relished the road's pitfalls – its stifling heat and swollen streams – its endless toil. Long stretches of road were but muck-mired animal runs. I recall a purblind rhinoceros (enamoured of the Land Rover, I imagined) who refused us passage for more than an hour. My father flapped newspapers. He blared the klaxon and fired his Browning rifle. At gunshots the beast bolted twenty yards down the road, only to return obstinately to a horn-to-bonnet ornament stance. By and by – ardour cooled by the Land Rover's cold heart and frigid response – the Rhinoceros lumbered away dispiritedly, but the road was ever chockablock with such impossibilities. I remember hours when my father – gripping the recalcitrant steering wheel – uttered but grunts and curses, all attention and energy focused through white-knuckled hands in which I vested all remaining confidence. Although my father's hands were sensitive hands that could craft a doll from a handkerchief, they were nonetheless possessed of an adamantine grip. My earliest memory is of those hands seizing me, defying gravity, hefting me to the aerie of his shoulders. My father's hands inspired several of my most successful sculptures. One may recall, perhaps, the black granite piece seen in Jaguar advertisements during the 70's – my father's hands as I remember them reining the bucking Land Rover.

Unlike my father, however, John shunned unfamiliar places and our single trip to Kenya was made not at his suggestion, but rather as a result of constant entreaties. I fancied that Africa would divert John's attention from the poor market that year, a turnabout that troubled his stomach, filled his mind with his stomach and his mouth with numbers – bid, ask, open, close, volume put, volume called. His litany of aches and integers – like any prayer, I suppose – signified much beyond the uttered sounds, but I heard only the droning numbers and endless requests for Maalox – his 'mother's milk.' Actually, the strain was long between us. At meals our silverware clinked in a lugubrious silence. I despise such silence! Much of what first attracted me to John had been his wit, his desultory conversations that played like some time-challenge chess match.

In contentious moods John argued for a more superficial base to that first attraction: his cowboy boots. Admittedly, they piqued my interest, particularly when I learned that, in a manner of speaking, John *was* a cowboy – his father owned 50,000 acres of cattle land in Wyoming where John lived until his parents' divorce. But really, does anyone ever truly fathom that inexplicable alchemy, that accidental chemistry of initial attraction? A fortuitous touch. A resolute timbre in an apology. A marble coolness in a handshake. A certain slant of light that deepens a brow or accentuates a chin. Perceptions, impressions, anticipations, and remembrance of things past, all jumbled, all rubbed together such that occasionally – ineffably – a spark is struck, an ember flares.

We met on a KLM flight from Djakarta to London. I was returning to my teaching position at Somerville College following a stay with my ailing father. John planned a fortnight in England after having inspected a small Indonesian concession in which his family held a percentage. He related this history while apologizing for brushing repeatedly against me. First-class legroom was insufficient for John – a lanky, Gary Cooper sort. Besides, an old wound had stiffened his leg, he said, and to insure my belief, he hoisted his trousers-leg above his boot to reveal a ragged scar where a wild boar had gored him when he was six years old. Later, I found less accessible scars which attested to the severity of the mauling, but at the time, I merely smiled and said that I, too, had been attacked by numerous bores from whom I also carried scars.

He laughed. We shook hands, spun our introductory tales, and dined the following night at Claridge's. Garrulous and innocently arrogant, John was quintessentially American. Pomp and custom ostensibly chafed, yet, covertly, he yearned for the security of tradition as a solo sailor yearns for the green light at a harbour entrance, at the end of a dock.

John had no numbers then. Words, laughter, stories – stories continued by post and telephone, via interludes on business trips and shared vacations – stories that sustained us during three glum weeks we endured in Wyoming after his father died. John's younger brother retained management of the cattle ranch, while John, residing near his mother in New York City, assumed financial oversight of the family holdings. Subsequently, I myself moved to New York, where we married.

John, also, served as model for my sculptures – several acclaimed, recent ones of lesser note. He disparaged my 'lies in stone,' but once I observed him stroke surreptitiously a small, unfinished carving as he might my thigh, comparing his hands of marble to those of flesh. I so startled him in his reverie that – insufferable clumsiness! – he fumbled the piece and cracked it. Seven months I had honed that stone to match my vision of what it contained.

His gaffe dated the rift that widened between us. Stories faded while numbers – this failing enterprise, that closed account – if not more strident, became more apparent. Dinners metamorphosed into solo affairs as did my annual pilgrimages to Djakarta where, upon my return, I detected the small signs – a disturbed lingerie drawer, a long hair on my robe, a laddered stocking of a shade I did not favour. John essayed petulant denials. Americans are so puerilely circumspect with what the world takes for granted. And, frankly, his lies offended more sorely than the deeds, since the deeds – so integral a part of my own world view – could mean nothing, nothing at all.

Thus, we came to opposite sides of a breach I hoped to bridge in Africa – a place away from numbers and accounts, away from pretense – a place where, once more, we might be who we were rather than what we had become. John protested, but I prevailed. We arrived in Mombasa early July, between the rainy seasons when the rivers run and the animals gather.

My father's old friend, Peter Mwangola, a Kenyatta clansman and mayor in those tranquil years before the Moi usurpation, insisted we lodge at his waterfront villa. Morning tea on the balcony overlooked the harbour, providing a magnificent view of moldering Fort Jesus. Afternoons, I prepared marvelously fresh Indian Ocean prawns the size of small lobsters and we drank champagne and Pimm's and Momba beer beside the fresh-water swimming pool, a sybaritic luxury for Kenya. John, conciliatory and enjoying the respite, nevertheless waxed obstinate against my plan to leave Mombasa and travel the road beyond. He pointed up the unpleasantnesses that can erupt anywhere in Africa. Offering compromise, he argued that the Park at Nairobi was a delightful place to view animals and that in Nairobi he might even conduct some business to offset the extravagance of the journey. Yielding finally to my inexpugnable persistence, he hired a Land Rover and outfitted us for a brief expedition south.

Outside Mombasa, Highway Two had become a dual carriageway! No dust cloud rose behind us. The air lacked its luminous, yellow quality – its bicarbonate of soda tang. And black flies swarmed. I did not remember flies. At Tsavo, we found costermongers hawking souvenir Masai postal cards and Kodak film. Disgusted, I demanded we press beyond the reserve. John urged caution, but taunts goaded him onward. We plunged into the rift between Hellene and Kilimanjaro.

And – as I had hoped – in the wilderness beyond the reserve, challenged by the primitive road, estranged from taxicabs and the Wall Street Journal, John rediscovered that quality inside himself that once gamboled in his speech. Despite the severity of the terrain and the cramped cockpit of the Land Rover, his limp abated. We ventured afield, unearthed rare stones, smelled exotic flowers, witnessed sun-blotting flights of birds. From a high ridge we watched waves of grazing animals ebb and flow through the valley below. Expansive again at last, John boasted of wonders he might show me on horseback. And with his boasts returned lovemaking – that celebration of self-in-other we had lost to physical coupling and release.

Three days outside Mombasa, somewhere between Namanga and Lake Natron, we camped beside a river and awoke to a pod of bathing hippopotami. Egrets chitted from the beasts' broad, glabrous backs. Tiny ears swivelled like radar dishes. *'Mu blati'* the hippopotami are called there – river pigs. Indeed, wallowing in the muddy shallows, they resembled giant, silent pigs. John lagged and urged me away from the water.

His reticence was wise. The river pigs kill more men in Africa than the lion or leopard – more even than the elephant. Unlike the often shy Rhinoceros, hippos attack remorselessly upon little provocation except, perhaps, propinquity. Those lolling, lumbering islands in the brown river water can, on land, gallop much faster than a man. If attacked, one is saved but by fortune.

As I crept forward, Nikon poised, one of the behemoths galumphed from a stand of tall reeds twenty yards away. Beast and woman – equally astounded, perhaps equally intrigued – froze until John's cry shattered the spell. The river pig lowered its head and charged. Futilely – since the beast would surely catch us – John and I sprinted for the Land Rover. Just behind me, thunder boomed and shook the ground. Gasping, I reached for John's hand.

Less than an arm's length in front, John scuttled away despite his game leg. My empty hand strained. I called to his back. Thunder upon me, I stumbled and covered my head with my arms as I had learned to do as a child in the air-raid shelters where – small and helpless – jarred by an ever-forever Boom! Boom! Boom! outside – my father held me safe in his hands.

Abruptly, the Hippopotamus veered away, having inexplicably lost interest. It slowed and waddled in a wide arc back toward the river. When it had vanished into the reeds, I lurched to my feet and scrambled to John at the open door of the Land Rover.

"I thought you loved me," I heaved, wringing the pressure from my chest.

"This was survival," John said sheepishly. "Love had nothing to do with it."

Unscarred and alive – now with time – we could laugh, but our excursion was spoiled. Breaking camp, John grew ever more pensive. Wrestling the steering wheel as we retreated through the wilderness to the safety of the tarmac at Tsavo, he uttered only monosyllables. I recall one time – neither of us had spoken for hours – when he blurted that the beast reminded him of the boar that had hurt him as a child. Despite my commiseration, he fell mute again.

I remember one other remark. Crossing the bridge into Old Mombasa – the green lights of crumbling Fort Jesus stark against the dark harbour – John sighed, "Guess I should've stayed where I belong."

Over the next year – before John and I separated – the hippopotamus returned a thousand times to bedevil us. Indeed, even recently while I cared for my father, the beast returned in letters, resurrected of John's intractable pain. And despite my assurances that the episode meant nothing, nothing at all –

The crowd buzzes. Umbrellas bob. The half-circle eddies and parts. Cowboy boots step into the no-man's land surrounding me. John, thinning hair rain-plastered in strands across his forehead, ducks under the canopy and squeezes my hands.

"The plane ... the rain delayed me," he whispers. "I am so sorry. So very, very sorry."

We stand clasping hands. The vicar concludes. Nods, condolences, chatter, and the crowd returns to its affairs. John holds his ground.

"I know how much he meant to you," he says, staring at the flower-strewn coffin. Relinquishing the coffin, we walk hand in hand toward the open door of a car.

"To ... to come all this way," I say. "I never ... I never expected it, you know."

"Yes, I know." John says, squeezing my hand again to share unreservedly what strength he has to give.

I enter the car. John slides into the seat beside me. Jolted by the closing door, I wheel involuntarily toward the rear window to see once more the coffin. Beneath the wind-flapped canopy, two laborers have appeared and stand waiting. The car groans and pulls away.

I look again at John. The seat is cramped. He kneads his bad leg. Still pained by my gaze, he lowers his eyes.

"John," I begin, "it meant nothing! Nothing at –"

"Please," he begs. "*Please*, don't say that again."

And he is right.

It *was* important. Undeniably important.

And he is wrong.

Because it is not the *only* important thing. It is not the most important thing in all the world.

The Girl in the Red 'Vette

The night I chased the girl in the red 'Vette, I was seventeen, already failing college, and about a year short of joining the Marines. It was 1962, early autumn, October I think – Detroit's *good* season; a brief, red-orange sunset before the bare, gray night of winter. And new car time back when new cars mattered.

I drove a red, unsafe at any speed, Corvair Monza with bald tires, a slipping clutch, and an overflowing ashtray. I worked evenings at the downtown News plant stuffing step-vans with wire-bound bundles of newspapers. The wire cut my fingers even through gloves, but Teamster jobs paid good money – plenty for gas back then, since I still lived at my parents' home, and three dollars filled my tank.

By midnight, my arms were heavy and my feet cold. I trudged from the clattering loading dock to the silent side street where I parked for free. Downtown was gray and deserted at night. Traffic lights blinked over empty intersections. Shivering winds whipped and whistled between the buildings. Sometimes I warmed myself behind the yellow, fogged windows of the Fort Street Coney Island where songless nighthawks perched on red revolving counter stools near the steaming silver coffee urns.

Other times I retrieved my car, stopped by the river behind Cobo Hall, and watched silent, graybearded men fish for pale carp that no one would eat. Driving away, I always prowled Brush Street where whores beckoned from dark stoops and shadowy recesses. The calling voices churned my belly with a murky yearning. But Brush Street was risky business, so I drove on.

Home was north out the John Lodge Expressway to Six Mile Road, then west until the spaces between houses grew so large the houses almost disappeared. Home was silent, my parents in bed. Home was scudding images on a flickering television screen – Fred Astaire tip-tap-toeing across a ceilingless ballroom pre-empted by bloated, deskbound Mr. Belvedere hawking aluminum siding. Home was poetry – since I didn't drink then – drivel eked out in longhand on yellow legal pads I still have somewhere. Home was Brubeck through earphones in the dark – album cuts selected in the dim glow of the tuner dial. I slept best when I was supposed to be in school, so most nights after work, I just drove until daybreak.

Those years now are indistinct, details gone, burnished, worn smooth like a rock in rapids, but on one of those nights, I chased the girl in the red 'Vette, a memory still sharp enough to cut. I was alone, waiting for a signal, idling in the slow lane at the intersection of Six-Mile and Greenfield. On the corner, closed for the season, stood a Dairy Queen, its windows frosted-out with Glass Wax. I remember the music on my radio – Brubeck's *Pick Up Sticks* – and the sudden catch in my breath when this brilliant, red 'Vette materialized in the empty lane beside me. The '63 'Vette was newly designed, and this was the first I'd seen – that first ever Sting Ray, fast-back, rocket car, car of the future, car like no other, car like I had *never* seen. Here was no dead whisper of the past, no Popular Mechanics, Art Deco future glutted with rounded corners and flying Fords. Here was the future as it was supposed to be. Singular. Coherent. A spare, clean, *angular* future that leaped out of itself in its eagerness to move forward.

In the cold, night air, the hot car shimmered like a mirage. The brilliant red body was a whirlpool of mirrored light, a swirling phantasmagoria of vague projections like the ice cube montages in whiskey ads. Engine gurgling, the 'Vette suddenly sang, idle to 4000 –

whhuum, whhuuummm – and sprang away. Breath locked in my throat, blinded to right or wrong or aftermath, I popped the clutch of my Corvair and lumbered after four receding taillights.

The 'Vette accelerated effortlessly to 50 in the 35 mile per hour zone, but *street* races were not always to the swiftest. Six Mile Road was straight from start to finish and deserted at three a.m. With road enough and time, the contest was one of *will*. I pulled even with the 'Vette before we reached Grand River.

A solitary girl was the 'Vette's perfect completion. Black hair fell to her shoulders. A narrow left hand, holding a smoldering cigarette, perched high on the steering wheel. She sat silhouetted in darkness, so I saw her face only once in the brief, red flare of the ember when she touched the cigarette to her lips. Gone like smoke, that moment, but like the smell of smoke the memory lingers and stings.

Constantly accelerating – the girl just ahead – we hurtled alone past Telegraph, Five-Points and Beech, my radio lost to the groaning of the Corvair's engine and the erratic slapping of its canvas top. Trees suddenly loomed in the swath of our headlamps as the road narrowed to two, unlighted lanes at Inkster. Near Middlebelt we passed my parents' dark house at 100 miles per hour.

The girl in the 'Vette pulled me along, remaining in the cone of my headlights only if I pushed my own car to its limit. I felt as if I were slipstreaming her – as if the girl's velocity drew me behind in the vacuum of her passing. The Corvair chassis dipped and swayed, teasing me with lethal possibilities, but the red, fast-back 'Vette, taillights blazing, swept me forward in a rushing roar toward some fantasy of girl and car and future.

Not far away Six Mile petered out, dribbled along several miles as a nameless dirt road between farms, then came to a *'T'* with some other innominate dirt road. I had gone that far one night, and before turning back, I'd wondered where the crossroad led. Nights of aimless driving had convinced me that roads never really ended, but intersected, forked, turned, circled about, became lost in a maze, but always continued – like tributaries to a river, like rivers to an ocean, like ocean merging with ocean. Names changed, off-shoots died, direction varied, while – how can I explain it? – the *Road* went on. It bothered me for some reason. Ends seemed important then. I quested at night for the end of the road as if at some mythic end, life would begin.

The 'Vette's brake lights burst in a cautionary flare. I coaxed my own brakes and slowed to seventy. A yellow diamond printed *Pavement Ends* blew by the window on the right like debris. The 'Vette shot from the blacktop onto the dirt road in a great fantail of billowing dust clouds. Plunging into the clouds, the Corvair shuddered as tires left pavement. Stones pinged and banged against the wheelwells and floorpan. My hands jerked at the steering wheel as the car rocked, lurched, and fishtailed.

Enveloped in a thick fog of dust, I took bearings from the diffuse red glow of the 'Vette's taillights and the elevator feel in my stomach each time the car began to sideslip. The red glow blazed suddenly when the girl tapped her brakes, then again, then again. We slowed – sixty – fifty – forty. She coasted now. The 'Vette's left turn signal began to blink – *off-on, off-on.* Six Mile was straight; I hadn't counted on a turn. Or – it dawned on me – a stop.

My mind gave sound to the silent, flashing taillights, the sound of the flasher mechanism as *she* would hear it, the faint tick-tock of the thermocouple – warming, bending, disengaging. *(Click-click.)* As the foggy dust settled to a low, misty wake behind her wheels, the road emerged. *(Click-click.)* Narrow and rutted, it was flanked by dry ditches and rusted barbed-wire fences tagged *Posted. (Click-click.)* Above me the sky was black, the stars blue and cold. A quarter mile ahead, the staring red eye of a mailbox post reflector marked a driveway. (Click-click.) Crawling now, I realized that – whatever I had guessed about the girl in the 'Vette, whatever I had imagined – one fact was *certain*.

She had signaled far too soon for the turn.

My right hand gripped the wheel at one o'clock. My left hand hovered over the turn signal. The mailbox post reflector glowed red hot. The brilliant, red Sting Ray, fast-back, rocket car, car of the future, car like no other, car like I had never seen, winked *(click-click)* and – *close enough to touch!* –turned.

A long, gravel driveway led to a dark, tree-shrouded house with one bright upper window. The 'Vette stopped, the brake lights dimmed, the car lights died altogether. I like to think that the girl glanced over her shoulder as I crept past, but, in truth, shadows spoiled my view and I sped away.

A mile or so ahead, at the nameless juncture where Six Mile ended while the empty *Road* went on, I doused my headlights and sat. Earth and sky, both black, fused at an indistinct, irregular line where trees obscured the stars. Later, when I circled back past the girl's house, I found the light in the window extinguished. The driveway was dark. I couldn't make out the car.

I never saw the girl in the red 'Vette on that road again, although – other places, other times, I thought I saw her racing by.

I never chased her though.

And I never felt again I could have caught her.

Friends

A freezing wind flapped loose scarves and hunched the shoulders of bundled people trudging past the restaurant window. Inside – insulated by the glass – a bearish man slurped his after-dinner coffee.

"Ouch! Hot!"

His delicate companion rat-ta-tat-tatted her fingers against the snow white table cloth.

"Men!" she huffed.

"What? What is it?" he said, clinking the porcelain cup back onto the saucer.

"I expected one of your little surprise scenes, Andy, but no! I think you *have* forgotten."

"Oh, Christ, Ginny! I must've ... Wait a minute. Your birthday was last month. Forgot what?"

"Six months since our first date! Six months today. I dropped hints all week."

"Women!"

"The past is important."

Andy patted the coat over his heart and produced a ribbon wrapped envelope from the inside pocket.

"So is the future, Ginny."

She seized the envelope.

"You're off the hook *this* time," she said.

Andy signaled the hovering, tuxedo-clad waiter.

"Will there be anything more, sir?"

"Ginny?"

Absorbed with the envelope, she shook her head.

"Just the bill," said Andy with a wink.

The waiter nodded and withdrew.

"You think men don't remember?" Andy said, blowing on his coffee. "You wore that shiny red dress I like so much."

"You *do* remember."

"How could I forget? Risky business, a cop dating a psychologist. Figured you for a mind reader."

"Male minds read like Dick and Jane books," she said, examining the envelope against the light.

"Insults!" Andy snorted. "Insults from a wench who scarfed up four – count 'em – *four* enchiladas."

"I like to eat."

"I like to watch you eat," Andy said, leaning forward.

"You like to watch. Period!"

Andy shot a red-faced glance toward nearby tables.

"Don't talk nasty!"

Laughter shook loose a single lock of hair from Ginny's perfectly constructed hairdo.

"Andy, you're priceless!" she said, brushing the curl from her cheek.

Outside a bedraggled, one-eyed man limped by the window. Black, unkempt hair spilled over the shoulders of his stained, Marine Corps field jacket. Glancing up, he smiled suddenly and barged inside.

"Wrong door, Pancho!" the waiter whispered coarsely, racing to block the way.

"Say *amigo*!" the man bellowed. "See you through the window! *Que paso?*"

Andy waved excitedly.

"Vamoose!" the waiter snapped.

Feinting right, the man lunged left and scrambled to the table despite his bad leg.

"Same old moves *GEE*-sus!" laughed Andy.

"*HAY*-sus, you *cabron*. *HAY*-sus, not *GEE*-sus."

Andy grinned at Ginny's bewilderment. "I've called him that since first grade. We–"

The waiter grabbed the man's arm.

"Keep your hands off me!" Jesus barked.

"S'okay, s'okay …" Andy said to the waiter. "He's my friend."

"Your *friend* is disturbing the other patrons."

Andy stood.

"I'll take care of him."

"A jacket is *required*."

"Field *jacket*," Andy said, pinching a faded green sleeve. "You don't want to argue with the Marines, pal."

"And a tie … *sir*."

"Well, maybe he left his tie somewhere," Andy growled. "Maybe in the 'Nam along with his eye and half his hip." He yanked off his own tie and draped it over Jesus' neck. "Happy? He has a tie."

"And now, sir, *you* do not."

Voice couched in a register felt as much as heard, Andy said, "I could wear *your* tie."

The waiter opened his mouth to protest, but something red and very ancient in Andy's eyes silenced him. He wheeled and marched toward the kitchen.

"Andy!" Ginny said curtly. "You're not in the jungle!"

"There's a world of things you might not know, Ginny," he replied.

Oblivious to the buzzing room, Andy dragged over an unused chair. "Huddle up, Gee-sus. *Cerveza*? Something stronger?"

"Strong as I need, *cabron*, they don't have."

"Sit down, man. You make me dizzy wobbling like that."

Jesus looked wistfully at the chair, then at Ginny sitting stone-faced.

"Naah, I'm no tent peg. Just eyeballed you through the window and figured, 's been most a year. Wanted to see your lady." He offered his hand to Ginny. "I'm Jesus Ramirez."

"Gee-sus. Call him Gee-sus."

"Virginia Steele," Ginny said, pinching the hand with her fingertips.

"Watch what you say, Gee-sus. Ginny's a shrink."

"Get out, man! With you?"

"Show him your license, Ginny." Andy patted the empty chair. "So whacha been up to? Still living off Uncle Sam's tit?"

"Barely get high on that check, *cabron*. Been shoving a mop at the Four-to Four … Look, man, this is bogus," Jesus said, glancing again at Ginny.

"What?"

"Me buttin' in. I'm gonna blow."

"Stay a minute, Gee-sus!"

"Hay-sus, you *cabron*. Hay-sus, not Gee-sus!" He bowed toward Ginny. "Good to meet you, Doc."

"Yes, of course, Mr. uh … Ramirez. A pleasure."

Andy stood, crushed Jesus against his chest, and pounded his back. Jesus broke free and staggered out the door.

"Andy, your tie!"

"He'll get it back to me," Andy said, dropping onto his chair.

Through the window they watched Jesus halt at the curb as if trying to choose a direction. The harsh wind whipped at his black hair. He tugged up the collar of his field jacket and – favoring his balky left leg – dodged traffic to cross the street.

"Who *is* that man?" Ginny said.

"Jesus Ramirez. He told you."

"Not his name. Who *is* he?"

Andy bristled at her smugness.

"He's a *friend.*"

"I think he was drunk."

"Bingo. He was."

"What can you two have in common?"

Taking a deliberate breath, Andy nodded toward the envelope in Ginny's hand.

"Anniversaries, Ginny. First grade. First beer. First date. We had football in common. God damn, he used to fly! We had our first win and our first ... We had the 'Nam, together, Ginny, but he left more behind than me, so he doesn't run like he used to, and they nail him now every time."

"So it's some *'man'* thing."

"He's a *friend.*"

"Of course, dear."

Andy turned away. Ginny waited.

"Are we not going to talk?" she said finally.

"I was."

He stared silently through the window. Ginny followed his gaze. Outside a young couple's voices made clouds in the frigid air.

"I'm sorry you're upset, Andy. I..I suppose I was a little shocked."

He sipped his coffee. Deliberating, Ginny opened her envelope and removed two tickets.

"Oh, Andy!" she said, wide-eyed. "*Eurydice*! How did you get these?"

"Broke a few thumbs," he shrugged, thawing. "You were dying to see it."

She examined the tickets. Her smile collapsed.

"Oh, no! *This* Wednesday?"

"Yeah, Wednesday. So?"

"Wednesday is my group night You *know* that."

"I do?"

"You *should.* Every month. My women's support group. You know what friends are, don't you, Andy?"

He looked down and traced the lip of his cup with a finger.

"*You're* my friend," he said as if speaking to the cup.

"And you're *my* friend."

"So what's the problem?"

The waiter appeared with a small cake bearing a single burning candle.

"Will this be satisfactory, *sir*?" said the waiter.

"Sure. Fine," Andy grunted with a go-away gesture. "So what's the problem?"

"Happy anniversary," the waiter said frostily.

"Beat it!"

Plunking down the cake and the check, the waiter retreated. Andy leaned across the table.

"So? What?"

"*My* place this month, Andy. It's all arranged."

"Oh."

"Andy, I'm sorry, I *am*, but–"

He sat back. "*No problemo.* I should've asked."

She paused. Melting wax formed beads on the candle.

"Well ... Can you get your money back?"

"Don't worry about it."

"An..dy ... I do have *other* friends, you know?"

"*Nooo problemo.*"

"Don't you have *other* friends? Not just, uh ... *work* friends. Once a year friends like what's-his-name. *Real* friends. Friends that *matter*. You *must*."

He looked at her. Although not one to police his feelings, Andy noted the sudden coldness he felt. Not like a cloud shadow or a passing front, more even than a wintry season. Something ageless, polar, and absolute.

"You do have friends, don't you?" Ginny persisted.

Her voice sounded strangely distant, almost as if she were calling from another place. Andy licked his thumb and quenched the candle flame between his fingers.

"A few," he said to himself. "Just a few."

He Rarely Thought of Her At All

He opened his eyes on golden bars of sunshine extruded through drawn blind slats. He had dreamed of *her* again. A lucid dream. A lingering dream. A tinted dream, its images suffused with the honeyed light of a solar eclipse.

He frowned. Dreams were alien. Dreaming disquieted his dreamless, melancholic heart. But what could he do? Dreams could no more be checked than the animated sparks of dust dancing in the sunbeams. And besides, he reasoned, he rarely thought of her otherwise.

The nightstand clock read six, its alarm set for seven. Disgruntled, he kicked aside the blanket and stood. Dreamless and melancholic, he was also a *night-person* by nature. Yet, suddenly, his rhythms were off; he felt jetlagged, as if some new time zone demanded accommodation – *but where had he gone?*

Dismissing the thought, he yanked the blind cord, and stood squinting for a moment, overwhelmed by the sunshine. *She* was the early riser, he insisted, not *he*. Already awake, she was sitting at her kitchen window, that same morning sunlight reflected in *her* eyes. He imagined the aroma of her cinnamon toast and coffee, the rustle of her newspaper, the lilt of her laughter as she read the comics.

He shook his head as if erasing an Etch-a-sketch. Daydreaming was even *more* unlike him. He was an engineer, for heaven's sake. A realist! A feet-on-the-ground, dreamless, melancholic, night-person who refused to indulge in vaporware spawned by an odd jetlag and nagging *dream*.

Commuting, he disciplined himself by concentrating only on the balky traffic, ignoring the surprising number of cars that looked like hers. Nor did he think of her at work, certainly not as he had when they met – the weeks she had spent at his company's offices redesigning the interior. *Then* her ever-presence had been a gravity that captured his thoughts – how her eyes seemed to reach out and encompass things she perceived like a child putting toys in her mouth – how words spilled from her gaily like water over stones – how her face could change like a landscape swept by cloud shadows. He recalled a silly squabble ... *What do you know from colors except wavelength!* How her face had darkened; how her eyes had flashed; how, just as abruptly, the sun broke in her smile with a rainbow promise, and – by God! – he had smelled *ozone* in the air.

Other times during those few weeks – watching her stand, walk, bend, sit, cross her legs – that same gravity had wrenched him in an earthier direction, bruising him with a jarring consciousness of her body. He remembered a hot day walking together at lunchtime on railroad tracks behind the building. As she knelt to free a struggling moth trapped in a spider's web, a glistening drop of sweat trickled down her chest beyond the drooping neckline of her shirt – a single, crystal bead, like a diamond on her breast – and he had prayed, profanely, that she would stoop an inch lower.

But that was *then*. Two whole months ago and mainly propinquity. Free of her gravity now, he could explore a universe of women, if he wanted – his boss' Amazon secretary (too humorless), the gypsy-eyed stranger in the elevator (too tall), the big-busted waitress at the lunch counter (too slow), the amorous, afternoon barkeep at Blake's (too hideously blonde). Securely unfettered, he chose not to call her before lunch.

Moreover, since he would see her Saturday, *that* call was simply administrative. Schedules and such. He scarcely dwelled on their first time together. How, as he lay above her, his weight braced on his elbows, she had traced the muscle of his arm and whispered, *you won't crush me, you know?* And how, when he relaxed, she had grunted loudly *ooof!* ... and rolling entwined, they had laughed, the sweet laughter distilling, becoming a syrup of silence that—

Quickly he diverted himself from her by recalling how she gazed at him sometimes with joy blooming in her face; how she touched him as if touching him pleased *her*; how she flattered his eyes until, reflected in *her* eyes, he felt – could he use such a word? – *pretty*.

At home that evening he called again and left a funny message on her machine to make her smile. Later he drank a beer and read a tough-guy detective novel. Now and then he looked up and imagined her sprawled in the opposite chair, also reading, also glancing occasionally at him. Such thoughts went almost unnoticed – beneath awareness, yet beyond any question – like his heartbeat.

Low in the purple sky, a faint, magenta glow lingered like a memory of day. Yawning, he closed his book, shed his clothes, switched out the light, and crawled naked beneath a sheet. How perplexing was this curious syncopation in their rhythms, he mused – a dreamless, melancholic, feet-on-the-ground, night-person retiring as early as did she! *I am just not myself*, he reflected, curling on his side, aware that she, too, was curled sideways between gradually warming, cold sheets.

The lament echoed. *Just not myself ... just not myself ...*

Through open blinds, a full moon washed the room with pale, silver light. He closed his eyes. His breathing slowed. His thoughts wandered.

Not just myself ... not just myself ...

And since it was *almost* Friday (the day before he would see her; naturally, a day he would think of her constantly), he permitted himself to savor the scent of her hair, the tang of her mouth, the softness of her skin, the sultry sigh of her breath against his neck. Reverie seemed safe now, because, come to think of it, he rarely thought of her at all.

Gift of the Maggie

Won't he be surprised? Maggie thought as she tiptoed across the darkened bedroom where her husband lay snoring. On a serving tray sat a pristine newspaper, a coffeepot, and an oversized mug. Fixed to the mug by a dollop of melted wax was a small candle.

She placed the tray on her husband's nightstand and glanced at his pocket watch, positioned (as always) between his wallet and keys.

"It's time," she said, lighting the tiny candle. "Wake up, now. It's time."

He stirred.

"Hen..ry! Oh, Hen..ry!"

He grunted, opened one eye, and closed it immediately.

"Wake up, Henry. It's time."

"Mmmph! ... Coffee."

"Right here, dear," she said, stifling a giggle. "As always."

The husband flailed like an overturned bug. He wriggled upright, squashed a pillow behind his back, and promptly slipped back into a noisy doze. Sleep clung to his eyelashes. His chins rested on his chest. A shiny line of drool crossed his cheek like a slug trail.

"Coffee, dammit!" the husband growled with a start. "Pour me ... pour ... coff ... Hooonnnnk! Ptwwwwwww ..."

Maggie watched his soft underbelly rise and fall beneath the blanket. He seemed so perfectly himself this special morning, so sweetly vulnerable. His hair, pillow flattened on one side, stuck out wildly to the other side like something caught in a wind. *He looks like a divi-divi tree*, Maggie mused, picturing the gay Caribbean getaway brochures she had gathered at the travel agency. *Oh, won't he be surprised!*

"AIEEE! CLOSE THOSE BLINDS!" the husband shrieked as Maggie yanked the blind cord.

"Sorry dear," she cooed.

He rubbed his squinched eyes with the backs of his hands and wiped his chin.

"Did you get my suit?"

Maggie shuffled to her side of the bed and sat.

"Yes dear. Your suit and shirt are in the closet. All ready."

"Not the brown suit. I've told you a million times–"

"No brown suit on Monday. *Blue* suit on Monday. Brown suit on Wednesday. Gray suit on Friday. I know dear. I know."

"Everything orderly. I've always told you how important that is. Haven't I told you?"

"Yes, dear. You've told me."

He reached for his coffee mug.

"WHAT IN THE NAME OF HEAVEN?"

Maggie's smothered giggles erupted.

"I am *not* amused!" the husband snapped. "This is … this is *inconceivable*! What if I had burned my nose? What then, Maggie? What then? A candle on a cup is absolutely unsafe. I've never heard of such a thing. Unsafe! Unsafe!"

"A surprise, Henry. For–"

"I hate surprises. *Orderly* is the way of things. A man picks up his cup. He drinks. A then B. *A then B.*"

He plucked the candle from the mug handle, blew it out, and dropped in onto the tray.

"You don't look first to see if the cup has a candle on it. Do you? Answer me, Maggie! Do you?"

The husband prodded the candle to see if it was smoldering. For good measure, he spit on his fingertips and quenched the wick under his thumb.

"Lift. Drink. A then B. Why ... *houses* burn down from these things. You think they're out, and then whammo! Film at eleven! Unsafe!"

One eye on the candle, he lifted his mug and drank.

"*Yaaaak*! And you're fooling with the coffee again! First this candle fiasco and now–" He thrust the mug at her angrily. "I've told you, haven't I? Haven't I told you? Chock-full o'-Nuts. *Period*!"

"You've told me, Henry."

"I've told you and told you! There's no powdered creamer in this, is there? You know how I–"

"Real cream, Henry. Just like you like."

"Real cream. *Period*. No chemicals."

"Real cream, Henry."

"If you think I'll get accustomed to this highfalutin', liquor-laced, flit juice, you've got another think coming."

Grumbling, the husband unfolded the newspaper and draped it over the mound of his stomach. Maggie stared out the window at a cloudless sky.

"Look, Henry! See how sunlight paints the grass over there? See? Just beyond the fence."

"Chock-full o'-Nuts. Nothing else."

"Mondays are always so gloomy, but not today."

Finishing a long drink of coffee, Henry snorted and snuffled like a pig. He held the cup at arm's length.

"Gawd, Maggie! *You're* chock full o' nuts! What is it this time? What? Kahlua-chocolate-mint? What?"

"For today, Henry. Special."

"Special my eye! Quit fooling with things."

He flicked at a wrinkle in the paper with his finger.

"What time is it?" he said. "Am I late?"

"Almost, you ol' grumbly bear, you!" Maggie twittered. And having discovered on this special day a new species of appreciation for his squinty, little, crusted eyes; his honky-snorty animal sounds; his wheedly-whiny Andy Rooney curmudgeonry, she pounced at him, tickling his potbelly.

"Oh, Henry! I could just love you to death!"

"Stop it!" the husband barked. "Stop it! You're messing up the paper. Stop it, dammit!"

Maggie sat back.

"Don't you want to know *why* I put the candle on your mug?"

"Could have blinded me."

"Why do you think I put the candle–"

"Menopause!" he muttered, head buried in the paper.

"The date, Henry..."

She waited.

"... Henry?"

"What is it now?"

"Don't you know what today is?"

"Monday."

"No, silly. The date."

He ignored her.

"Oh, Henry! It's our anniversary."

"Um..hmmm."

"Do you remember our wedding day, Henry? Twenty-seven years ago."

He rustled the paper loudly.

"You wore ... Let's see, it was a Saturday, so Friday's suit. Gray. You wore–"

"I am trying to *read*, Maggie. Pour me some more coffee."

Maggie pattered around to the nightstand, refilled the husband's mug from the pot, and returned to her own side of the bed.

"May I have part of the paper?"

"How many times have I told you, Maggie? When I'm done, you can have it all."

"A then B."

"Exactly! I hate it when you mess up the paper. I tell you that every morning. How many mornings have I told you that?"

Maggie picked up a comb and drew it through her long, graying hair.

"Nine-thousand-eight-hundred-sixty-two."

"What?"

"Nine-thousand-eight-hundred-sixty-two mornings," she said matter-of-factly. "Twenty-seven years. I checked with the calculator. I had to consider leap years, of course – add the extra mornings."

"Foolishness!"

"Yes, dear."

Maggie returned the comb to her nightstand and ran a hand over the bed sheets. A tired rut scored the mattress where her body had lain so many, many nights.

"I think I need a new mattress," she said.

"Hrumph."

"This is a very old mattress."

"Hruummph!"

"It's not our first, of course, but it is old."

"Paper, Maggie! PAPER!"

She waited. The husband took another drink of coffee and puckered. Maggie snickered.

"Did you spit in my coffee again?"

Maggie burst out laughing.

"Oh, Henry! I'm not mad at you today. I'm happy, don't you see?"

"Then let me read my paper!" he demanded, swirling his mug and eyeing the liquid suspiciously.

Maggie waited.

"Paper is the first, you know?" she said after a time.

"First what?" the husband mumbled.

"Fifth is wood."

He lowered the newspaper. "What *are* you babbling about?"

"Twenty-fifth is silver. Remember? I gave you your silver watch fob and I bought myself the silver comb. From *you*, of course."

"Can't wait to see what I'm getting you this year," he muttered. Folding the completed section of the paper neatly, he placed it out of Maggie's reach and opened the Sports pages. "So today is … what did you say? Twenty-seven, right? What's a twenty-seventh?"

"Mineral," she giggled.

"Mineral? What the hell is mineral?"

She smiled.

"Just what kind of smile do you call *that*?" the husband said dubiously.

Maggie examined her face with a hand mirror.

"Why … a rather inscrutable smile, don't you think? A riddle wrapped in a mystery inside an enigma smile."

"You'll be the death of me yet, Maggie."

"Finish your coffee, dear. A then B. A then B."

He downed the rest of the mug, stuck out his tongue, and gave a shiver.

"Well? Am I supposed to guess the flavor again?"

"It's special, Henry. Special for our anniversary. I call it Amaretto."

He sniffed his cup.

"Amaretto? Isn't that made from almonds?"

"Yes, Henry. Almonds. Almonds soaked and soaked and soaked until all the essence is leached from them."

"Well, never again," he said curtly, but suddenly began to cough. A *wet* cough.

Maggie observed a small bye-bye tremor in his right hand. Her book had said the end would come quickly now.

But not *too* quickly.

"Never again, Maggie! Do you hear me?" the husband brayed between coughs. "Chock-full-'o nuts. Nothing else! This stuff tastes like poison! It's too damn bitter! Bitter, I tell you, bitter! It's—"

With a swan-song of honky-snorty animal sounds, the husband collapsed.

"Yes, dear," the wife said, reaching across his body for the paper. "*Very* bitter."

Hedge Fund

Jeremiah Jacobson – having mourned recently the passing of his
51st year – weathered now the autumn of his life, a season he mulled
dolefully each night despite a genius for repression. His ruminations
began as scattered images he assembled in his mind like jigsaw puzzle
pieces atop a table. Inevitably, he overturned the table with a single,
sharp shake of his head.

The images were of his father, Jacob, a custodian at Vassar College.
At 52, late in an unexpectedly wintry Fall, puffing beside the ice-strewn
Hudson with Jinx, his aged Cocker Spaniel, and Jinx Jr., as he dubbed
eight-year old Jeremiah, Jacob had belched an ugly grunt, gnashed his
tongue, toppled onto a patch of gritty snow, and flailed as if making an
angel.

Many years later, having chosen a career in heart surgery,
Jeremiah came to know death in every guise. That first death, however,
his father's death was the nidus around which all subsequent
conceptions had crystallized. Thus, despite any outward manner, *dying*
was at core thrashing arms and kicking feet, a kind of blue-lipped,
blood-sputtered hokey-pokey, the *do-si-do macabre* of small, white
hands clutching a jerking fist while a braying concertina expelled an
abruptly final lungful of crisp, November air.

In the confusion of policemen, paramedics, solicitous Samaritans,
and gawkers, Jinx Sr. had vanished, a loss Jeremiah soon came to see
as ironic. Since Jacob had judged life insurance a bad investment,

Jeremiah's mother lost hold of their Poughkeepsie duplex. She and son hard-landed in a rundown, downtown, basement apartment where – and this was the irony – dogs were *forbidden*. Able to seize at last upon the dog's loss as a kind of desperate, ill-wind fortune, Jeremiah sensed an inkling of some fundamental truth. Words to perfect that inkling, however, had lain dormant in his psychic substrata, buried like a seed awaiting its requisite number of freezes and thaws. Time come round, several years after he married Sommer Leyden-Jacobson, those axiomatic words had germinated, sprouted, and blossomed articulate as credo – *loss is gain, and vice versa.* On the arbor of Jeremiah's mind, the fruit of that blossoming now hung full-sweet and overripe, pendulous and overdue like late harvest grapes destined for some post-prandial wine whose ambrosial sip would complete and make immortal the Thanksgiving repast of which it was to be the culmination. That fruit – perhaps a sweet salvation in Jeremiah's fleeting Fall, that season of loss – was the Jacobson Hedge Fund.

* * * * *

Although the Jacobson Fund was fully subscribed, time and circumstance, as parents of decision, had conceived Jeremiah's selection of a *final* partner. Standing with his wife beside the marble staircase of the Newport Beach Four Seasons, he watched his choice cross the lobby.

"I'm Charles," the man said, offering his hand. "We've met, but you wouldn't remember, Jerry."

"I forget very little, Dr. Gardiner." He clasped the outstretched hand. "But please call me Jeremiah. I loathe sobriquets, don't you?"

"Loathe sobriquets? I don't know. I'd have to look it up."

Jeremiah dismissed the insinuation of affectation, confident that his words were simply an organic abhorrence of lazy or devious approximations that terms such as *nickname* seemed to exemplify. Formal words were solid assets, casual words mere shinplasters.

Assiduous study of topics ignored by his public school educators had forged for Jeremiah a prodigious vocabulary that he wielded to advantage against opponents who began with superior socio-cultural armamentaria.

Jeremiah brushed at a stray thread on the sleeve of his gray suit coat.

"I'm the fund's managing partner, of course, and this is my wife, Sommer Leyden-Jacobson."

Although two years Jeremiah's senior, Sommer's sunshine hair and blue-sky eyes radiated a warm, lazy timelessness. Transplanted, but grown thoroughly Californian and insouciant to season, she wore a flowery, silk sundress despite the November chill. Her outré choice was mediated by the obvious cost of the designer piece and a five-carat diamond on her left hand.

Born to the green but not to the purple – the spoiled, only-child of a prosperous Poughkeepsie merchant – Sommer was used to money, but *never* bored by it. Having tasted, if only via her parents' *impoverished childhood* harangues, both satiety *and* want, she relished wealth, savored its desires and temptations, its anticipatory glows and doomed consummatory blazes.

"Don't question the woman's hyphen, Charles. She'll take your head off! Leyden was her mother's maiden name."

"Not her father's name?"

"She adopted her deceased mother's name after her father shot himself. Take a lesson in the value of insurance, Charles. Sommer inherited a tidy fortune, and I know just what you're thinking. You're crediting Sommer with all hers and half mine. Everyone does. What a hedge *that* would be," Jeremiah chuckled. "Actually, you two are acquainted, aren't you?"

Sommer glanced at both men knowing that one or the other had hatched this meeting for reasons she could only guess.

"What's it been, Chuck?" she said breezily, squeezing Charles' hand. "Oh, I hate to *think* how long! Nine, ten years?" She turned to Jeremiah. "We met at Seaside, shortly after we moved here. Back in my nursing days before I became addicted to leisure. I used to terrify him with lurid tales of New York winters. Chuck is an Orange County native. He'd never seen snow. Imagine!"

Jeremiah filed Charles' failure to defend his proper name in a mental personnel folder where already were logged the man's ludicrous Hawaiian shirt, frayed jeans, and scuffed cowboy boots.

"I *can't* imagine. I detest snow," said Jeremiah. "We moved to escape it. California is always green, always growing."

"Seaside certainly grew," Charles said.

"My first hospital purchase, you know. Back in New York I realized that surgical practice was a dead end. My hard work served mainly to enrich the hospital owners."

"I realized the same thing," said Charles.

"You should have seized your opportunity. Seaside was ripe for picking back then."

"Oh, I was thinking it about *you*," Charles grinned.

"Were you? ... Well, I'm delighted to be free of hospitals now. Another dead end. Bricks and mortar and goods and services, that season is over. But my Hedge Fund, this Hedge Fund is the harvest, Charles; the harvest of the experience we've sown. Knowledge capital, don't you see? Who knows more than doctors about the medical field?"

"Don't you have a little urology practice in Santa Ana, Chuck?" Sommer interrupted. "Indigents, immigrants, itinerants and whatnot?"

"Yes, Mrs. Leyden-Jacobson, I practice in Santa Ana."

"Then I'm ashamed of you," Sommer mocked with a luminous shake of her head. "Bilking us for free cocktails this way! You can't possibly qualify for a highly leveraged Hedge Fund."

"I think it's time I get rich. It sounds like fun."

"It *is* fun, Chuck. But only the *rich* get rich. Tell him, Jeremiah. Hedge Fund partnerships are limited to *accredited* investors – net worth, repeat annual income. Besides … the buy-in is a half-million. Sorry, Charlie."

"Sommer!" Jeremiah snapped.

Her blue eyes flashed at his tone, but abruptly she laughed with a lazy indolence, the laughter almost liquid, like a hot, August rain.

"Don't get your boxers bunched, Jeremiah. Chuck once had a keen sense of irony. The humor he saw in things kept him young. Is that still your secret, Chuck? I swear, you look as young as ever. Younger! There's something ever-fresh about you, isn't there? The perpetual boy."

Jeremiah knew that his own boyishness – if ever he had it – was long gone. His hair was the color of gritty snow.

"Let's have that drink," he said. "It's chilly here."

Two marble risers separated the Four Seasons' lobby from its lounge. Jeremiah, a tall, large-boned, and generally deliberate man, bounded the steps, briefcase in hand, reclaiming his mood with the action of rising. Leading the *melange a trois,* he bored through the maze of the lounge to a reserved nook that overlooked a tropical garden. Jeremiah maneuvered Charles onto a beige love seat and took the opposite spot across a low, glass table. Sommer chose a mauve-cushioned side chair facing the bar. A waitress appeared.

"*Vin du glaciere.* Signal Hill," Jeremiah said.

"Sapphire martini, dry," Sommer said absently, gazing through the tall lounge windows.

"Tell you what, Melodie," said Charles, his glance sliding from the waitress' golden nametag to her cleavage. "How about a Bud? Or is a sobriquet like Bud too plebian for such a regal joint?" His contagious smile sparkled like the first good day in April.

"Why, it's the *king* of beers, sir," Melodie said cheerfully.

Jeremiah opened his briefcase. He dealt spreadsheets and a prospectus onto the cocktail table.

"Peruse the yellow folder first, Charles. Net capitalization and two-year performance, alpha and beta. And keep in mind the Jacobson Fund credo," he said, tapping the words printed in red across the glossy prospectus. *"Loss is gain, and vice versa."*

"I like that," said Charles, drawing a folder from the stack. "Your idea?"

Jeremiah nodded. "It's everything you need to know."

"Not truth is beauty?"

"I gather you've read Keats," said Jeremiah. "Perhaps you should appear on *Jeopardy*. The point to consider now, however, is the inherent contingency of mutual funds. Each has its season, to be sure, but sooner or later, they sputter. Why? Because the life's breath of a mutual fund is a rising market and the higher the market soars, the thinner the atmosphere. A hedge fund, on the other hand, has hedge tactics – short sales, puts, calls. We hedge the downswings and leverage the upswings. Autonomous, don't you see? A hedge fund rockets *above* the market, propelled by the engine of gain in loss."

"To infinity and beyond," said Charles with a twinkle.

"You can be quite ridiculous, you know? Study the spreadsheets. The numbers speak for themselves."

Settling in for the wait, Jeremiah eyed the lounge windows and congratulated himself on the perfect venue. What better reflection of perpetual growth than a garden awash in greens and reds despite the November twilight. Oceanfront hotels – perched on palisades angling downward toward gritty, white sand –were contingent things that *needed* the ocean as some *primum mobile*. The Four Seasons, however – rising a half-mile inland – rebuffed the ocean. Just beyond the garden path and sparkling Koi pond stretched a priceless vista, Newport's golden coast. Exercising the extravagant option of caprice, however, the Four Seasons sold short the ocean, interposing a soaring, foliage, spite-fence that blocked the view and channeled eyes toward limitless sky.

Imagining the ocean stymied by a simple hedge, Jeremiah recalled God's boast to Job of His authority to command the sea. *Just so far and no farther*, Jeremiah recited inaudibly, as if within this walled arena, he himself could hold back the tide. Or the seasons.

Trailing wet footprints on the white cement, a towel-wrapped couple, returning from the swimming pool, darted hand-in-hand down the garden path. The man stopped short, whirling the woman to plant a kiss. Wet and almost naked, the couple stood engulfed in deep shadow cast by the hedge. Thinking them chilled, Jeremiah gave an involuntary shiver. The couple giggled and disappeared into the hotel.

Sommer amused herself by challenging the peek-a-boo glances of men in the lounge. One smarmy, olive-skinned specimen eyed her with a reptilian indifference to her privacy. She knew such eyes, having been raped twice. The first time, at fourteen, was a confusing, shameful experience she had revealed to no one for years until a college counselor encouraged her to talk about it with someone she trusted – a designation she reserved for Jeremiah alone. After the second incident, however – she was attacked by a rebuffed high school boy on her sixteenth birthday – Sommer had taken immediate action.

Already turning to Jeremiah with every wound, her first instinct had been to enlist his aid in revenge. She was blocked, however, by the fear, almost a certainty, that Jeremiah's knowledge would mean the boy's death. And while she thought Jeremiah capable of *any* accomplishment, including successful murder, she dreaded the nuisance of an investigation and trial. Instead, she seduced three tractable varsity linemen to variously abuse the rapist while she slaked her blood-thirst on his wet pleas and blubbered regrets.

To her annoyance, the boy's copious tears soon brewed an infusion of pity, and then, from pity over-steeped, a bitter decoction of contempt. She might have anticipated that result. Eighteen months earlier, not long after her mother died, her father – lurching through one of his drunken mood swings – had knelt beside her bed and rocked and prayed and sobbed interminably. That, too, had been a most unpleasant experience, all that sobbing.

Feet on the floor, high-heels elevating her knees, Sommer reclined slightly – the resulting angle of body and long legs falling just off-square, slightly obtuse and cocked like the lines of a Corbusier chair. Holding the swarthy man's eyes, she crossed her legs with the languorous furling motion of bedroom curtains billowing in a warm breeze. The dark man fumbled with his change and retreated.

Sommer laughed silently and sipped her martini. She watched Jeremiah slide another spreadsheet across the glass table. Charles swiped it up and grinned as if holding a pat hand. Jeremiah's face was the stone mask she had known since childhood.

Actually, although they had shared an elementary school, Sommer recalled little of Jeremiah from *those* days. She was two years older and lived in a wealthy neighborhood. Light-years had separated two worlds whose orbits rarely crossed.

Moreover, the years following her mother's death remained a blur. Sommer's adolescent rebelliousness had at that time flared from insurrection to all-out civil war. Her father consulted psychiatrists who – in the manner of bestowing a name such as *junior* – labeled Sommer manic-depressive because other psychiatrists had so labeled her father.

As often happens, the name eclipsed the persona it caricatured, obscuring whatever meaning informed Sommer's drug abuse, runaway hitchhiking treks, arrests, and half-drunk, strange-room awakenings with nameless men or women. The mud she tracked across her slip-covered existence was dismissed as disturbed brain chemistry, a paternal inheritance for which *why* was irrelevant. Thus, the tumult of the years preceding Sommer's final estrangement from her father, his apparent suicide, and her immediate marriage to Jeremiah remained an unexamined swirl of runny, wintry halftones. Miraculously, however, either the suicide or marriage had acted as a mordant, fixing her mood in a kind of casual, tropical tie-dye. Basking in the eternal sunshine of her adult disposition, she rarely recalled that roiling, gray season, but when she did a single, solid element stood apart.

In high school – Jeremiah had placed out of several grades – worlds collided. Sommer's fiery turmoil cast a kind of chiaroscuro illumination on Jeremiah's icy reserve. Sommer abhorred solitude, yet treasured the clarity of distinct boundaries in the way success is counted sweetest by failures. Jeremiah – always alone – was discretely outlined by an unpeopled margin that seemed as tranquil as the eye of a storm.

With the feral acumen of pubescence, Sommer soon discerned how improbably often Jeremiah's isolation occurred within *her* radius. Impudently, she crossed the no-man's land surrounding the boy and made contact. Expecting some display of gratitude, joy, anger, relief, guilt, surrender, or even triumph, Sommer found only that now familiar stone face.

She *needed* stone.

Cold. Impervious. Durable.

What captivated her, however, was the unmistakable energy burning *beneath* the stone. In rare moments when Jeremiah lowered the shields of his eyes, Sommer felt exposed, almost irradiated. Moreover, she had witnessed that inexhaustible, inner force power Jeremiah's fearsome intelligence through sleepless weeks to incredible accomplishments. In strange contrast to her father's frenzied moods, however, Jeremiah's mania was an icily controlled paradox of light without heat, of fire that did not burn. With a single, sharp shake of his head, he became as cold and impenetrable as a containment vessel.

Thus – even for Sommer who alone had so closely approached his core – Jeremiah was an unnerving presence. The discomfort people felt explained his isolation. While Jeremiah was a constant, *others* shied from him. They shrank from the tangible paradox of an irresistible force immovably controlled. They shunned Jeremiah as they might a nuclear reactor – less from fear of explosion than from the more complex disquiet of awe.

Yearning for awe and finding little else to inspire it, Sommer took Jeremiah as her nucleus. Spinning through the mad years before her father's death, she was held by Jeremiah's sharp boundaries and perfectly regulated energy, kept by his fire-that-did-not-burn paradox, the contemplation of which became a koan. Soon – at those dark apogees just shy of death-spiral, at those urgent nadirs when crash was imminent – a telephone call to Jeremiah rescued her from whatever distant motel, clinic, or police station she found herself in. Always afterward – returning as a falcon to the center of its gyre, to the surcease of an upraised gauntlet and the nepenthe of a hood – she remained with him.

For a season.

Concealed beneath Jeremiah's stone face, however, was the quantum relativity of their bond: the need of a nucleus for its electron. Somewhere in his childhood, Jeremiah had transmuted a trifling smile into a golden perception of Sommer as his opposite yet perfected equal. She was rich, he was poor. She was blonde, he was dark. She was hot, he was cold. She was mercurial, elevated, remote; a star that outshone all around her. Jeremiah was earthbound, a quintessence of dust who in apprehension and action aspired to heaven.

For years, unnoticed, he had studied Sommer's wandering light – gazing across what felt to him a galactic distance, peering as he imagined his father might have peered at the alien Vassar girls through some telescope-like knothole in his custodian's shed. In ninth grade, however, Sommer's contact ignited an accelerant of fulminant longing. Launched, he fell not so much in love with Sommer as *into* her with the meter-per-meter-squared acceleration of gravity.

Sommer perceived Jeremiah as a fixed star. Introspection might have imploded the notion, leaving a black hole to consume her universe. Hence, the nature of their bond – a strange chemistry that transcended Sommer's incendiary flights and betrayals as well as Jeremiah's outward frigidity – remained veiled to her. Only once had she peeked; a moment ten years earlier when first began her continuing affair with Charles Gardiner.

Their initial coupling had been an impulse. Although little more than a work acquaintance, Charles was attractive and shamelessly eager at a moment Sommer was prone to lust. Following him from the Seaside Christmas party to the on-call doctor's sleeping room, she had spread her white thighs beneath a hiked-up, scarlet, evening gown and ardently reciprocated his sweaty stoking. A seemingly incidental moment of mutually gasped climax, however, had transpired as some strange smelting experienced as a boiling amalgam of sensation and emotion that spilled over both like molten metal poured from an crucible. Curiously, Sommer had sobbed. It was as if that brilliant process had assayed something unknown but elemental within her – the adamantine bond of her marriage.

Jerimiah's conjugations were infrequent and near arctic. The bond they shared was not forged in fire, but rather proven through repeated tests of perennial dark nights – Sommer's own quarter-to-three maydays, but also rare nights when, impossibly, Jeremiah, too, seemed to totter. She suspected such moments occurred when Jeremiah's, sharp, shake of his head failed to silence what he had once described to her as the plosive raspberry his convulsing father had sounded like an alarm buzzer. He offered little explanation during these moments, however, merely stony, disjointed assertions and baffling decisions such as a Thanksgiving night choice to abandon heart surgery and purchase Seaside.

"I won't go on losing like this," Jeremiah had said in answer to her every question.

"But you're a surgeon!" Sommer had protested in their dark, Manhattan bedroom. "Not a hospital administrator!"

At the time Jeremiah was, indeed, a renowned cardiac surgeon. He had perfected a procedure for pained and stifled hearts that married a microscopic web of patent vessels to the three, half-occluded arterial lifelines. The Jacobson technique was a desperate recourse – losses were inevitable – but its superiority to alternatives had earned him fame and considerable wealth. Nevertheless, despite substantial risk, Seaside and subsequent hospitals had proved sound financial and emotional investments. The new work had been a bulwark against Jeremiah's dark nights.

For a season.

"You can't abandon all you've built!" Sommer pleaded when returning dark nights gave rise to Jeremiah's hedge fund. "You're a hospital owner, not some Aga Khan!"

"It's not the principal, Sommer, it's the interest. Don't you see? It's the *principle* of the interest." She felt his invisible shudders in the trembling bedsprings. "Interest is ... it's *progress*. Growth. Upward movement. I can't lose that, don't you see? I don't want to lose interest. I ... I don't want to *fall*. Don't you see?"

In every other realm, Jeremiah was exactly what Sommer required, a man of perfect linearity – impervious, immutable, inexorable. She recoiled from his infrequent, bedroom moments of *depth* as she might cringe at the lip of a chasm. At heart, however, Sommer remained the trueborn progeny of merchants – her penchant for loopholes demanded the sanctity of contract. Thus indentured, she *kept* Jerimiah during such slips. Wrapping him with her arms and legs like a safety harness, securing him as to an anchored piton, she held fast till daybreak.

Lying with Charles that first time, Sommer had drifted in the afterglow of their white-hot smelting, loathe to wrench herself back to the Christmas party. Idly, unconsciously, she had summoned those dark nights with Jeremiah.

"Cold fusion," she had blurted.

In subsequent years, she and Charles would mine amusement from her quirky non sequiturs. Just then, however, he slept or drifted on his own thoughts. *Cold fusion* was, therefore, hers alone, an oracular pronouncement whose Delphic obscurity suggested a clue to some pregnant question, some intimate mystery she had entertained. In her warm languor, however, she allowed the question and the mystery to evanesce. Nevertheless, the *words* remained, as if an eerie alchemy of sexual fire had transmuted the raw ore of recollection into two exquisite nuggets, rare and pure. Sommer prized the cryptic words as a secret, hoarded possession. They became an arcane mantra whose spoken toll of *cold fusion* she savored only when alone.

"In loss there is gain. And vice versa," Charles said, reading from the red-lettered prospectus on the cocktail table. "So we can't lose!"

Melodie returned carrying a tray of drinks. She stooped to place the drinks on the table, paying special attention to the arrangement of Charles' glass and napkin.

"We'll lose," Jeremiah said, inspecting his icy-cold wine glass before sipping the sweet and sour *vin du glacier*. "But when old age shall this generation waste, *it* shalt remain, in midst of other woe than ours."

"What's that from?"

Jeremiah chuckled softly; his gaze was merciless.

"Death closes all, Charles, but until then we *hedge* our losses, financing the hedge with large gains on the upside." Jeremiah clinked his small, stemmed glass back onto the tabletop and made a see-saw motion with his hands. "Win ... Win! Don't you see? That's the ripe perfection of a hedge fund – whipsaw techniques that Mutuals can't use. And what's your alternative? Stock picking? Day trading? Mere roulette and, count on it, luck runs out. Besides, where's your leverage? The fund has *leverage*, Charles. Your half-million buys *no limits*. Do the arithmetic."

Charles smiled at an irony. Arithmetic was itself a limit and he detested limits. Time clocks, for example. Deadlines, schedules, budgets. *Particularly* budgets. Limits were harsh discipline for a boy whose favorite childhood board game had been *Clue* with its delightful, secret-passageways.

Consequently, Charles had invested much of his life in a quest for shortcuts. Not criminally – he was neither thief nor embezzler except with regard to his own assets. It was merely that he viewed certain *lesser* principles through a lens of entitlement polished by an only child's guilty parents who granted his every material wish. Blue-collar and penny-conscious, however, they satisfied their son's desires with floor samples, returns, knock-offs or unknown brands, honing a curiously astigmatic lens – entitlement to wishes that *almost* come true, entitlement to an *also ran* finish just out of the money.

Also-rans *do* run, however, and Charles was successful in his fashion. He was bright, with a Roman candle kind of brilliance, ever bursting with potential. He would be a poet! He would be a scientist! Writer! Architect! Lawyer! Philosopher! As each exploding blossom eclipsed the previous burst, the sound and fury attracted oohing and aahing patrons and mentors, especially in Charles' salad days when he was green ... no, *gold* – that ephemeral *first* hue. Yet even now – his dawn gone down to day – people saw resurrected in Charles' childish dress, springy step and mischievous grin some long interred part of themselves. They overlooked his stumbles with the impulse that plants a kiss on a scraped knee.

At some midpoint of his beginning, Charles had settled on a career in Medicine because a bright lad with potential could prolong the always-growing, never-grown, state of boyhood with college, medical school, and years of specialist training. Discovering upon completing a gynecology residency that gynecology bored him, Charles opted for additional years of urology. And while he found clogged prostates as humdrum as uterine fibroids, a life is budgeted with but so many false starts, so many seasons. Consequently, Charles began to contemplate the balmy indolence of vacation.

He had loved many women. In truth, a part of him loved *all* women, but especially ignored, well-to-do, older women who coddled him.

Surprisingly, however, he had remained faithful to Sommer through much of both residencies and the five years since.

Their affair began at Jeremiah's black-tie Christmas party for hospital staff the year he purchased Seaside. Charles – merely a rotating, resident-in-training – was not invited. On-call that night, however, he crashed the hospital dining room celebration.

Charles was instantly smitten with the hospital's new owner. Jeremiah hummed with power. He was formidably direct with precise words, a cool handshake, and a stone-faced gaze. He was a tall man, too – not giant, but, unlike Charles and most men, larger-than-life. Stature awed Charles, although – constantly whetted by impossible yearning – his awe had a cutting edge.

The owner's wife, Sommer, despite obvious wealth, worked as a nurse at the hospital. Charles knew her as a deliciously warm, somewhat older woman who playfully returned his flirtatious banter. Stripped of her professional garb for the party, however – she wore a red-sequined, front-slit, satin sheath and ruby-red, fuck-me heels – Sommer was as stunning as Jeremiah. Tall herself and raised on the stilettos, she sashayed with him shoulder-to-shoulder, equal yet strangely opposite complements.

Cavorting among the tuxedos and evening gowns in his green, resident's scrub suit like a pajama-clad child at a grown-up affair, Charles leered unabashedly at Sommer's long, white legs. She challenged his stare with a haughty glare that reminded him of Miss Scarlett, always his prime suspect in the game of *Clue*. Confronting her reproach with a wink, he converted Sommer's sneer into the stealthy smile of an accomplice. Exchanging glances, they began to play.

Jeremiah, completing a circuit of tables, rapped a spoon against a glass. "This has been a winter of discontent for most of you," he intoned. "Seaside's former owners saw managed healthcare as a long, dark night. You had your hiring freeze. Dwindling reserves. No more!" He waited for polite applause. "Under my stewardship, we've entered a new season. We're tightening our belts to expand!"

Jeremiah's tone, one that tall, rich men seemed to share, tickled Charles. Eyes twinkling with *watch this!* ... he grinned at Sommer as if showing off atop a fence.

"If we tighten our belts, how can we expand?" Charles shouted.

Sommer flinched. She had seen Jeremiah unleash nemesis upon hubris. The brash, young fellow in his green pajama scrub-suit was so boyishly disarming, however, Jeremiah merely chuckled and addressed serious questions from adult faces.

Sommer's smile applauded Charles' derring-do. Applause had always been his favorite aphrodisiac. Waiting for a few chairs to become vacant at the Jacobson's table, Charles popped into a seat beside Sommer as if materializing from a secret passageway. Across the table Jeremiah sat declaiming to a few rapt guests his preternatural grasp of past and future. Emboldened by the man's self-absorption, Charles snaked a hand beneath the tablecloth onto a naked thigh exposed beneath the slit of a shimmery red gown. Sommer, too, watched Jeremiah, knowing that were he less preternatural and more grounded in the present, were he a man for whom sex was noteworthy, he would have discerned the flare of her pupils and the delicate catch in her breath as she opened her legs to the insinuation of Charles' hand.

Completing his monolog, Jeremiah bit absent-mindedly into a cookie. A tiny flurry of crumbs and powdered sugar fluttered like snow onto his black tuxedo vest. Jeremiah looked down and fell silent.

"Well ... good times, all," Charles announced, standing. "But *some* of us work tonight. The call room beckons."

Brushing distractedly at the white flakes, Jeremiah seemed deaf. The dowager to his right badgered him for conversation. When finally, he looked up, he gave a single, sharp, shake of his head, and expounded anew his vision for Seaside.

Certain that Jeremiah would overlook her absence, Sommer slipped away. Although marriage had cured Sommer of both mood swings and *overt* promiscuity, her sexual appetite remained a torrid mismatch to Jeremiah's polar indifference. Faithful in her fashion, however, she practiced discretely what she called *serial bigamy*. Two recent episodes in that serial had taught her that the back hallway was deserted after midnight save for on-call doctors using the sleeping rooms.

Charles waited in an open doorway. He took her wrist, yanked her inside, and rose onto his toes to kiss her lips and neck. Tiring of tiptoes, he fell to his knees and spread her slit gown with his hands.

Back braced against the wall, Sommer pictured Jeremiah regaling the partygoers, a cornucopia showering them with his abundant self. But *this* one – she looked down and clenched Charles' hair in her fists – so empty! So needing to be filled. She raised a foot to kick off a stiletto, but Charles grabbed her ankle, looked up, and shook his head.

They had fucked rapaciously with a perfect communion neither veteran had experienced. And while, over time, the inexhaustible passion of the act had become lovemaking, the bond she shared with Jeremiah remained impervious and strangely untarnished.

Charles picked up the Hedge Fund prospectus and tapped it against the glass table.

"No limits, Jeremiah?" he said. "I do like the sound of that."

Abruptly he slapped the prospectus across the pile of black numbered spreadsheets like a card player trumping a discard. *Loss is gain, and vice versa* proclaimed bold, red letters, as if the declared suit were hearts ... or perhaps diamonds, the two sometimes confused.

"But you may change your mind ... *JJ* ... when you hear what I have to say. What *we* have to say."

The men turned toward Sommer whose cryptic expression was that of a bridge partner reacting to a foolishly bid hand.

Jeremiah tidied the table. "Charles, I must insist on Jeremiah for us to continue harmoniously as partners. Partners to be and, of course, the partners we've *been* these last – what is it, ten years? When exactly *did* we incorporate? Oh, yes! The Christmas party."

Charles lacked heart for games with *surprise* secret passageways. "Y.. You've known about us?"

Sommer sat silently, as if accepting some auction come round to her at last.

"I acquired the language of my wife's face in childhood, Charles. I knew before *you* did."

Burned by the dry ice in Jeremiah's voice, Charles rose. "She loves me!" he declared, glaring down from his modest height.

"Stipulated, Charles. Nevertheless, Sommer is indispensable to me. I would say *vital*. She keeps me, uh ..."

Jeremiah found his words swamped by a wave of images – dirty snow, a yelping dog, a whimpering boy trying to hold fast, a flailing father slipping again and again from two small, clenched fists. He gave a single, sharp shake of his head.

"Suffice that she *keeps* me. She won't choose otherwise."

Grown desperate in his Neverland, Charles ached for a permanent playmate, for the change of season and vacation Sommer could provide.

"I suppose your money *might* come between us," he feinted, savoring the irony of a climactic thrust. "But California is a community property state."

Jeremiah sighed.

"You are, indeed, the quintessential imbecile, Chuck! No, wait ... that was beneath me. *Chuck* was gratuitous. It's just that – well, Charles, I have *yet* to underestimate you." He looked at his wife. "Sommer, dearest, dearest, Sommer ... you do see it's the money, don't you?"

What Sommer saw in Charles' pouty scowl was the teapot tempest of a foiled prankster, a stormy child's thunderhead gloom that blows over, leaving sunshine and rainbows.

"Chuck is Chuck," Sommer acknowledged. "But it's more than money."

"We shall see."

Jeremiah turned back to Charles.

"Consider the clues, Charles. The wife of an extremely wealthy, *self-made* man employed as a nurse. A hyphenated name. A long-term lover despite a bedrock marriage. And surely you've discovered in my wife's mercurial heart that contrary vein of consummate practicality. Ask yourself, then ... having just inherited a substantial fortune from that *despicable...*" Jeremiah's clenched fists seemed to squeeze out the word like a gunshot. "*...BASTARD* of a father ... would so practical a woman marry a janitor's son without an iron-clad prenuptial agreement?"

Charles sank back into the love seat.

"Our assets have never been commingled, Charles. And Sommer's *independent* portfolio had no hedge-way when the market bottomed years ago. Actually, her lifestyle – I'm sorry dear. I know you detest the word – is completely contingent upon me. She has jewelry, of course. Credit cards. *Some* cash. Enough, perhaps, for a brief season."

"It ... *might* be alright," Sommer mused aloud, her hollow tone of foregone conclusion that of a woman addressing a fitting-room mirror.

Charles looked away.

Melodie, the waitress, reappeared. She carried a silver tray holding a candle warmer, three snifters and a half-filled or, perhaps, half-empty crystal decanter.

"I took the liberty of ordering Armagnac when I made our reservation," said Jeremiah.

Melodie splashed luminous amber liquid into each snifter, warmed the glasses over the candle, then arranged them on the table in a scalene triangle. Shimmery vapors rising from the warm Armagnac condensed halfway up each glass in a ghostlike ring from which drained tiny spectral rivulets. Charles stared into his crystal glass as if transfixed by some augury.

Jeremiah pulled a sheaf of papers from his briefcase. He dropped the papers atop the prospectus and spreadsheets as a final discard.

"A contract deserves a toast," he said.

Charles picked up the papers and scanned the first page. "You ... you're buying me in? A full share?"

"A *preferred* share. No voting rights and a number of contingencies."

"I'm *not* going away, Jeremiah."

"Today? Probably true. A ten-year investment in this oddball enterprise attests to something in you. But face it, Charles, you *can't* be counted upon. Realize that the boy in you is draining away and who knows what you might do. I intend to secure what future I have."

Charles glowered, but, indeed his anger was the fickle bluster of an April storm. He laughed at himself and turned to Sommer.

"Ironic, isn't it?" he said.

Although Charles' bright eyes demanded *See me!* with the petulance of potential, Sommer had always felt in their mirroring sheen a *See you* reciprocity. She knew from the first those eyes would never, *ever* be boardroom eyes. Nor, in truth, were they bedroom eyes. They were *playroom* eyes.

Jeremiah remained businesslike, a financier for whom cost yielded earnings, investment bought returns. His stone face showed only a flicker of annoyance when he glanced down at his coat sleeve and noticed again the long, unraveling thread. Plucking the thread, he sat impassively, twirling it in his fingers.

For once Sommer yearned for some chink in Jeremiah's stone-wall visage through which she might see the person within. Her sigh of futility disturbed the candle flame of the brandy warmer. A wavering shadow scudded around the table, silhouetting for an instant the adept fingers of Jeremiah's right hand tying unconsciously a chain of one-handed surgical knots in the coat thread. The staccato flitting of the fingers reminded Sommer of a desperate spider repairing its fractured web. And suddenly, as if the fingers had signed some *open sesame* that

Jeremiah could never *speak*, Sommer saw revealed in his face not only a wily financier hedging his bets, but a terrified boy creating a holdfast, and a healer whose knots had once married half-occluded lifelines and permitted stifled hearts to beat.

"I will, of course, demand discretion because –" As if sensing the threat of some surging tide, Jeremiah wheeled toward the hedge he had imagined a dam. In the window pane – a reflection limned by the falling star evanescence of the sputtering candle – he saw his eyes welling. Mentally mouthing once again the sacred words *just so far and no farther*, he needlessly he cinched his tie. "... Because I am not without feeling."

Frozen in the chill shadow of the season's early dusk, the courtyard garden lay dormant. Its vital greens and reds appeared now as frostbitten grays and black. The white cement path glimmered dimly like gritty snow on a moonless night. The pond shone lifeless and flat, its crystalline reflections like light on ice.

"Cold fusion," Sommer blurted.

The men wheeled, but nothing else escaped her. Charles shrugged and pocketed his contract. Jeremiah gave a single, sharp, shake of his head, and raised his Armagnac, no longer warm.

"To our Hedge Fund!" he announced. "In loss there is gain!"

And vice versa.

Birth

＊

Grunion Hunt

Relinquishing city lights, Pete and Mara crested the sea cliff and faced a black expanse of ocean. A hot, offshore wind – a Santa Ana – beat against their backs, whipped their hair, fluttered their clothes. Mara stopped to knot her baggy, tropical blouse beneath her breasts. Impatiently, Pete scuffed a sandal against a tuft of dry grass and coaxed her forward. Single file, they picked their way down a rock-strewn path toward a vague crescent of sand one-hundred feet below.

"Ouch!" cried Mara.

"What is it?"

"My toe! I stubbed my toe! This is dangerous, Pete Sheridan. It's dark. I can't even see the ocean."

"If your shorts get wet, you've gone too far. Here, give me your pail."

"We could fall! We could –"

"Hold my hand. We're almost there."

He nudged her down the path.

"This is silly, Pete! Californians *don't* hunt Grunion."

"Sure they do. I saw it in the movies when I was a kid. There was a character called Moon Downer ... Moon Dogger ... something like that. Fred MacMurray was the dad."

They squeezed through brush blocking their way.

"In the *movies*? Did you *personally*, in real-life, ever do this? You didn't, did you?"

"Well ... you have to go at night and all."

"I see. Listen, Pete, I grew up on the beach and I wouldn't know a Grunion if I saw one."

"They're small and long, I think. Silver-ish. Like little silver bananas only with eyes."

"Bananas with eyes. Great! Tourists do this, Pete. Californians do *not*."

"Sally Fields did," he said. "Annette Funicello did."

"And Fred MacMurray, I suppose."

"No. He stayed home."

They clambered over a small boulder and scrambled down a mound of talus at the base of a tiny cove carved in the sea cliff by tide and time.

"Pete, I hate to burst your bubble," Mara said, halting when her feet sank into sand, "but Sally and Annette probably grew up in Pittsburgh or Nebraska or somewhere. Honest."

"Look, Ms. Lamb, you can put on Eastern airs if–"

"Eastern airs?"

"Exactly. But the annual hunting of the Grunion is part of our California heritage. Yours *and* mine." Pete lifted both arms. "The untamed Pacific crashing against these rocks."

He swept his arms emphatically, grazing her with the empty bucket.

"Oww!"

She squinted her eyes, pursed her lips, and slugged him in the shoulder.

"Hey! It was an accident," he complained.

"That was, too. I was aiming for your nose!"

"Where was I?" he said, massaging his arm.

"Sea against the rocks, I think."

She ducked as he again swept his arm in the dark exclaiming, "The *brooding* rocks!"

"Oh, much more expressive," she said. "Brooding. Yes, I like that better."

"The dark of March's moon. Primal stirrings –"

"*Your* primal stirrings."

"Primal stirrings impel star-crossed grunion onto this lonely strand where *we* await, bucket in hand. The convergence of the twain."

"English teachers!" she muttered. "Look, Pete, what if there are millions of them? *Billions*? What if the beach is teeming with shiny, sex-crazed, silver bananas? Eyes bulging! Razor-teeth clacking like castanets!"

He dropped the bucket and shrugged a gym bag from his shoulder.

"Here. Far enough. It is not good for a man to go out too far."

She chuckled. "Wise move, Santiago. Now how about some light? It's scary here at night."

"I'm here."

"'Nuff said."

Pete knelt to remove a blanket and a Coleman lantern from the gym bag. Mara spread the blanket and sat cross-legged while Pete primed the lantern.

"Should I rub two sticks together?" he said. "To impress you?"

"Technology impresses me," she replied, removing a pack of matches from the bag. "Here. Close cover before striking."

"I bet you read that somewhere."

A scratched match sizzled, flared, and ignited the hissing lantern. Bathed in blue flame, the delicate mantles glowed red then stark white, animating the encircling cliffs with a wavering light. Pete planted the lantern in the sand and rummaged through his bag for a bottle of wine and a box of cheese crackers.

"Open the crackers," he said. "You have nails."

"Which I'd like to keep," she grumbled.

Pete unscrewed the cap of the wine bottle, filled two plastic tumblers, and raised his cup in a toast.

"Here's to—"

A wave hurled itself against the strand.

"Listen to that surf!" he said. "*Boom!*"

"And then a sigh. The wave's regret," Mara reflected. "We're very close, aren't we?"

Pete hoisted the lantern. Oblique sedimentary layers of black and gray striped the ancient cliff.

"Rocks to rollers about a dozen yards," he said. "Caught between the devil and the deep blue sea."

Mara hugged her knees. "How do you talk me into these things?"

"What things?"

"*Things!* Scary, dangerous things."

Pete tossed back his wine and poured another. "If you're still carping on that Knott's parachute ride, I suggest–"

"THAT! Don't even mention the parachute fiasco. I can't believe I went out with you again."

"It hardly ever gets stuck like that."

"An hour! An HOUR we were up there."

"They didn't charge us extra."

"An hour listening to you sing show tunes."

"I was trying to calm you. Weren't you calmed?"

"Calmed is not exactly the word that comes to mind. Something more, uh … *gastrointestinal*." She sipped her wine and chuckled. "Remember that huge, yellow pillow they dragged beneath us?"

"The air-bag?"

"It had a bulls-eye on it."

"A coincidental circular pattern."

"A *bulls-eye!* Comforting or what?"

"Fear of flying," Pete intoned.

"Flying is fine," Mara said. "*Falling's* a bitch!" She shook her head. "How *do* you do it."

"Animal magnetism," he said.

Wordlessly they drank wine and listened to the suspiration of the sea.

"So where's Annette?"

Pete pointed north. "See the fires? Probably up that way with everyone else."

"Uh … Pete? Why is everyone else someplace else?"

"They don't know."

"Oh, I see," she said. "Know what?"

"That *this* is where the big ones come."

"The *big* silver bananas with eyes. Great!"

"Stay alert. I think they sneak up on you."

"Well, let me know," she said.

"Oh, you'll know," said Pete.

Mara lay back on the blanket to gaze at the sky. The Santa Ana wind had blown aside the veil of smog to reveal a thousand stars.

"Look. There's Pisces."

Pete scooted closer. "Uh-huh."

"And Andromeda … Over there."

"Really! Andromeda, you say!"

Pete trailed his fingertips over her stomach, bare between the knotted, tropical blouse and the top of her shorts.

"The sky is a calendar," she said. "The sky is a clock."

"Science teachers," he muttered.

"The stars, the moon. How do you think the Grunion know that the time has come to –"

"Uh-huh."

"Stop it!" Mara said, wriggling away. "That tickles."

"Very sexy that hard, flat stomach. Not bad for someone your age."

"My *age*?"

"No stretch marks. Not bad for thirty-five."

"NOT until TUESDAY! And don't remind me then."

"What? You want to live forever?"

She turned her back and began to scratch in the sand with her finger.

"Maybe ... maybe ..."

Pete inched closer.

"What are you drawing?" he said.

"*P.S.* plus *M.L.* and a—"

"Heart with an arrow through it. Aww!"

Mara glanced at the cliff face. The striped eons seemed to writhe in the flickering lantern light. She turned to stare at the hard, black ocean. Catalina was a dark mass on the new moon dark horizon. A single point of light winked at the tip of the island.

"Do you think they're out there?" she said. "Waiting?"

"Who?"

"Who? The Grunion, that's who! Are they just floating around waiting for some exact moment to wiggle ashore, or what?"

"You're the encyclopedia."

"And you're the philosopher."

"... They're waiting, I think ..." Pete mused. "The moon, the stars. Something in the blood urges them forward, but holds them back at the same time, and then, splash! The heroes go for it."

"Right into the bucket."

"We..ll ... they don't know about the bucket. And *some* of them make it. The one's that stay in the water are–"

"Smart!"

"They die out. That's dumb."

"Really? Ask the ones in the bucket."

A breaker boomed. Mara flinched as a tongue of foam and whitewater lapped her legs and the blanket.

"Ooooh! That's cold!" Pete laughed. "There goes your heart and arrow."

"The tide is coming!"

"Probably."

"Let's go back, Pete."

"We have time yet."

Mara sat abruptly, her anxious frown etched by the lantern light. "No! Look! The line on the cliffs."

"We have time yet."

"No. See? This cove floods. The rocks, too."

"I bet you're right. Like *Toilers of the Sea*. He who sleeps must die. What's the French? *Qui*–"

"Damn it, Pete! The tide is coming. I'm scared!"

He rose to his knees and straddled her legs. Leaning forward, he forced her down onto the blanket. His weight pressed her hips into the sand.

"Pe..te? Not *now*. The tide!"

Deliberately he began to undo the knot of her blouse.

"I said we have time."

Something Borrowed, Something Blue

Hidden behind drawn blinds, a naked man and woman sprawled across a rickety bed. A crooked web of sunlight, woven by the blinds, crisscrossed the rumpled sheets. A muffled garble of Spanish words and music filtered through the shared wall.

"The walls here might as well be paper," said the man. "We make too much noise."

"You think that old lech cares?"

"He *lives* here. We're hourly."

"So what?"

"He turned up his TV. He can't *hear*."

"Oh, he hears us fine. Jostle the bed."

"We *were* jostling," the man said, rocking the noisy bed. "That's why he–"

The music fell.

"See? He turns it up when we *stop*," the woman gloated.

Rising on one elbow, she glanced at a white drug store bag sitting on the nightstand amid a clutter of change, keys, cigarettes, jewelry, and a strip of condoms.

"Let's get this over with," she said, sitting abruptly and reaching for the bag.

"Not yet," he said, grabbing her hand.

She swiveled to hike one knee up on the mattress.

"Everything will be the same," she whispered.

He nodded, tracing the muscles of her thigh. Her pose excited him with its open-legged contrariness.

"You look like an actress in an old black-and-white movie," the man said.

"Jane Russell?"

"No. Definitely not Jane Russell ... One foot on the floor. A Hays Code pose. Still quite proper."

"Proper? I'll give you proper!"

Tunneling beneath the bedclothes, she crouched animal-like on all fours and straddled him. The sheet, splashed with daubs of sunlight and shadow, arched over them like a tent.

"This reminds me of the girl next door when I was little," he said.

"Ooooo ... tell me more!"

"*Very* little! We used to play Pretend."

"Better and better!"

"Not this way. Out back. Under the clothesline. You know ... tents made of sheets. Sunlight through the trees made dappled patterns. Like this. Like camouflage."

Hunched over him, the woman trailed her dangled hair up his belly. "Want to play house?"

His face tightened. "I played soldier."

She bit his nipple. "Doctor?"

"Some..times ... robbers. Oh! Too soon!"

"Since when?" she laughed, throwing back the sheet. She crawled over his legs and immediately retrieved her blouse.

"You don't like to be naked, do you?" he said.

She perched on the edge of the bed. The bed springs squeaked as she wrestled her blouse over her head and wormed her feet into her shoes.

"That's silly, don't you think? You're in a funny mood."

"No. Even in bed. If I want you naked, I have to undress you."

"That's silly," she said, tugging on a shoe.

"Still afraid you'll stick to the floor?"

"Better safe than sorry!"

"This room hasn't been so tacky," he protested. "It's clean. Check the paper ring on the toilet seat."

"Right! They re-use those here."

She grabbed the white bag and stood. He stretched to catch her, but she was already marching toward the bathroom, her wooden heels clacking on the floor. She disappeared. The light clicked on.

"Your voice changed. Did you hear it?" he said.

He knew her changes; her sultry squalls, her lightning ire.

"What?"

"Your voice," he shouted. "A sudden chill. I felt it. Like a … like a front passing."

"You're crazy."

The man pulled the sheet over his chest.

"I know you," he whispered to himself. "I know you like a weatherman knows the weather."

The woman's distorted shadow played across the bathroom door.

"Why are you doing this?" the man said. "Why not with a girlfriend? Why not–"

"I want *you* here," she interrupted. "*Just* you."

The man heard the sound of rustling paper, tearing paper, periods of silence, and finally the tinkling of her urine. A toilet flushed.

"Four minutes," the woman called from the bathroom.

"Four minutes," he repeated, buckling on his wristwatch.

"Check your watch!"

"I did, I did."

She shuffled through the doorway carrying a small, clear vial at arm's length.

"You're holding that thing like nitroglycerine," he said.

"I'm sorry, what?"

"Like nitroglycerine," he repeated. "The vial."

"Not supposed to jostle it," she said, her thoughts elsewhere. "Make some room."

He cleared a space on the nightstand, dropping the strip of condoms onto the bed. She positioned the vial meticulously, then skittered around the bed and burrowed between the sheets. Facing away from the vial, they nestled like spoons, his arms ringing her.

"So what happens now?" he said.

"Yes is blue."

They waited.

"I can feel your heart fluttering against your ribcage."

She said nothing.

He pinched her blouse. "Take this off."

"I'm cold."

He said nothing.

"Sooner or later, right?" he said at last.

"How long?"

"Couple more minutes. Sooner or later, right?"

She sighed wearily. "We've discussed this. I'm almost forty."

"Right?"

"I'm almost forty. I–"

"Right?"

"Everything will be the same," she repeated, her face turned away.

The muffled Spanish from the TV set in the next room grew louder.

"The lech got tired of waiting," she said.

The man sensed some urgency in the Spanish words. "Is that a newsbreak?"

She cocked her head. "Paper towels ... soaks up spills. Nothing."

He shrugged. "Sounded important."

"How long?" she said.

"Almost time."

"You knew all along," she declared brusquely. "I mean, you knew *someday*."

"I know."

"What are you feeling? Tell me what you're feeling."

He nodded toward the shared wall. "I wonder if he can hear us now. Talking."

"That old man?"

"Yes, that lonely, old man. Do you think he understands what we say, or just listens to the other?"

"Tell me what you're feeling! I have a right to know!"

"I wonder what it's like for him – borrowing whatever life spills through a shared wall from a couple in another room?"

"What are you talking about?"

"Just thinking," he said.

"How long?"

"It's time."

He felt her shoulders tense.

"Y..*you* look."

He released her and rolled toward the nightstand.

"It's blue, isn't it?" she whispered, eyes squeezed shut. "I..I know it's blue."

"Very blue."

She looked.

"Congratulations," he said, kissing her cheek.

"That's the bluest blue I ever saw," she mumbled dazedly, as if battered by implications and possibilities.

"Very, very blue," he repeated softly, almost to himself.

Silently they stared at the nightstand. Sunlight through the vial cast a faint blue shadow over his loose change, their keys, her jewelry. Jerking upright, the man reached for his cigarettes, but glanced at his watch and changed his mind.

"We should be going," he said.

"I have time yet."

He handed the woman her Rolex. "I can't afford it."

"I ... I could pay this once."

He took a gold necklace from the nightstand and fastened the chain around her neck. "Pretty," he said. "New?"

She sighed. "No ... I've had it a while ..."

"Does *he* know yet?" he said, retrieving the woman's wedding set.

"*We* just found out!"

"You know what I mean."

She took the rings from his hand, slipped the wedding band over her finger and anchored the large solitaire above it.

"I told him I would know today."

"He'll be happy now?"

"For a while. He – Look, I *had* to! You know that. You know what he–"

He placed a finger over her lips and cradled her in his arms. A new program was beginning in the next room, the same foreign words, but different music.

"What is that?" he said.

"What?"

"I recognize that music. It's a game show, you know the one, only it's in Spanish."

"Everything will be the same," she said.

He shrugged. "'A shudder in the loins engenders there the broken wall' ... Funny. I remember that from high school. Yeats, I think."

"'*Yates*'" she said. "It's pronounced '*Yates*.'"

"Well, it *looks* like *Yeats*."

She touched him. As always, he responded, but when she tried to duck beneath the sheet, he stopped her.

"Not that way," he said.

She lay back. He fell onto her, kissing her throat as he groped for the condoms.

"You don't need those anymore," she said huskily.

He rose onto his elbows, suddenly mindful of her belly,

"We should be careful. I'm pretty heavy."

"Silly man. Everything is the same."

Her stared into her eyes – deep blue, *steel* blue – and rolled to sit on the edge of the bed.

"You won't break me," she said.

He stared at the shared wall.

"I know."

"You *won't*."

"I know."

Last Train

A train was coming.

Close now. Coming fast. A headlight beam slashed the darkness. A horn moaned. The ground trembled. The air exploded in a tornado of clattering wheels and flickering coach cars. The caboose clickity-clacked past. A red marker beacon shrank and dissolved in a pink glow lining the horizon. Loneliness lingered in the air like smoke. Joey closed his eyes and woke.

Curled on his side, clutching his wife's pillow, he heard the rustle of her newspaper from the kitchen. Scraping his tongue over dry lips, he pumped a sleeping fist and eased his legs over the edge of the bed. Motion set the room spinning, but Joey's gut was a gyroscope that could correct a yawing Motocross bike 50 feet mid-air and his gut was intact. The accident had broken only his backbone.

Joey's pajama bottoms lay coiled on the floor like a shed snakeskin. Fused vertebrae fired a warning shot as he wrestled them over his legs. He stood cautiously and trekked across the bedroom to retrieve his wallet from greasy coveralls draped over a hamper. Compelled to check yet again, he removed the carefully folded credit card receipt his wife had dropped on the bathroom floor yesterday morning. A single purchased item was printed plainly above Susan's signature.

The receipt was *not* some imagined nightmare. He shoved the slip into a pajama pocket and limped into the kitchen.

Dressed for work in an outfit well beyond Joey's means, his wife glanced up from her newspaper.

"I figured you for a horizontal day, baby."

"I have to finish a Kawasaki I'm tricking out for Tomlinson."

"Can you?"

Joey poured himself a tall glass of milk and sat. Susan reached across the dinette table to brush at his wild, red hair. Joey shrugged her hand away.

"The birthday boy is cross this morning," she said.

"I wasn't expecting that surprise party, Susan."

"Hence the term *surprise*."

He downed half the milk.

"I must be fifty years older. What was I drinking there at the end?"

"Listerine."

"No way!"

Susan touched his cheek, allowing her fingers to drift down his smooth chest.

"I could tell you anything this morning, couldn't I?"

"We, uh ... we *did it*, didn't we?"

"The drug that heals our sorrows," Susan said.

"Is that a yes?"

"It's something someone said about forgetfulness."

"C'mon, Suz. You got years of schooling on me."

"And years of years. Fifteen to be exact."

"Did we or not?"

"Would you like to see my carpet burns? ... You were possessed last night, Joey. I couldn't have stopped you if I wanted to and I didn't. It's been a long time."

Joey looked away. "It's the medicine. It ... it happens."

"Especially to young men with old women."

"Bag that crap, Suz."

She crossed to the sink and gestured with the coffee pot. Joey shook his head.

"It felt good again, Joey," she said, refilling her cup. "Good being *us* again."

"I didn't, uh … use anything, did I?"

"Quite the Alley Oop."

"What's Alley Oop?"

"Nothing, nothing … a caveman in an old comic strip. You wouldn't know it."

"Then why say it?"

She replaced the pot and gazed through the kitchen window at the California sunshine. Their house – *her* house before they married – perched high on an Orange County hillside blanketed with yellow mustard and orange poppies. At the base of the hill the San Diego Freeway and the railroad tracks ran together for a mile before they parted at San Juan Capistrano. The morning sunlight was like a honeyed glaze on the tile roof of the Capistrano depot and the dome of the Mission church. The sunshine was a lie, Susan thought, but a good one.

"I'm no Science Guy," Joey said. "But I know what I learned in Health. One time bareback is all it takes. You might be pregnant, you know?"

She turned. "Would it be so bad? As bad as you've made out?"

Joey swirled his milk and said nothing.

"I guess that's my answer," she said.

"I had a dream, Suz. I can't shake it."

"Try," she said, returning to the table.

"You know how a dream can make you—"

"I'm not into dreams, Joey."

"God, I hate this feeling."

"There's Maalox in the cabinet."

"The feeling from the dream."

"It's just a feeling."

Joey studied her face. "Have you been crying?"

She shrugged. "My period is due."

"That makes you cry?"

"It can … Look, you have *your* chemical imbalance, I have mine. Maybe I should take some of your Prozac."

"Go ahead. But try to get a woody." He waited for a wisecrack that never came. "That was funny, Suz."

She smiled. "… Yes, baby, it was. Thanks for trying. I'm preoccupied, I guess. My boss is in town."

Joey had already noticed her red stilettos.

"Are the heels new?"

She extended a leg. "Do you like them?"

"They look like the ones you wore when we met."

"Where are the Choos of yesteryear?" she said.

They had met at a Perris, California Motocross track where Joey was racing and Susan was pitching radio time to the promoter. Her red stilettos had clinched the order, but, later, as she scouted the track alone, the spiked heels proved as dangerous as they looked. Stumbling in the soft dirt, she fell into Joey's arms.

"Are you here posing for *Easyriders*?" he said.

"Sure," she teased. "A MILF spread – Mom's I'd Like to Forgo."

She asked Joey for a lesson in Motocross to help her with the promos. He showed her around, but insisted she wear his work boots.

"The devil wears Pravda," she said, striking a pose.

The remark left him behind, but Joey wasn't competing in that game. He enjoyed *her* enjoyment, her laughter and the playful way she clomped about. He asked her to stay for the race.

Throwing her arms around him after he won, she gushed, "How in the world can you do that?"

"Do what? … Ride?"

"Fly! You can *fly*. You roar up those slopes and suddenly you're 50 feet in the air."

"Flying is the easy part, Suz," he had replied. "*Landing* is the trick."

Susan glanced at the kitchen clock and stood. "I'll miss my train," she said.

Joey dodged a kiss on the head and grabbed her arm. "Let's meet in L.A. tonight."

"I have a few late calls to make."

"Make 'em."

Stalling, Susan checked her keys and purse. "Okay," she said finally. "It's been ages since we went out. Call me later."

The front door slammed. Immediately Joey pulled the receipt slip from his pocket. He gave no thought to his compulsive scrutiny. Actions spoke for themselves, but motives were mysteries, and Joey was a reluctant detective. When the therapist his surgeon ordered him to see began harping on *unconscious motives,* Joey had bailed. The idea that another mind haunted his own mind like some bitch-seat ghost driver whispering in his ear was a fruitcake notion Joey couldn't swallow. The depression pills his doctor gave him, he *could* swallow. Chemical imbalance he could picture – like the sour lemonade his mother made when he was a boy before she died – not enough sugar when just-right was sour-sweet.

Joey hobbled to the refrigerator, poured more milk, and stood staring at the trash compactor. After finding the receipt in the bathroom, he had ransacked the house and finally discovered the crumpled pregnancy test under garbage Susan had used to hide it. The result of the test had been unreadable, but the meaning was perfectly clear to someone who had passed health class.

Apart from last night, Joey had not slept with Susan since his accident.

Strangling an urge to root through the trash, he stared out the window and refolded the receipt, unconsciously passing the paper creases between his fingernails again and again until each was razor sharp. Blind to the sunlit hill and the vibrant yellow and orange wildflowers, Joey saw only the Capistrano depot and Susan's northbound train at the station.

Leaving.

* * * * *

Craving a glass of wine with lunch, Susan watched Todd gulp half his martini. He parked his glass and reached across the table.

"Bummer, Susie-Q. What'll we do?"

The *we* was smooth and typically Todd. Susan squeezed his fingers, then plucked a thin lemon slice from her water glass and dropped it on a bread plate. The yellow circle on the white china reminded her of an egg. She looked away and sipped the water.

"I don't know that I've decided yet," she said.

Todd toyed with his butter knife.

"Well … is there any chance? I mean … at all?"

"Drug store tests aren't perfect, but—"

"Not the test."

Susan stiffened. "You mean a chance it's not yours?"

"A man has to ask. You're *married*, you know."

"It's not Joey's, Todd."

He nodded noncommittally.

"Or anyone *else's*, okay? Let's just call it mine."

"Don't get your back up! I wasn't saying anything."

"And I wasn't *asking* anything. I thought you should know. My bad."

"You're starting to talk like the kid, Susie-Q."

"Joey. His name is Joey."

"My bad," Todd said.

A teen-aged waitress in orange Day-Glo hot pants and tee-shirt brought salads.

"Ground pepper?" she said to Susan.

Susan shook her head.

"Spice it up?" she said to Todd.

"Some like it hot, sweetie."

The girl jiggled with each crank of the pepper mill and swayed as she sashayed away.

"Looking to fill an opening, Todd?" Susan chuckled. "She'd probably be happy to work under you."

He yanked his eyes from the waitress's behind and laughed.

"Kid has potential. She sold the hell out of that pepper mill."

Susan found Todd's laugh particularly attractive, despite having seen him practice it in front of a mirror. The laugh was easy, open, disarming – part of an affable camouflage that had helped make him corporate vice-president of marketing for AllTalk radio and Susan's New York boss. He liked to say that selling Farm Report airtime to some Boonieville tractor repairman was ardor not Arbitron. He urged his people to 'give the rubes a laugh or two. Show some leg … a little tit if you're blessed. Your real product is *you*.'

Susan began reporting to Todd shortly after her wedding, mere weeks after she and Joey met. Her wedding shower was replete with *cougar* and *boy-toy* jibes from her friends, but the passionate urgency she and Joey felt was something other than lust. Joey was awkward, even reluctant sexually. Nevertheless, for Susan he was a sublime *lover*. Some deep and timeless libidinal energy drove a fervent adoration that penetrated her untapped core.

Thus, for almost three years, she had tolerated Todd's shoulder rubs and occasional gropes, while bluntly rejecting his propositions. The sponge-like resiliency with which he absorbed each 'no sale' was as much a part of his charm as his relentless persistence. Although Todd was no threat to her *marriage*, Susan did miss the kind of cave-man sex to which she had always been drawn. Having dinner with Todd the night of Joey's accident, she realized that her choice of outfit that morning – new lingerie, her *"maybe-you'll-get-lucky"* red stilettos – suggested fantasy morphing into plan. An emergency call from the hospital had interrupted, but not squelched that progression. When

Joey's post-traumatic pain and depression rendered him not merely physically impotent but emotionally unreachable, she had finally settled upon Todd as a convenient, partial solution. Todd was bright, good-looking, and funny. Pre-sold, he required no bothersome ramp-up. Frequent trips to the L.A. office made him available, but not annoyingly so. Happily married himself, he was unlikely to become a millstone. It turned out, too, that, while certainly a caveman in bed, he was also a salesman and, thus, eager to please.

"The mystery to me, Susie-Q, is why on earth you'd consider keeping it." Todd speared a forkful of salad. "You're not the mom type, you know?"

She shrugged.

"The ol' tick-tock?"

"Maybe ... Okay, sure. I'm almost forty."

"Your forty still looks twenty. Wait until you're fifty."

"You are one glib bastard, Todd."

Todd wore his necktie loose and collar button open, flashing a peekaboo patch of chest hair. The overt testosterone of his display reminded Susan of markings on a dangerous snake, a kind of biological *caveat emptor* she found sexy although deep-down she preferred Joey's boyish physique.

"You want *more* than glib, Susie-Q?" Todd said. "Then riddle me this. If you keep it, what do you tell the kid? Can you come clean? Is he *that* stuck on you?"

"No ..." she mused. "He *might* weather a surprise baby. It's iffy, but possible. Another man? ... No. Never."

"Get out! He thought you were a virgin? He can't be *that* dumb."

"I love my husband, Todd. Don't insult him to my face. And no, he didn't think I was a virgin. He *did* think I'd be faithful."

"Tiptoeing around the *D-word*, why would he think that?"

"Because I promised him."

"And you meant it. At the time." Todd twiddled with the wedding band on his ring finger. "It's not who you dance with, Susie-Q. It's who you *leave* with – that you always go home with who brung ya."

"Joey's a possessive type, Todd. Not crazy so, but so. That's why he never raced for a team. The bike was his or not. It's hard to explain, but ... he *doesn't* share."

Todd pushed aside his empty salad plate. "So, I guess you either go it alone or put one helluva spin on it. Will he buy immaculate conception?"

Susan picked at her salad, remembering last night and Joey's "so you could be pregnant" remark this morning. A baby coming early wasn't rare. It wouldn't be a hard sell.

"Or maybe," Todd continued, "this is a perfect excuse for you to move on. If things were hunky-dory you wouldn't be seeing me, you know?"

"I think that's obvious, Todd. His accident—"

"You were already itchy. Face it. You're mismatched. You should have carded him when he proposed."

"*I* proposed, Todd!" She took a drink of her water. "... Oh, you may be right. It's not the fifteen years, though. Not yet, anyway."

"So what is it?"

"He thinks I look down on him."

"Don't you?"

"He was U.S. Motocross champion three times."

"Good for him. He earned a first-round bye. In *this* round, however, he's just a mechanic while you're as educated, bright, successful, and attractive as ever. And, I might add, *still* the money-maker."

"We're more than what we *do*, Todd."

"Can't say I buy that, but if so, problem solved. Embrace the inner *non-doers* who found each other to begin with."

She picked out several baby ears of corn from her salad and dropped them on the bread plate beside the lemon. Todd waved for a refill.

"Very perceptive, Todd. Try it on yourself."

"Haven't seen a need."

Chewing a bite of salad, Susan spit an olive pit onto her fork and dropped it beside the lemon and baby corn. The arrangement had a faintly disturbing still-life quality to it.

"You're ruining a good thing, you know?" Todd said.

"Neither of us saw it as a *thing*, Todd. It was just good sex when you were in town."

"I, *myself*, am what I do," Todd smirked, eying the waitress again as she brought his martini.

Susan asked the girl to remove the bread plate.

"But it's never *just* sex, Susie-Q. If that's all you need, you masturbate. Safer, cheaper and guaranteed."

"More insight, Todd?"

"The doctor is in. Why, for instance, would you think *good thing* meant *us*. You're my top producer – a *real* good thing."

"That won't change."

"Sweetie, you have a gift, but watch your minutes nosedive when you're waddling around big as a cow. And how about those weeks or months of maternity leave you'll need to discover how much you hate changing diapers?"

"Sprawled on a *pin*, am I? But what if I've been hustling you all along, Todd? What if my inner-self is really a mom?" She sipped her water. "Tell me something. I told you I couldn't take the Pill. Why didn't you use condoms?"

"You didn't make me."

Susan pushed away her picked-over salad. Todd upended his martini and signaled for the check.

"I never made Joey either," Susan said finally. "He did it because he didn't want a child."

"He *is* a child."

"I'm meeting him in town for dinner tonight."

"Plan to tell him the truth?"

"I have to, don't I?"

"You're a salesman," Todd said.

Outside on the sidewalk, Todd held her loosely, his hands on her waist. Strangers swirled around them.

"I know all this is a downer," Todd said, "But ... my plane isn't till five ...?"

"Why lock the barn after the horse escapes?"

"Or maybe I was thinking you needed to talk. Just cuddle for a while. But what do I know? Women are mysteries."

Susan knew he didn't mean it, but she was sure he meant it *some*. Holding his gaze, she found herself wondering if the thing inside her had Todd's blue eyes. Like sunshine, blue eyes were a lie, but a *good* lie.

"Do you know who Alley Oop is, Todd?"

"The caveman."

She touched his cheek.

"Never change, dear. You're perfect."

They shook hands and went separate ways.

* * * * *

The motorcycle throbbing between Joey's thighs was unfamiliar, but felt good – like first-time sex. After his accident, he had dismantled his own bike and sold the parts piecemeal. This was a work bike – he had built it for the team he worked for now and signed it out for a shakedown run. It was sound; ready to do whatever he asked.

A brief shower had raised oil residue on the pavement so Joey was riding deliberately. Perhaps *too* deliberately. A flash of high beams from behind jarred him. In his handlebar mirror, Joey saw an onrushing semi veer into an outside lane. Rumbling past, the truck blasted an air horn. Joey shrugged. An untimely accident would spoil his plans.

Eyes watering from the wind, he blinked away tears and glanced at his watch. Susan would have two hours until the last train at ten o'clock. He exited the freeway at Flower, spiraled up the circular ramp, and weaved between stalled lanes of cars, zigzagging down side streets to a block near Susan's office.

Joey had always chafed at the constraints of street riding. On dirt he felt free. On dirt – breaking loose the rear wheel with a goose of the throttle – he glided over the track, steering with the throttle, with the variable traction rpm's imparted to the spinning wheel.

And jumps!

Plowing into a slope, he was squashed into the saddle, a thousand-pounds heavy. And then, as wheels left earth, weight dropped away like balloon ballast. In those weightless, airborne moments – he and the bike hurtling as one – Joey had often felt an impulse to push away and fly off on his own. He knew, however – knew *absolutely* now – that while he might separate himself from the bike, their freefall arc was predetermined. Hard or soft, they landed together.

Landing was a moment when the sin of flight was punished with the same crushing weight as the launch. Landing demanded life or death choices – angle of the frame, alignment of the wheels, posture in the saddle, position of his feet on the pegs. Racers who made it to Joey's level alive and intact were extremely good at landing, however. He hadn't made a mistake in years.

The restaurant was on a street clogged with fancy cars disgorging well-dressed passengers. Squeezing the clutch with his left hand, Joey toed the bike into first and wrenched the throttle. Almost disappearing in a blue cloud of burnt rubber billowing from the screaming rear wheel, he leaned precariously to power-slide the bike, cock-eyed, into a gap between two parked Mercedes. Startled pedestrians shook their heads sourly. Joey kicked the bike-stand and killed the engine.

Unzipping his leather jacket, he removed his helmet. The air was filled with the smell of wood-fired ovens, garlic, cigarettes, marijuana, and tire smoke. Music spilled from clubs to mix with jabber on the sidewalk. Susan stood just apart from a long line of people inching in twos or fours past an ogreish bouncer raising and lowering a red, velvet rope. Joey watched her scan the crowd, searching for him, and noted how often her eyes lingered on some stranger.

Susan rushed forward.

"You're riding!"

"You're not mad at me?" he said.

"I'm not! Not at all."

Dismounting, he clicked his helmet into the helmet lock beside the passenger helmet. "Hoping to get rid of me, Suz?"

"I'm hoping to *keep* you, Joey. You've been down so *long*. But ... last night? This? Maybe things are looking *up*."

"Sure ... I'll be racing soon."

She hugged him and held on.

"No ...not soon, but why not *someday*? Braces and therapy and a different kind of racing, perhaps. The surgeon never said it was *impossible*."

"I'll wish real, *real* hard."

"You have someone to love, Joey. You also need something to do and something to hope for."

Any disappointment in her voice was always an arrow in Joey's heart. "Okay, you're right, who knows?" he said quickly. "So, what's for dinner?"

Susan led the way to a quiet, candlelit, Italian restaurant and asked for a rear table. As soon as they sat, Joey automatically ordered root beer for himself and Chardonnay for Susan.

"Why here?" Joey said, eyeing stucco walls covered with old religious paintings. "It's dead."

"Because you love spaghetti, silly. Besides ... we can talk."

The prospect of talking kept them quiet. They studied menus until their drinks came. Joey ordered spaghetti with meatballs and downed half his root beer while Susan chose Chicken Piccata.

"No swordfish this time?" he said when the waiter left.

"I'm not in the mood for it."

"Problems with your boss?"

"No. That went fine," she said, circling the rim of her wine glass with a finger. "Performance review, next year's targets…" She took a deep breath and looked up. "Joey, we need to start a family."

"We're *already* a family."

"Of course, but–"

"*Again* with this? I'm not enough for you?"

"No, you're not," she blurted, rushing on, uncertain where the leap had landed her. "No one is enough for *anyone*. Oh, baby, baby … It's *time*."

Joey upended his drink and signaled for another. It came with the food. They ate for a while.

"Say something, Joey."

"Time for what?"

"We have things we're meant to do, things we have to choose before time runs out on us."

"Keep it simple. What are you driving at? Like, uh … the change or something?"

"Not *just* that."

"All I hear you saying is you want me to share you."

"I want *us* to share, baby. A *child*." She hesitated only briefly. "*Our* child. Us together. And who knows? You said it this morning. We may already be pregnant."

Joey felt played by the *we*. He snorted and grabbed up his mug sitting across from Susan's still untouched wineglass. How he knew, he didn't know, but suddenly he *did* know the result of the test in the trash. He knew that Susan was pregnant and planning to lie.

"Talk to me, baby," she said.

It didn't change anything, he thought, swirling his drink. Nothing could change the way he felt about Susan.

"Okay … okay, Suz. Sure. Let's do it."

Susan pounced, pulled Joey to his feet, and kissed him. "If last night *wasn't* the beginning, Joey, tonight will be."

"You, me and baby makes three."

Trying but failing to read his face, Susan signaled for the check. "Give it time, Joey."

"Who needs time? Let's get the party started."

"Okay ... I understand," she said slowly, signing the credit card receipt. "Good enough for now."

Joey tapped his watch. "You missed the last train, Suz."

"What? Oh, great! What'll we do?"

"I've got wheels."

She smiled. "I don't know, Joey ... You've had quite a few root beers."

His face was flat.

"C'mon, baby, make this fun. You haven't taken me riding since—"

"Since the last time you wore red spikes."

She glanced at her feet and looked up puzzled. "Since your accident."

"Yep. That was the day."

Outside, Joey climbed on the bike. Susan waited for his kick-start.

"Just hop on. I have to use the starter now," he said, handing her a helmet.

"You brought two?" she said, buckling the chin strap.

"You're not the only one who throws surprise parties."

"*Quite* a surprise, considering my outfit. I'll have to hike this thing up to my panties."

"Are you wearing any?"

"Don't be such a man, baby. Okay ... All in." Hitching her skirt high enough to spread her legs across the saddle, she drew whistles from the sidewalk. "Like an *Easyriders* photo-shoot," she giggled, scooting forward and squeezing her stockinged thighs against Joey's hips.

A Santa Ana wind had nudged aside the rainclouds. Palm fronds shimmied in a warm breeze. The engine caught with a growl when Joey pressed the starter button. He jockeyed the bike into traffic, toed the shifter into first, and zoomed away.

Engine roar and helmets made shouting necessary, so they said little for almost an hour. Crouched in the lee of Joey's back, her arms clamped around his waist, Susan was content in her thoughts. Occasionally she squeezed her arms and legs, saying everything she wanted to say. Too soon, she heard the low moan of a train, looked up and saw – harshly rendered in the full-moon light – her familiar hillside and the stretch of tracks running alongside the freeway. The oscillating headlight beam of an approaching train swept like a scythe across the track-bed.

"Right on time," she heard Joey yell. "The last train."

A violent swerve might have ripped Susan from the saddle if not for her arms locked around Joey's waist. The bike angled into a dirt slope. For an instant she was squashed into the saddle, a thousand pounds heavy, and then ... weightless.

"NO! I CAN'T!" Joey bellowed. "DON'T LET GO."

Through clamped thighs and locked arms, Susan felt Joey strain and the bike respond – not with a change of trajectory, which was predetermined, but with a change of aspect ... like a bird about to light. In that momentary assertion of control, she experienced a giddy promise of delivery broken instantly by an impact so crushing it seemed as if their bodies had merged.

* * * * *

Susan stepped back from her front doorway.

"Come in, Todd," she said. "Good to see you again."

He peered into the house as if expecting an ambush.

"You've been missed, Susie-Q. The office is eager to get you back."
He eyed her cane. "Leg still bothering you?"

"The cane? I use it for sympathy. Better each day. See?" She raised
her hands and turned in a circle. "The doctor says I'll be running
marathons soon."

"Really? ... You don't run."

"Still all figured out, am I? Well, maybe I'll start."

Todd followed her into the living room. Susan sat on the sofa.

"Look at all this stuff," he muttered. "Medals and pictures and ..."
He touched a trophy timidly.

"You need a hat to stand hat-in-hand, Todd."

"What? ... Oh, I get you. Look, uh ... I thought it best not to visit
given the circumstances."

"Don't worry about it. I'm glad you don't have to remember me that
way."

He took a seat on the edge of a facing chair. "Feels odd ... first time
here and all."

"Would a drink help?"

"No, I'm good. I'll wait for the restaurant."

Susan watched him study her.

"People said you were a real mess at first."

"Gee, thanks, Todd."

"I'm just saying how great you look now. No scars."

"Under the dress," she said. "Two drink minimum for the show."

His eyes dropped to the hem of her short skirt.

"Everything else is, uh ... okay?"

"I lost my womb along with the baby, Todd." She crossed her legs.
His eyes registered a flash of panties. "The rest is intact and fit for
duty. I can get a doctor's note if you like?"

"I'm not *all* ulterior motives, Susan. *You* called me. You say you
want to come back to work. I need to know you're ready."

"Ready and willing, Boss. Our good thing, right? I'll milk the cane and double my minutes."

"Maybe ... maybe ..." he said thoughtfully. "But why? I hear you're not going hungry."

"Not for money. Joey had a good accident policy. A comp settlement, too, since, technically, he was road testing a work bike. Our lawyer says that Amtrak and the Highway Commission will cave sooner or later. Negligence at the construction site."

Todd glanced toward a closed door. "So, tell me, how *is* the kid."

"Stable."

"This setup *has* to be exhausting."

"Insurance wanted him out of the ICU so they provide round-the-clock nursing."

"But how long can you—"

"As long, Todd."

"Aren't there ... uh, places? Homes?"

"*This* is his home."

"Easy, Suzie-Q. Easy. I'm just wondering, okay?"

Susan looked at her hands clasped in her lap.

"I lied to him that night, Todd."

"So? Lies are like lubricant. Besides, guilt only stretches so far. He almost got you killed."

"No, Todd. He *saved* me."

"Really? This should be good."

"It is. His team helped reconstruct the accident. I know exactly what happened that night."

"Me, too. He head-butted a train."

"Joey swerved. Tire marks say something was in the road. He used an excavated dirt pile to jump a construction barrier. Hitting the train was inevitable, but Joey was a champion; he *chose* how."

"Didn't he break his back with one of those choices?"

"Would you listen! He shouted *don't let go* and I felt him wrench the bike around. Everyone agrees that he glanced off the train at the perfect angle ... for *me*. *He* took the full impact. His body was my air bag."

Todd glanced again at the bedroom door. "Well ... give the kid props for trying, I guess. Look, can we blow? This is too weird."

"I understand. Let me tell the nurse."

Susan stood and opened the door. A bosomy, black nurse occupied a large chair next to a hospital bed enclosed in a traction crib. Joey lay half-suspended; his torso and both legs in casts; his head and neck immobilized in a halo collar. Surrounding the bed were monitors, oxygen bottles, suction equipment, nebulizers, IV bags.

"Can I help with anything, Etta? Bring you back something?"

"We're good," said the nurse, patting Joey's motionless hand. "And you've been moping around here too long now. Go enjoy your evening. We'll be fine."

Todd peeked over Susan's shoulder.

"He looks asleep," he said.

Joey's eyes gaped open.

"Damn!" Todd exclaimed. "They told me he can't hear."

"He hears, Todd. He just doesn't understand."

Todd stared with the fascinated revulsion he might show toward road-kill whose mysterious insides lay exposed.

"This is it for him? Like ... *forever?*"

Susan wheeled. "All his needs are met, Todd."

Although Joey's body was paralyzed and his head and neck fixed in the halo collar, the muscles of his face and throat were intact. He began to grimace and growl. The motives for such displays were mysterious, but often they seemed to communicate instinctual pleasure or, more often, frustration such as hunger or soiled bedclothes. Etta stood, felt the bed sheet, and then began to stroke Joey's cheek with her fingertip. His lips puckered and he quieted.

"What's she doing?" Todd whispered.

"Infant reflexes reappear after brain damage. Stroking his cheek stimulates the suckling reflex. It's soothing."

"See?" Etta said. "We're fine."

"Okay," Susan said. "I'm leaving."

Joey's eyes went wide. Through clenched jaws he screeched and moaned. His teeth ground together with the strident creak of a stretched anchor rope. Todd staggered backward as if shoved from the room.

"What in hell is *that*?"

"He's crying," Susan said matter-of-factly. "Probably your voice, Todd. It's unfamiliar. Can you wait in the car?"

"No freaking *problemo*! I'll be the guy doing a joint."

He retreated. The front door slammed.

"Let me," Susan said to Etta. The nurse sat down. Susan craned through the traction crib, positioning her face just above Joey's face so he could feel her breath. "There, there … there, there," she cooed, gently petting his head with one hand while she stroked his cheek with her fingertip. "There, there … there, there …"

Joey's face relaxed. The keening and the grinding subsided. His mouth puckered.

" … I'm here. I'm always here," Susan droned, her voice drifting into a soothing, lullaby purr. She placed the tip of a baby finger between Joey's imploring lips. He sucked it in; his eyes closed.

Susan's breathing and Joey's contented sighs came together as a single rhythm. Her heart pulsed in tandem with the insistent throb that milked her finger. Suffused with a satisfaction beyond understanding, she felt fulfilled, as if in the consonance of so primal a physical bond, the two, as one, were perfected.

"I'm always here for you, baby," she whispered. "My baby. My precious, precious baby."

Death

†

True Believer

The pew of barstools sat empty save for Socks, a daytime regular whose immediate excuse was the sweltering summer heat outside. Lost in thought or, maybe just lost, Socks rotated his beer mug and muttered to himself. His litany was a soothing white noise. Mind at peace, I polished glasses and waited for the evening congregation to assemble. Behind me, a back-lighted arch of colored bottles rose like a stained glass window.

"Jiminy Christmas!" Socks yelped, slapping his arm. "Damn black flies! Worst I ever seen. You 'member worse, Marlow?"

"Nope"

Socks pinched the swatted fly between his fingertips.

"It's the *heat*, man. A hunert 'n two out there. Blacktop's like chewin' gum. My tenny shoes stuck!"

"Umm-hmm."

"Flies *love* heat. Sexes 'em up or somethin'. Never *ever* seen no worse."

"Yep, it's the heat, all right," I said.

"One-oh-two ..." he mumbled, scrutinizing the dead fly. "... Phew! Nasty lookin' boogers. *Nasty*." He looked up. "Why would God go and make a fly, Marlow? Why?"

"Meanness, maybe?"

He flicked away the fly and resumed his beer mug ritual until a figure appeared silhouetted in the doorway.

"Don't let them damn flies in," Socks barked, squinting against the light. "Oh, say, Tommy, it's *you*. Marlow, it's Tommy!"

A small, frail man – poor match for the hellish weather – shuffled in and climbed on a stool. Swallowed in a baggy, borrowed suit, wayward hair greased in place, the little man mopped sweat from his forehead, propped his elbows on the bar, and cupped his face in his hands as if praying.

Socks switched stools to pat the man's back. "Sorry, Tommy. I feel plain rotten."

Tommy nodded dumbly.

"I'da come," Socks continued, "but, well … you know, you said … *don't*"

"You guys were the old life," Tommy sighed into his cupped hands. "Didn't seem right, you to be there, her not knowing you."

In the empty space held by his hands, Tommy's breath whooshed like wind in a cave. Socks shot me a raised-brow glance.

"You okay, Tommy?" I said.

Nodding as if deliberating, he lowered his hands.

"Give me something, Marlow."

"Sure thing. Soda? Coke?"

"No. Give me something."

Socks winced. "Tommy! Tommy! One day at a time," he admonished. "One day at a time, man."

"Southern Comfort," said Tommy. "Straight up."

"I know how you're hurtin'," Socks persisted, "but that's no reason to—"

Tommy wheeled on the stool.

"Know how I'm hurting, Socks? When did you bury a wife? When?"

"Ain't buried nobody lately, Tommy."

"Then stuff a cork in it!"

Socks squeezed Tommy's shoulder. "C'mon, man! Time was, figured we'd bury *you*. You got two years now. You got your job back at the mill. Got your license back. Lemme call whoosis. Your sponsor."

Tommy shrugged away the hand.

"You serving, Marlow, or you preaching, too?"

I selected a polished old-fashioned glass, chose a bottle from the back-bar, and poured.

"Fill it!" Tommy said, gesturing impatiently.

I topped off the glass and left the bottle sitting on the bar.

"Two years," Tommy said, eyeing the glass. "Two years for what?"

"Two years you ain't in the tank, all pixilated. Two years you ain't bringin' up blood."

Tommy peered into the amber liquid as if at an augury, hesitating as if some truth in the glass, partially revealed, frightened him.

"Grace did that, Socks! Like ... like she fished me out of Hell."

He bowed his head. His shoulders began to shake, but he made no sound.

"She believed in you," I said, reaching across the bar to touch his shoulder.

Tommy reared back, his eyes red and wet. "She's not *here*!" He raised the glass. "One day at a time? Well, here's to this day and the next day and all the days in Hell to come."

"That don't drown the flames, man," urged Socks.

"Says the captain of the bucket brigade."

"You ain't never dragged *me* out from under the pinball machine!" Tommy turned away.

"I guess Grace was a fool," I said.

Glass almost to his lips, Tommy froze.

"I mean, you had her thinking you were a believer, didn't you?"

"What's to believe?" Tommy said. "I believe in death!"

"So that's that, I guess. She's gone to worms."

Tommy lowered the glass, sloshing liquor onto the bar. He pounded the bar with both fists.

"You sonovabitch, Marlow!"

I tugged the towel from my apron belt and blotted the spill.

"Is that what you believe, Tommy?"

"NO! Not ... not like *that*."

"Then where's the belief?"

Tommy slumped forward as if some prop inside had toppled.

"It went with Grace."

"And now there's no sense to life. Is that it?"

"Where's the sense of cancer?"

"God is dead? Maybe never was?"

Tommy teetered, ancient prohibitions warning him back from some abyss.

"We..ll, didn't say *that*. Gotta be a God, but –"

"But what? He bungled this one? What?"

Tommy bowed his head. "I just ... don't ... *understand*. Why Grace? Why Grace and not—" He pounded the bar again. "I was nothing! I'm still nothing!" He raised his head and stared into my eyes as if at an augury. "Why not *me*? Grace was ..." Not one to know his feelings or squeeze feelings into words, he flailed his arms. I slid the old-fashioned glass out of reach. "She was ... She was special, Marlow. She was ... she was an *angel*!"

Socks opened his mouth, but I held up a hand. He shrugged and drank his beer.

"So, maybe she's home now, Tommy," I said. "*Really* home."

Tommy looked down, his eyes drawn to the church-window pattern of bottles reflected in the polished bar top.

"Wish I could believe it, Marlow."

"You said you believe in God, right?"

Tommy's answer echoed from so far back, from a well so deep, he could never know the source.

"I ... I believe in God," he said.

"Then somehow, some way, things make sense."

"*Gotta* make sense!" he whispered.

"Sensible thing is she's with Him now, right?"

"I can't believe she's just ... *gone.*"

"If she's with Him, maybe she's still watching over you. *Believing* in you."

Tommy looked up. A note of hope returned to his voice.

"You think? You think it's true?"

I nodded.

"You read books, Marlow. You went to college. You *know* things." His voice grew stronger like words from a parched throat after a cool drink of water. "You think? You really think?"

"What I've learned, Tommy – what I *know* – is you need to believe."

"I *want* to believe," Tommy said, closing his eyes. "I want to believe so bad!"

"Believe it."

Tommy opened his eyes and pulled himself straighter.

"She's with God now, Marlow."

I nodded.

"All that pain is gone. That medicine that made her so sick. Gone! She's home now."

I nodded again.

"She's watching over me, like she always did. Helping me do better. One day at a time!"

"Your higher power," I said.

Tommy smiled.

"I almost lost it there, Marlow. Thanks."

"Thank Grace," I said.

He stood, leaned over the bar, and grasped my shoulders with both hands, as close to a hug as he could come with the bar between us.

"God bless you, Marlow."

He dug in his pocket, withdrew a few bills, slapped them on the bar, and headed for the exit.

"God bless both of you!" he repeated over his shoulder, pushing open the door.

The outside air washed in like heat from a furnace. I scooped up the money and dinged the register.

"Well looky-looky here!" Socks snickered. "Teacher says every time you hear a bell, a' angel gets his wings!"

I separated my tip from Tommy's bills, stashed the tip in my shirt pocket, and deposited the balance in the register. I slammed shut the drawer and turned back to Socks.

"You don't believe it, Socks?"

"Jumpin' Jesus, Marlow!" he said, pausing to drain his mug. "You don't believe it, neither."

"Umm-hmm."

"All that learnin'. Them books. I've heard you bad-mouthing religion with my own ears."

"Your own ears," I said, automatically refilling his mug.

"She's home now. She's watchin' over you." Socks slurped the head off the fresh beer and downed half to chase the heat. "C'mon, Marlow, we all feel bad, but HAW! You don't believe a word you fed him."

"I don't?"

"I've heard you preach it *ain't* no God! You're no believer, man. You was puttin' him on."

I lifted Tommy's untouched old-fashioned glass.

"Maybe I was putting *you* on, Socks"

"Shee-it! Maybe you don't believe *nothin'!*"

I swirled the Comfort and stared into the tiny whirlpool.

"More's the pity, Socks," I said, upending the glass and swallowing the whole.

The liquor burned like dry ice. For an instant I saw a face before me. A face like a vision, like an augury. But it was only my own face reflected dimly in the bottom of the upturned empty glass. I banged the glass onto the bar and poured another drink from the bottle close to hand.

"Say, uh ... easy there, Marlow. It's hardly noon. You got a long spell till closin', man."

"More's the pity," I said again.

Don Juan in Iowa

Author's note: this piece was published during my final year of psychiatric residency. Pursuing a full-time academic career, I had to consider leaving the promised land of southern California for realms marked on the maps of my nightmares "Here be tigers." I include this personal fantasy as sketch of a universal dread: striking out from a familiar rut and losing one's way.

part the first

"Dr. Howard ... *Joe!* You're working yourself into a tizzy. Relax!"

"No. This isn't *right*, Jeb. That patient needs treatment!"

Jeb's face was sunbaked and leathery. His overalls were threadbare from tractor seats. A spot of manure marred the toe of his left boot. He was Chief of Psychiatry at Iowa State Hospital and Joe's new boss.

"Of course he does, boy. That's why we're getting him out on the hospital farm. Nothing like tending crops to bring the mind around."

Joe stopped pacing and leaned across Jeb's desk. "He needs more than ... than ..." Finding no match in the psychiatric lexicon, he invented a word. "More than *agritherapy*. The man needs dopamine blockade. A third generation, high-potency agent and a GABA adjuvant."

"Lordy, lordy, lordy, Joe, you *do* go on!" Jeb chuckled. "Words just a-poppin' like popcorn. *Exactly* why we hired you from that fancy school."

"He's delusional, Jeb. Hallucinating. Psychotic."

"I'm the last to tight rein a new Ward Chief, Dr. Howard. But, jumpin' Jehoshaphat! That man is no more delusional than the rest of us."

"He's talking to the Corn God!"

"Don't be sayin' nothin' 'bout corn," Jeb warned. He jiggled the phone on its cradle and lifted his desk blotter to glance underneath.

"Corn is irrelevant!"

Jeb sprang from his chair. "Ixnay on the orncay," he whispered, finger over his lips.

"Jeb ... the man has a genetic diathesis for hyperdopaminergic syndromes."

Jeb laughed, relieved to be back on unfamiliar ground. "Now *that...*" He threw an arm around Joe's shoulder. "That there is *just* what I'm talking about. Another one! Do another one."

"Drugs, Jeb. We have to consider drugs."

"That patient doesn't use drugs. Where would he get drugs in Iowa?"

"*Psychiatric* drugs. Neuroleptics. Psychotropics ... *Treatment!*"

Jeb sighed.

"Seein' you're a stranger, yet, I'm tryin' to make allowances for your *Cali-funny* notions, Joe. But sooner rather than later you need to get your mind right. Folks to these parts are plain and simple. We help people the old-fashioned way, the way God intends."

"The Corn God?"

"What's that, boy?!"

"Nothing, Jeb. Nothing."

"Good ... I don't relish failure to communicate." With a firm hand on Joe's shoulder, he urged him into a chair. "Now tell me ... how are your other patients doin'?"

"What other patients?"

"Ward empty again, is it? Fine work. Mighty fine."

"I haven't *had* any other patients."

"No need to fret. One'll come along, wait and see. Besides ... we academicians need time for teachin' and research. Right, *Professor?*" Jeb winked. "What's the story there?"

"The medical student plowed the back forty yesterday. Out sowing now."

"Midterms already? Mighty, mighty fine," Jeb purred. "And that study you're doing? I've heard good talk about it."

"It's only preliminary, but I've shown a definite correlation between the Lottery in June and the corn being high soon."

"Gol-dern! You're close, boy. *So close!* Prove *causation* and you change the game. I'm talkin' the Prize! The *DeKalb*, Joe. Des Moines ... *Des Moines.*"

"Dr. Jeb! Dr. Jeb!" The medical student burst through the door. His nose was sunburned, his forehead beaded with sweat. "Clouds out yonder. She's fixin' to rain!"

Clasping hands, Jeb and the student began to prance in a circle.

"Rain, Joe!" Jeb chortled. "The Golden Bantam is saved!"

"Thank the Lordy," Joe said.

"Louder, Dr. Joe!" the medical student whooped. "Let Him hear ya!"

Jeb dropped one hand to beckon. Joe grabbed hold and joined the circle.

"Thank the Lordy," he bellowed. "Thank the Lordy. Thank the Lordy."

part the second

Nothing happened in Iowa. Nothing, nothing, nothing, nothing at all.

part the last

Specks on an unchanging landscape, a boy and girl moseyed hand in hand along a narrow country lane. The road stretched flat and straight.

The summer sky was serene. A tepid breeze fluttered Billie Mae's gingham skirt and ruffled the baggy legs of Thurmond's overalls.

"Let's eat over by the corn field, Billie Mae."

"Oh, Thurmond! You're such a crack-up," she giggled. "Ain't naught but corn fields for 200 miles."

They crossed the gravel shoulder to a strip of grass verge shaded by elephant-eye high cornstalks. Handing Billie Mae a wicker basket, Thurmond spread a blanket, lay back, and savored blue sky and birdsong. Billie Mae arranged paper plates of cornbread, corn-on-the-cob and succotash on a red and white checked table cloth and poured two plastic cups of sweet tea from a silver Thermos. They ate and made small talk.

"What's that, Thurmond?" Billie Mae said, noticing a narrow mound of dirt about twenty rows ahead.

Thurmond peered in the direction of her outstretched arm.

"That? Just some old grave."

"Let's go look!" Billie Mae said, scampering off.

"It ain't nothing" Thurmond said, trailing. "Not even a marker."

Billie Mae took Thurmond's hand.

"I wonder who it was?" she said somberly.

"Some Doc, they say. Used to be a State Hospital here."

"What kinda Doc?"

"A Doc's a Doc."

They looked down at an insignificant blemish on the surface of the earth. Billie Mae scraped at the weeds with her toe.

"Well ... he must've had a name," she said.

"Not no more." The boy tugged at her hand. "You brung some of your momma's sweet corn cakes, didn't you?"

"Course I did," Billie Mae chuckled as they turned away. "I don't rightly think you could live without corn cakes, Thurmond Dillford."

Quarter

Jeff Hardy, 55, *Los Angeles Times* staff writer, white-knuckled his rented Ford Escape down a slush-covered Detroit Expressway. Beneath a gray blanket of clouds, the air temperature hovered near thirty-two. A fresh snowfall – alternately melting and freezing – rendered the trek from the airport skid and go. Jeff was years-rusty maneuvering such minefields of slop.

Lhude sing Goddamm, he said to himself.

For the umpteenth time –his OCD quirks were raging lately – he glanced at the seat belt of the surly, 13-year old girl scrunched against the passenger door. Soundlessly she lip-synched whatever hip-hop or head-banger poison spewed from her earbuds. His daughter's "music" – one tactic in an ongoing six-month insurgence – was as brutal a brainfuck as the 24:7 noise PsyOps employed to torture detainees at Abu Ghraib and Gitmo. For five of the last six months, entering the car, Jennifer had slashed at the radio until it hemorrhaged with screeched obscenities.

Exasperated, but terrified she might run away again, Jeff had floated earbuds as a don't ask, don't tell alternative to *no*. Inexplicably she had yielded the radio. All else remained a battle red-in-tooth-and-claw. No common ground.

No mercy.

No quarter.

Exiting the Southfield Expressway eastbound at Joy Road, Jeff sensed something amiss. On his left were boarded, burned-out storefronts, but that was just Detroit. To his right was ... No! A half-mile square, barbed-wire enclosure of urban prairie, the leveled footprint of the former Herman Gardens Housing Project. Blanched foundation pads poked through the spotty snow cover like stripped bones.

Fresh out of Wayne State as a rookie *Detroit Free Press* reporter, Jeff had come to know every city project well enough to count its razing, whatever the date, as overdue. His feelings toward Herman Gardens, however, were personal and mixed. His wife, Crystal, had spent most of her childhood there.

The exposed decay of something once alive and human – whatever its former corruption – was disturbing. One buries the dead, he thought, his mind seizing on swaths of dormant grass showing through the snow.

Good. The grass would have this one, too.

Give it time.

Let the grass do its work.

The spectacle recalled desolation he had witnessed as a correspondent in Somalia and Iraq. Save for a mere handful of childhood moments, however – Tiger games, junk yard safaris, back-yard ice rinks fashioned with a garden hose – Detroit had *always* seemed bleak. The day he and Crystal boarded a plane for L.A. was a gleeful beginning. Helplessly, he pondered yet again why she had returned, knowing that Crystal's whys were unfathomable.

Now *forever* so.

Jeff looked again at his daughter. Beneath her disguises, she favored him more than her mother – a lack of maternal inheritance he prayed ran deep. This week her persona included black, zombie rings of eye shadow and an ironed veil of blonde-root, jet-black hair. The straightened hair reminded him suddenly of her hair press and how immune she was to his Cassandra scenes punctuated with the popped spark of a yanked plug. He imagined the infernal thing still smoldering in her room 2000 miles away. This time, perhaps, she *would* burn down the house. He pictured his life as smoldering ruins and fumed, although, actually, he fumed continuously like an underground coal fire. He suffocated in the hot stench of a buried anger whose squelched but unquenchable combustion slowly turned his heart to ash. Anger at his daughter's spiteful recklessness; anger at her surly litany of fuck this, fuck that, fuck *you*; anger at her daily getup of torn, no-rise camo pants, whale-tail thong, lupine eye makeup and purple lipstick that made her look like a ... he jibed toward the adjective "indecent" to avoid the looming rocks of a noun.

"Why are you staring at me like that?"

Jennifer tugged out her earbuds. An audible chirp indicated a volume set to lithotripsy. Jeff moved his lips.

"What?" she snapped.

He repeated the pantomime. Her sullen scowl yielded to bewilderment.

"You're going to go deaf," he explained.

"You want the *radio* on?"

"Then we'll *both* go deaf."

"So what. You don't hear me anyway."

"I hear you, Jenn. I wonder if you do."

"What an ass-hat!" she grumbled, turning away.

"I wish you wouldn't swear."

"You swear. All the time."

"Because I'm an ass-hat."

She rolled her eyes. "You're just janked cause I'm making you do this funeral thing."

He almost blurted that she couldn't *make* him do anything, but caught himself since that was Jennifer's universal response to *him*.

"I'm janked – if that means sad and angry and hurt – that we never have a civil word anymore. I'm the same Daddy I was for 13 years."

"I didn't know the *real* you. The one that kept me from knowing *her* at all!"

Helplessly Jeff felt his anger vent in a pyroclastic rush of words – an obit written in his head long ago like the advancers editors keep handy for ex-Presidents and old movies stars.

"Crystal Hardy, 52, no known address, died December 8, 2006 of AIDS and a final overdose. Services: 3 p.m. Friday, Mt. Zion Memorial Park, Detroit."

"Shut up!"

"Born August 16, 1953 in Detroit, Mrs. Hardy suffered a refractory, post-partum psychosis. Fleeing Los Angeles for the streets of her hometown, she rebuffed every attempted rescue, existing cock-to-mouth as a stripper and crack whore."

"Fuck you!"

"Survived by her husband, Jeffrey, 55, and abandoned daughter, Jennifer, 13, Mrs. Hardy had remained a benign myth until she placed a single, malignant phone call ... Now you know her, Jennifer. Unfortunately, the pleasure was all hers."

Arms across her chest, the girl pressed into the door as if to withdraw every molecule as far from Jeff as possible. He readied to grab her, although self-harm and running away again were so far merely constant bluffs. Jennifer's three lost days on the streets had scarred her. Chlamydia was one scar – nothing more serious physically. Other scars she kept secret, even from the therapist she refused to talk to.

The cemetery was a mile farther. This part of the city had been Crystal's ... Jeff substituted stomping-grounds, refusing to call it her home. The side streets were lined with shabby, decayed, or abandoned two-story flats separated by vacant lots like missing teeth. Tall, winter-bare elms arched over rusted cars. Here and there, lone, hoodied figures picked their way along untended sidewalks. The absence of children slip-sliding on icy patches, Jeff attributed to the school day, since children were the one, certain bounty of impoverished places.

Jeff had chosen Mt. Zion because the unfamiliar aunt who had handled details said it was convenient for Crystal's *friends,* meaning fellow patrons of Joy Road bars, frequenters of the side street crack houses, denizens of nearby hot-sheet motels. Such was Crystal's life each time Jeff went looking for her, and such was the life she re-embraced after each hospitalization.

Mt. Zion was also cheap. An elaborate funeral had seemed absurd. In retrospect, however, Jeff regretted that decision. His daughter's acquaintance with funerals had been filtered through the cool medium of television – Princess Diana's, Reagan's perhaps. The occasional belly-up goldfish, having lived the life, made the passage with a weepy *we liked you fish, go back to the ocean* and the flourish of a flush. When Jeff's old, blind Retriever died, he buried the dog himself before Jennifer woke for kindergarten. His "ran-away" lie cost him a day of work as, hand-in-hand, daddy-daughter papered trees and light-poles with crayon-rendered missing posters. Useless, but sacrosanct, the posters yellowed until the tape let go, and one by one the pages blew away, expunging the dog from their hearts incrementally with no ultimate good-bye. A few relatives had died, but faraway in Los Angeles, Jeff had always sent flowers and regrets. His obligatory appearances had preceded Jennifer's birth – Jeff's parents had died in an automobile accident while he was embedded in Iraq: the Prequel. The sole death formative in Jennifer's life had been the fabricated death of her mother in childbirth.

Jennifer yanked out her earbuds again.

"I hate you, you know. I really, really hate you."

"So you say. Really, really often."

"And look how much you care. You hate me, too."

Hate? Love? ... Jeff could summon *no* simple formulation to express his emotions of 13 years. Rather he was suddenly awash in all of them at once – the euphoria of Jennifer's birth; the roller coaster of dread, grief, over-solicitousness and guilty distraction he felt through Crystal's psychosis, her disappearances, her mental deterioration, her adamantine refusal of any help or connection; the agonized flip-flopping he experienced over an ultimately final decision to raise Jennifer with the lie that her mother was dead. He felt, as he frequently did, flashbacks of the soul-strangling panic that had gripped him when Jennifer became lost at Disneyland on her fifth-birthday; the delirium tremens that wracked him for days when she ran away earlier this year; the liquid terror that choked him whenever he acknowledged that Crystal's illness might also claim his daughter. Jeff saw his feelings as tangible proof of something unseeable, unknowable, and essentially unnamable: a weld forged when a spark of eternity leapt from Jennifer's tiny finger to his own at their first touch.

"You have no idea what I feel, Jenn," he said solemnly.

She started to replace her ear buds, but Jeff grabbed her hand.

"Listen, I'll say it again. You have every right to be angry that I lied. I regret it every day. But it was stupidity, not perfidy."

"All those words no one knows! You *try* to make me feel dumb."

"We infer intentions, Jenn, often mistakenly. Maybe the truth is simply that we share a pretty good vocabulary and need all the words we have. Perfidy means deliberate—"

"I know what it means. Treachery."

"Lying was wrong but not treacherous. I wanted to protect you."

"By robbing my history?"

He ignored the grammar, glad to have *any* words, any way.

"You still have a history, Jenn. It's worth remembering."

"Why remember lies! I just want to say good-bye to … to *her*. I'll say good-bye and get gone to that jail you're sending me to."

"It's a *school*."

"It's juvie detention."

"No, it's *not*. It's a school for troubled kids. And..." Jeff squeezed the steering wheel. "And you're *troubled*, Jenn. You know you are. You're slipping away from people you used to like, things you liked to do. From your education. From *yourself*. I don't know what else to do."

"Who's complaining? I *want* to go away. I just want to get *over* you."

Jeff found the sudden ache in his chest as inexplicable as phantom pain from a missing limb. He considered that part of his heart – the part that could so grieve spurned love – ablated in his own fierce campaign to get over Crystal.

"You won't get over me, Jenn. We'll have family therapy and weekends together. They'll help us work this out and then you'll come home again where you belong."

"Just stay away."

"Your mother abandoned her family. *You* can't. Not *yet*, you can't."

"Shut up!"

"Crystal couldn't help herself. She was sick. You're not."

Jennifer jammed the buds in her ears and stared through the passenger window.

"I have to pee," she said, half-shouting.

Jeff ignored a two-pump gas station whose garage bay doors were coated with grime. A block farther he spotted a white-tiled mini-mart with a half-dozen pump islands. He pulled into a parking space reserved for the restroom.

Jennifer sat braced in the seat, staring at the restroom door as if it hid a monster.

"I *hate* these places," she said through clenched teeth. "They're filthy and scary."

"Well ... can you hold it five minutes till we get to the funeral home?"

She wriggled in the seat. "No."

"Let's check it out then. Come on."

He piled from the car. She trailed him to the door. A coin lock barred the way. Jeff felt in his pocket.

"I'll have to get change."

"I'm coming with you!"

At the cashier window, Jeff slid a dollar beneath the greenish, bulletproof glass, heard the tinkle of coins in the metal tray, and scooped out four quarters. Returning to the restroom, he plugged a coin in the lock and opened the door.

"Look inside!" Jennifer said, bouncing from foot to foot.

Jeff flipped a wall switch and stepped inside.

"Check behind the door, " she said, eying the flickering light fixture. "And the stall."

He pushed the door all the way back to the wall and opened the stall. The commode was intact. Dispensers held toilet paper and seat covers. He surveyed the graffiti-smeared walls for peep holes and spy cams.

"Disgusting, but functional and safe. Just make sure you wash your hands."

"Check the door lock. Make sure it works."

He flipped the lock several times and stepped outside, holding the door for her.

"You'll stand here, right?"

"I'll wait."

"Right here!"

She slammed the door. He heard her trip the lock and jiggle the handle.

Snow was falling heavily again. Large, clumped flakes. Jeff's breath made clouds. He regretted leaving his overcoat in the car. Stamping his feet, he jammed his hands into his pants pockets and toyed with the remaining three quarters. From habit he removed the coins to look for new finds. One was an old quarter with an eagle reverse; another an

Ohio which they already had. He flipped the shiny third quarter on his palm and smiled.

Such was luck. Faraway you find home.

He heard the toilet flush and the sink run. Drying hands on her blouse, Jennifer flung open the door, darted past him to the car, and piled inside. Jeff slid beneath the wheel.

"I found a California," he said, still clutching the quarter.

The words were a reflex like the twitching of a dead thing. Instantly he grieved the remark's forlorn hope. Jennifer yanked out her earbuds. Jeff braced for the derision that would snap a last, stretched connection.

"Let's see," she said, holding out her hand.

He dropped the quarter into her cupped palm. She turned it in her fingers.

"Who is this guy with the stick?" she said.

"John Muir. He persuaded people to save wilderness land in California."

"You know everything, don't you?" she said snidely

"No, Jenn. But I read a lot in my job and learn things."

"You don't learn everything from reading, you know?"

"I agree. It's good to be reminded of that sometimes."

"When did we start this dumb game?"

"Your fifth birthday. We bought the blue album at Disneyland after you got lost. We scoured the house for quarters and found a Rhode Island, a Maine, and a Virginia."

"They wouldn't fit in the slots," she said. "You used that roller to squish them in. Why do you even have that thing?"

"The rolling pin?"

"Yeah, that. All you use it for is squishing quarters and they don't stick anyway."

"It ... it was Crystal's. She got into baking for a few weeks. *Really* into baking. A hundred pies. It was sort of funny. At the time."

She swiveled in the seat and leaned toward him. "What's this mountain?"

"Half-dome. In Yosemite."

"We went there once, didn't we?"

"Camping. You were four."

"I think I remember it was fun."

"It was great. I'm sorry we never went back."

"You said you went there with … with *her* once."

"Our first year in California."

"Did *she* have fun?"

Jeff hesitated. "Do you want to call her Mom, Jenn?"

She gave a tiny, sharp shake of her head.

"Camping was not Crystal's thing. At all."

"Is that why you gave up on her?"

He felt an atmospheric change in her tone, like a passing front. He weighed each word.

"I don't think I did, Jenn."

"That's a fucking lie!"

Jeff knew that *any* response would draw lightning. He hunkered down, weathering her glare, hoping that she might find some safety herself, something to clutch tightly until the storm passed. After a moment he saw her open her fist and examine the quarter again.

"She gave up on *me*," he said cautiously. "And … and then I couldn't hospitalize her anymore. I had to stop chasing after her. She kept calling the police. I was arrested. *Twice.* But every time she *asked* for my help, every time she *accepted* it, I was there. Soon … she didn't ask anymore. That's the truth of it "

"Did *you* make her crazy?"

"I hope not. I … I don't think so. The doctors said it was a chemical problem in her brain. Manic-depression."

"Why did you marry her then?"

"Because I loved her and she loved me. Besides we had no way to know until it happened. It works that way sometimes. No warning. Most people get better because they try, but sometimes they can't or they won't. Crystal couldn't. She refused medicine, therapy, any help at all."

Jennifer pored over the quarter, rubbing the stamped image with the tip of one finger.

"You said post-partum. That means after birth, right?"

"... Y..yes ..."

"Did ... did *I* make her crazy?"

A beeped horn startled them both. In the mirror Jeff saw the driver of an old Chevy gesturing that she needed the rest room. He waved her off.

"Absolutely not, Jenn. Crystal's chemistry was something she was born with. The illness it caused was mostly bad luck. The doctors said hormone changes like puberty or menopause or pregnancy can set it off the first time, but that's the *only* connection."

"But if I hadn't been born ...?"

"The world would be a darker place. And what happened to Crystal would have happened anyway."

"Like fate or something," she whispered.

"What do you mean?"

"Like those myths in school, you know? Fate."

"Well ... a *little* like that, I suppose."

"... Will it get me, too?"

Jeff scooted close to put an arm around her. She buried her face in his chest. For a time outside of time Jeff relived thirteen years of nightmare scenarios his unconscious had scripted from experiences with Crystal. He felt himself enduring an adult Jennifer's hatred, her physical assaults, her disappearances; he saw himself wiping Jennifer's chin of drool from the wrong medication, holding her arm as she shuffled about dopily after electro-shock; he imagined himself chasing her from city to city, failing to rescue her from shelters and jails and gutters just as he had failed miserably to rescue her mother.

"Myths are about how we deal with what we're given and what we know," he said, stroking her hair. "Crystal's chemistry was fate, but she had a say in what she did with it."

"But maybe I'll get the Goddamn thing too, right? Maybe I have it already!"

"No, you don't. The psychiatrist doesn't think that at all."

"You both think I'm nuts."

He tilted her chin up so she would see his face.

"We think you're *thirteen!* ... We think your world was flipped upside down because *I* made a stupid mistake not telling you the truth. We think you're trying to figure out who you are again, but you're angry and mistrustful and feel you have to do it alone. We *don't* think that you're sick."

"But I could *get* sick!"

"*Anyone* can. Like getting cancer or hit by a bus. But it's a small chance, Jenn. Your mother makes your chance a little larger, but nothing you'd place a bet on. Being prepared and not giving up makes that small chance even smaller."

Jennifer looked at the dashboard clock.

"We're late."

"This is more important."

She rotated the quarter in her fingers, studying both sides.

"She gave up on both of us, didn't she?"

"All *three* of us. It helps me to remember that mostly it was her illness."

"Are ... are you giving up? On me?"

"Absolutely not."

"You're sending me away."

"That's *not* giving up. It's trying to make sure neither of us does."

"Why didn't we go back to Yosemite if it was so fucking great?"

Jeff made himself hear the feeling, not the words.

"I don't know. I regret it, too."

"Am I too old now?"

"Of course not. We can go."

"Could I bring a friend? Jess is pissed at me, but we could make up."

"Sure. Jess is a *good* friend. She'll stick."

"I liked camping, I think." She paused, staring at the quarter. "How many more states to go?"

"Ten, I believe."

She handed Jeff the coin. "Squish it in the book when we get home. I still like Tennessee best, though. So far anyway."

"Me, too." Jeff said, squeezing the quarter tightly in his fist. "Elvis and the guitar are way cool."

"You sound bogus when you say things like *way cool*."

"I suppose so," he said, tucking the coin in his billfold to save and protect. "But sometimes things that sound phony are real and things that sound real are false."

"Like that ... crap *she* told me."

"Yes. But there's *some* truth in most stories, Jenn."

"Do we *have* to do this funeral thing? It's gross!"

"Not if you don't need it. Try to be sure, though."

"Won't people be disappointed?"

"I doubt it. We're strangers they'd never see again and wouldn't want to. I can call on our way back to the airport."

"Let's ditch it then."

"Done!"

Jeff fastened his seat belt. Waiting for the click of Jennifer's buckle, he circled around the building and turned west onto Joy. Jennifer inserted her earbuds, but tugged them out and sat listening to nothing.

"About that school, Jenn ... If we work with the doctor, all of us together, it's not *necessary*, you know? He told me that and I ... I don't *want* you to go."

"That doctor is a creep. He looks like a child raper."

"We'll find someone else then. Someone who doesn't look like a creep. Would a woman be better?"

She shrugged and stared out the window.

"Detroit is fu–" she caught herself. "… Way ugly," she said.

"Some parts are better, but you're right. It's ugly."

"I'm glad home isn't here."

"Me, too."

His daughter sat with her thoughts. Finally, she turned and said simply, "The quarters will end."

Jeff felt a catch in his throat.

"Someday, yes … they will," he said.

"It's fun finding them first. I like squishing them in that dumb book." She smiled. "You get so mad when we take the book down and quarters spill all over."

"That is funny, isn't it?" he said, his voice breaking.

"What do we do when the quarters end, Daddy?"

"We've got a while yet."

"But when they do?"

"We'll find something else to share, Doodlebug."

Infinity

Night at the Institute

*Authors note: many years ago Psychiatric Times published this personal account inspired by a true story of a struggling psychiatric resident finding what **wasn't** the way.*

The invitation included dinner, and for years after my night at the Psychoanalytic Institute, I insisted that the dinner was why I went. Understand, I was a first year psychiatric resident then, and residents are always hungry – always gleaning sealed, germ-proof cartons of milk or covered cups of mushy, melted ice cream from patients' trays; always scurrying first chance after midnight for the sack lunches set out in the on-call lounge, hunger-driven to swallow almost anything, even rainbow-streaked ham splotched with some Vaseline-like goo that had to be scraped off with a finger and wiped on a paper napkin.

Inevitably someone had rifled the bags and plundered the cookies by the time I got there. The brown bags gaped like dumb mouths. I crammed my cheeks with ham sandwich, mumbled crumb-punctuated curses at the cookie thieves, swore I would pop them if I caught them, and schemed to reach the sacks earlier next time to get the cookies myself before the thieves did. Hunger makes you crazy like that. Once I brandished a fork at a bovine, blank-faced hash-slinger husbanding an on-call meal as if each potato were a rare truffle. Honest, I did. Hunger makes you desperate, and residents are always hungry, always stuffing their gullets like a surgeon packing a wound, as if food could staunch some leak midway of their chests.

Consequently, I might have consorted with Scientologists for a free dinner at a good restaurant, but, fact was, I was intrigued by psychoanalysis and was in analysis myself, because analysts *knew.* No one else knew. Is it cancer, Doctor? Doctor, will I walk again? Doctor, where's the pickled peppers Peter Piper picked? God knows I didn't know. But analysts knew. They knew it all. They knew why you sneezed and why you had arthritis and why you thought you were in love. They knew why you hated calculus and why you wrote poetry and even why you fancied yourself as someday knowing, too. Besides which, Psychoanalysts had a club – *The Institute.* And while I supposed it wasn't the kind of club where potted members donned tasseled hats and tore around town hanging from fire engines, I knew that it was a special place just for them with a clubhouse and rules and officers and everything! Maybe a little like an *Our Gang* for grown-ups where Spanky and Alfalfa gave lectures and sometimes they all got together to make a circus or put on a show. I pictured the Institute something like a posh library – all dark woods and red brocade walls, tall shelves filled with leather-backed tomes, oil paintings of sea battles and hunting dogs. I imagined analysts nestled in cozy, wingback, clubhouse chairs; the clubhouse toasty-warm from a crackling fire, everyone smiling and warm and just chock-full of knowing.

The invitation to the Institute came from the token analyst at my residency program, a man who hustled new residents like a time-share salesman extolling to lucky so-and-sos the vacations they had won. Rumor was, Institute politics had held up the token analyst's card or decoder ring or whatever, and that recruitment was his way to promotion, like a Ponzi scheme.

The token analyst was a lusty, big bear of a man, a good curser whose phone was cracked from frequent angry battering. During supervision music from *A Clockwork Orange* boomed from his tape player while he flossed his teeth. Once he twanged a piece of corn stuck between his incisors onto my jacket. He was a character. I liked him.

His classes, however, were as devoid of life as the waterless moon. He prefaced his lectures each year with an ultimatum that psychoanalysis be treated with respect and he ousted people who made jokes. His evaluations of residents often included the criticism *lacks seriousness,* a deficiency which could be corrected only through *long-term, intensive, insight-oriented, individual psychotherapy,* i.e. psychoanalysis. Senior faculty ignored this foible, so I did, too. Besides, he was an analyst who had been analyzed, so he knew. What did I know?

Halfway through my first year, the token analyst invited first- and second year residents to a monthly scientific meeting at his Institute and offered to buy dinner afterwards. On the psychoanalytic issue, polls were pretty much closed by third year, so campaigning there was a waste. But to young residents, psychoanalysis was grandly historical, like ancient Egypt, and analysts and institutes, like mummies and pyramids, appealed to a youthful room for wonder. Wondering, we all accepted the invitation. And, well ... there *was* the dinner, the free dinner.

The night at the Institute was a complicated proposition for me, however, since I was in analysis. For psychiatrists, psychotherapy is a reasonably harmless initiation rite that avoids physical barbarisms like branding and subincision. Hence, most residents participate in the ritual although few choose formal psychoanalysis with four sessions a week as I did. The complication was that, on the night we were to go to the Institute, the panel leader was my analyst!

His name was Lansky, a common name, so you won't know who I'm talking about. Frankly, I don't think I remember his first name. In session I always called him Dr. Lansky which may seem strange since nowadays therapists let you call them Pete or Pookie or whatever. But this was formal psychoanalysis, the real deal, and the analyst was Dr.

Lansky. Damnedest thing – every time I did use his first name, which I think started with an "M", I stumbled and called him Meyer. Years later, I thought the error was significant, but I never completed analysis, so I wouldn't know.

Anyway, Lansky led the panel the night I was supposed to go, a tricky situation that analysts have written papers about. An analyst, you see, is supposed to be an unknown quantity, a blank screen. The patient never sees him outside the office. Never knows anything real about him at all.

Oh, it's difficult at first, but believe me, after a while you don't *want* to know him. I mean, what if I went to the Institute and saw Lansky with canapé crumbs in his beard? What if he passed gas? What if he smiled or laughed for once?

For weeks I stewed. I would go. I wouldn't go. In analysis you learn immediately that the last person you ask about *anything* is your analyst. The night after my evaluation session with Lansky, I had this magnificent dream in which the elevator to Meyer's office was the old freight elevator at my Dad's business, and his office was my Dad's office. Next morning, I realized that in relating my history the day before I had never once mentioned my mother. Analysis was phenomenal! Already I was hot in pursuit of my unconscious.

At my second session, when the actual analysis began, Lansky intoned a flat "good morning" and sat blank faced. I bubbled out the dream, and the discovery that I hadn't discussed my mother. Struggling to clear the roiling ideas, I talked and talked and talked, and then I waited. I waited for the knowledge. Lansky said, "Our time is up now," stood, and opened the door.

Hurt and confused, I stopped at the lobby coffee shop and gobbled a cheese croissant. That croissant became a habit. Wasn't long, I was wolfing croissants before *and* after sessions. A couple of weeks into analysis, I started smoking.

Whenever I mentioned the croissants and the smoking, Lansky merely nodded like a psychiatrist. I finally asked him outright what he thought.

"You seem to want to know what I think," he replied.

"Indeed! Yes! Yes! I want to know what you think."

"Our time is up," He said.

I tried other tacks. Like ambush.

"Why do you think Freud abandoned his incest theory, Dr. Lansky?"

"You seem to be neutralizing affect by removing yourself from the discussion."

Discussion???

"Okay," I said, "Do you think the incest theory applies to me?"

"Our time is up," he said.

I tried tears.

"I'm so sad (boo-hoo). Do you think (boo-hoo) there's hope for me?"

"Our time is up," he said.

I tried anger.

"Do you think you can give me one straight answer?"

"You seem angry."

"Goddamm right, I'm angry you – "Luckily I wasn't holding a fork.

"Our time is up," he said.

Yes, he was a master. I can't recall a single break in form, not one direct answer to a question except for the time I caught him sleeping. Truth be told, in the years I myself practiced psychotherapy, I dozed occasionally and once fell out of my chair. Lansky saw me at the Godawful hour of 7 am so he could get to his real job at the state hospital by 8:30. And, honestly, a psychoanalyst has a particularly tough lot anyway, sitting with someone 50 minutes at a time without ever responding humanly. So the first few times I noticed him napping, I let it slide. I mean, he always woke up in time to say "our time is up" so I figured I still got my money's worth. But one morning (I think I had missed my croissant) I asked him, "Are you sleeping?"

He woke up, wet his mouth, and gave me the only direct answer he ever gave.

"No."

For goodness' sake, I'm a physician. I recognize sleep when I see it! Deciding whether people are asleep or dead is part of my job, and I knew Lansky wasn't dead. He was snoring!

I said, "Really? Your eyes were all fluttery and rolled back in your head, and your mouth was hanging open. It looked like you were asleep."

"No," he said. "I was not asleep."

"What were you doing then? Because you were making this snoring noise and, look, there's a spot of drool on your necktie."

"Freely hovering attention," he said sternly,

"What?"

"An analyst adopts a freely hovering attention to become empathically attuned. You'll learn more about that later."

Shortly after this exchange, Lansky gave his only therapeutic directive. He told me that to break through my entrenched resistance and more fully develop the therapeutic alliance, future sessions would occur with me on the couch in the traditional analytic position – facing away so I couldn't see him.

Since I was on the couch as the night at the Institute approached, Lansky was more useless than ever. To go or not go? That was the question, but of course there were no answers from Lansky, and I couldn't even watch his face for an unconscious nod or raised eyebrow. I confessed my predicament to the ceiling above the couch and tried to squeeze guidance from the tone or timing of his *Go on's*, *I see's*, and *Our time is up's*. The first two, I came to understand, were more or less random remarks like "uh-huh" or "I hear you, man," delivered, however, without the customary nuances of emotion. (Years of training, that trick. You try it!). The "Our time is up's" were dictated by the second hand of the wall clock and often came in mid-sentence.

"What should I do?" I finally blurted two days before the night at the Institute. I felt wretched asking since any desire for the analyst to reveal right and wrong except with regard to payment of fees and penalties for missed sessions is proof of primitive, unresolved oralism.

Lansky replied sagely, "You expect me to be withholding like your father."

He was right! My neurosis revealed. I *did* expect him to be withholding.

"Dr. Lansky!" I cried out. "This is the crux! Do you think—"

"Our time is up."

Bolting down an extra croissant after that session, I reflected on the ugly distortions of transference. Lansky was right (chew, chew). I was projecting (chew, chew) withholding onto him (chew, chew) from my father (swallow), whom I erroneously remembered as a hugging, kissing, generous man. Next morning, proudly relating my new insight to the ceiling above the couch, I felt embraced by Lansky's hovering analytic attention, so empathic, so free. So sonorous.

Insight is not enough, however, and the day of the night at the Institute broke cold and brooding with no end to my waffling. I should go. I must go. I can't go. Be bold! Yes, I'll go. But reaction formation is not boldness – it's cowardice *disguised* as boldness. So, to prove I could go, I won't go. And if I don't go, I can go, so I will go! But what if he does pass gas, contaminates the transference, and botches my analysis, condemning me to dark years of not knowing? No, I won't go. But I must go. Yet I can't go. Six o'clock came. I went. I was starving.

The city where I trained (which I'll identify only as L.A. to preserve anonymity) boasted several Institutes. Our invitation came from the Crips (not their real name). The token analyst rounded up the residents outside the Crips clubhouse and herded us in for tally and credit. The foyer was stark and cold – blank, white walls and a white, slab floor. Although crowded with milling analysts, it was a place of whispers and strangely quiet.

The older analysts I saw all wore beards, but surprisingly many younger analysts did not. Ignoring a smattering of female analysts – who were also, for the most part, clean-shaven – I wondered if, perhaps, beards were earned like Clarence's angel wings in *It's a Wonderful Life*. A phrase oozed from my id: whenever you hear a snore, an analyst is earning his beard. Hunger was cracking my defenses. I needed food quickly! What if I acted out and was demoted to *pre*-analysis?

Looming in my vision like Tony to Maria across the West Side Story gym, Lansky stood surveying the gathering throng. I prayed that he hadn't noticed me yet, since I knew he could read my thoughts and feelings from my face, although he had never actually demonstrated the ability. Oh, to hell with it, I decided. I'll walk up, stick out my hand, and if Lansky doesn't shake, it's his problem. I started toward him and saw them.

Cookies!

Lansky's bulk had obscured a small folding table upon which sat a doily covered tray of cookies and a pot of coffee. I lowered my head and charged. Lansky, it turned out, was no problem – shake his hand, not shake his hand, what to say or not say – all irrelevant because, quite simply, he didn't see me. I mean it. He didn't *see* me. *At all.* I might have been one of Topper's ghosts. Perhaps he saw cookies being snorked up by an invisible Hoover, but he didn't react to it, and he didn't react to me.

Chocolate chips, quickly absorbed, bathed my brain cells with salubrious nutrients, allowing me to relax and observe. My first observation was how *freely* I observed because I was a ghost to all the analysts. The other residents were, too. Not a second's attention was paid to any of us. I watched one gray-bearded analyst approach the token analyst and his huddled brood of residents (who obviously had not yet spied the cookies). The token analyst, still dark-bearded, said nothing and kept his eyes lowered. The gray bearded analyst – looking as stiff as a proctology patient with 25 cm of surgical steel sigmoidoscope rammed up his bunghole – simply began talking. I could tell he wasn't addressing the residents, but it took me a moment to understand why. *He didn't see them.* As I struggled to make sense of things, another analyst reached for a cookie (which, incidentally, he *broke in half*) and bumped me unapologetically. Realization dawning, I saw that his behavior was not from rudeness, but blindness. He didn't know I was there.

Physicians learn that healthy organisms respond first to novelty, to the new or unfamiliar in the environment. Yet, here were organisms responding only to the *familiar*. The rest was unseen, unacknowledged, unimportant. They responded only to themselves.

Made bold by a bellyful of cookies, I studied Lansky. His breaths were quick, shallow, chest breaths. White showed above and below the irises of his eyes. His pupils were dilated and his corneas glistened. He was *scared*.

I could see how talking might throw him, but ... on Crips turf? Chillin' with his homeboys? In fact, however, *no one* was chillin'. Faces twitched. Voices whispered. Backs stiffened. Eyes darted. No one joked, no one laughed. Younger analysts jockeyed next to older analysts, but said nothing unless spoken to – eager to be seen, loath to be heard. Unseen *and* unheard, I drifted ghostlike through the crowd, eavesdropping.

"Doctor, your brilliant remarks of last month were—"

"Ach, you youngsters. Talk, talk, talk. But who listens?"

"I...I listen, Doctor," squeaked an unbearded analyst. "All the time."

"But do you *feel*. Here," said the older analyst, tapping his chest.

"I do. I do," yipped the first analyst, thumping his own chest hard enough to start a stopped heart. "I listen and I feel right here."

"*Empty* feeling!" snapped the older analyst, coldness suddenly spilling from him like the exhalation from a deep cave. Other analysts felt the chill and circled. "Empty feeling without knowledge. Perhaps your analyses were incomplete that you do not see your countertransference."

The two younger analysts lowered their heads and froze like opossums. The older analyst began to nod and the circle, also nodding, drew tighter.

An even older, white-bearded analyst elbowed through the pack.

"You, Doctor, were always flirting with Jungian nonsense," he snarled and *everyone* studied their shoes.

"Jung? W..why ... never!" the gray-bearded analyst stammered with an oblique glance. "Our great mentor taught—"

"*Our* mentor, Doctor? *My* mentor, but you seem to have found some new inspiration. Perhaps you will enlighten your colleagues how mistaken was the genius Freud."

The crowd gasped. The two younger analysts smiled crookedly at the floor.

Frightened by the gasp, the gray-bearded analyst sputtered, "P..please, Doctor ... Freud's infallible genius has been conclusively acknowledged by all. I would merely bore those here with my exposition of our one, true, great knowledge universally accepted."

"Of course, Doctor," purred the white-bearded analyst, handing the gray-bearded analyst his business card. "Sometimes, in haste, we misspeak, but fortunately recognize an incomplete analysis. Additional work with a qualified supervisor will—"

Talk ceased as the oldest analyst of all hobbled by and even the even older analyst looked down. Curious, I followed the oldest analyst to a crowded sanctum. Shoulder-to-shoulder no one spoke there and all eyes looked upward. Analysts squashed themselves against the porcelain urinals and no one shook it more than twice. The oldest analyst alone seemed unashamed to stand back, but could not make much of a stream, and dribbled on his shoe. At the sinks, analysts wash-wash-washed; rinsed; inspected the hands and lathered again. They wash-wash-washed; rinsed and re-inspected. Blot-blot-blotting with paper towels, drying carefully, completely, they folded the towels into neat little rectangles with crisp creases and placed them in the trash receptacle. Moving to the door, they turned to check that the towels had remained in the receptacle. Inspecting the hands once more, they opened the door, glanced again toward the receptacle, inspected the hands a final time, and left. A particularly conscientious few poked their heads back in a time or two to keep tabs on those damned, elusive towels. When the oldest analyst left, I trailed behind to the conference room. When he sat, the scientific meeting began.

The topic that night escapes me. Actually, the topic was irrelevant since it never came up. The meeting immediately devolved into a free-for-all, like mud wrestling at the Tropicana – senseless, chaotic, and one hell of a show.

Lansky: So, as the farseeing wisdom of Freud's great genius predicted—

Middle-aged analyst: (rising) Yes, yes. Dr. Lansky, all well and good, but with regard to maternal introject libidinal cathexis, our great mentor proved, as I myself have observed—

Older analyst: (also rising) You yourself observe nothing, Doctor. Session length is multi-determined, as I noted previously when—

Second older analyst: (shooting to his feet) What has this to do with furniture in the waiting room? I have discussed how waiting room furniture may contaminate the transference and —

Older analyst: (still standing) Have you discussed with a qualified supervisor how contaminated and prematurely terminated was your analysis? Furniture, bah! Chairs are vaginas. Conclusively! I have written—

Other analysts interjected. Half the room was immediately standing, shouting, gesticulating. It was like some bizarre saloon brawl minus the piquancy of fisticuffs, breakaway furniture, and gun smoke.

Lansky: Perhaps we could return to our topic of—

Unbearded analyst: (remaining seated, looking down) Dr. Lansky, could you comment on fees?

At length silence fell and everyone sat when the oldest analyst of all stood. The oldest analyst was the Institute patriarch, a repository of tradition and source of wisdom. He had been analyzed by Freud himself, or by someone who had been analyzed by Freud, or knew someone who knew Freud, but definitely had something to do with Freud or at least Vienna because he had a Bela Lugosi accent. At first, he merely stood, wise and silent, his head bobbing, his upraised right hand oscillating with a coarse tremor. He opened his mouth.

Caesura.

As God is my witness, like Irwin Corey, he began with "Furthermore." He rambled and muttered and halted, omitting subjects and verbs. He made sounds until he tired of making sounds, and then sat. All the analysts nodded, peeked to make sure others were nodding, and when they saw others nodding, all nodded more forcefully.

Lansky: Our venerable president, who in his youth was an eager receptacle at the very seat of our mentor, showers us once more with Freud's issue and again demonstrates the indubitable truth of our science.

Applauding politely, the analysts looked around guiltily to discern whether they should stand and applaud. This time, apparently, the remarks warranted only sitting applause. The oldest analyst picked at non-existent flecks on his sleeve and stared at his hands. Shortly, his attention began to freely hover.

I sneaked out to the foyer for more cookies, but the cookies were gone. The analysts had provided only one small tray of cookies anyway. In retrospect, they were not even good cookies; they were small and brittle-crumbly instead of chewy. Too few chips. Too many nuts.

Gazing at the barren cookie platter, I mulled the words *"our science"* spoken as if science were property, as if science for one were not science for all, as if what they did were science. Next visit I would tell Lansky our time was up.

On that night, however, we all kept the token analyst to his bargain. He took the residents to a Chinese restaurant – the tourist trap on Wilshire with the pagoda façade and the two scary Foo Dogs out front. Sub-gum chow mein sounded deliciously exotic to me, but it had no meat, and an hour later I was hungry again.

End Zone

"Find my boy, Mr. Pinel. Please."

Richard Manning flicked his cigarette against the lip of a half-filled Styrofoam cup.

"I'm a good investigator, Dr. Manning," I said, swiveling a little in the hard-back chair next to Manning's desk. "And runaways usually come home on their own anyway. Still, it's easy enough to hide if you're motivated. And Ricky's what? Eighteen? You can't force him back. Not in California."

He drowned the cigarette in the cup and rubbed the dark hollows of his eyes with his palms. "I know that. It's just ... I want a second chance."

Was that all? ... Manning was a psychiatrist. He should have known about second chances.

"I used to teach down there at UC San Dismas." He nodded toward the fifth-floor window behind him. "Private practice isn't as easy as I once thought it was. I suppose I've been ..." He lowered his head. "Too busy lately."

Manning's new practice consisted of leased, Maalox-bland furniture, a silk fichus that required no water, a sofa-sized sea gull print that demanded no thought. A diploma, hung carelessly like a sales tax license, seemed the only personal touch in the office, until I noticed the easel-framed photograph of Manning's boy on his desk.

"When did he go."

"Last night. We were asleep and thought he had left early for an extra practice, but my wife found a note in his room and he wasn't at school. His friends just shrugged and the police were useless."

"Too little, too soon."

"My lawyer, Bernie Welles, said you have fewer limitations."

"I'll have to send Bernie a thank-you card."

"Can you find my boy?"

"I can *look* ... Let's start with why. Some run *from*, some run *to*. Any ideas?"

He clenched his hands. "If only I knew, Mr. Pinel. Why didn't I see something? He's a good boy, I know that. Never in trouble."

"Drugs?"

"Beer now and then after a game, I'm sure, but not drugs. Too conscientious about football. The team has been his obsession this year. Do you follow local high school sports?"

My head was starting to throb again. Frankly, I had one hell of a hangover. I fidgeted with the ring on my right hand to still the tremor.

"A little," I said.

"Ricky's school, Vista Viejo, is new. Part of the south County building boom. No one expected much from the football team this soon, but they won the league title, and since Thanksgiving they've trounced three favorites in the Division playoffs."

"They play Woodbridge for the Championship tomorrow," I said.

"Ricky graduates in June. He wouldn't miss that game for *anything*."

"If he did, would it change the odds?"

"You're not suggesting ...?"

"I don't know enough to suggest anything. I'm asking.

"No. Ricky is second string. Shares the fullback position with another boy. And besides, this is high school, Mr. Pinel. Kids."

"Steroids are news these days even among kids."

"No, not Ricky, I'm sure of that. When he joined the team, I scared hell out of him about overbuilding. Cancer, psychosis, heart failure. And I know the signs." He smiled faintly. "I wrote a paper on the topic two years ago."

"Could I see it?"

The smile faded. "I haven't really sorted through my files since I left the university. So little of use here, you know. Everything's still in boxes in my study at home."

It was almost noon. My empty stomach churned, and my head pounded from squinting to read Manning's back-lighted face.

"Excuse me, Doc, but would you have some aspirin?"

"Headache, Mr. Pinel?"

I squeezed the bridge of my nose. "Yeah."

Manning rummaged in the top drawer of his desk, withdrew a bottle of Beyer, popped the lid with his thumb, and shook two tablets into my palm.

"Chaser?" he said.

"Straight up," I grumbled, acknowledging the accusation. "Birthday party last night. The big five-oh."

He nodded silently.

"It doesn't interfere," I said, tossing the tablets in my mouth and swallowing.

"Bernie says you're good man. Just find my boy."

Runaway cases. I sighed.

The window behind Manning framed a view of southern California you could use to sell land. Almost Christmas, and – what's that phrase? – another perfect day in paradise? The orderly, San Dismas tracts embracing the University campus merged with distant orange groves and strawberry fields. To the east rose mile-high Saddleback, snow frosting the twin peaks. Across the southwest stretched beige ranchland and, between the hills, scallops of sun-speckled ocean. Above it all, soared a blue, cloudless sky. Manning paid extra for that blue sky, for a window facing south, away from the rust-colored curtain of smog to the north that hid a hungry, straining Los Angeles.

"Let's say three days, Dr. Manning. Likely he'll come back on his own before then, probably for the game. After that, I'll keep looking if you want, but not full time, not without good leads. You'd be wasting your money."

"I have to do *something*," he said, pressing white knuckles against the desktop.

"Waiting *is* something, Doc. If I find him, I'll try to get him to talk to you. If he's in trouble, I'll do what I can to help."

Manning nodded slowly, then reached into his inside coat pocket and handed me papers. "Bernie suggested a $1500 retainer check. I also made a list I thought might help – Ricky's car and license plate, friends, teachers, hangouts."

I skimmed the names and addresses.

"What else do you need?" asked Manning.

"I'd like to see his room first. That's where he was when he left. Then I'll talk to some of these names, especially the coach. Boys are usually pretty close to their coach."

His gaze dropped at the last part. "I'll call my wife to tell her you're coming."

"Have a picture?"

He nudged the framed photo across the desk. "From the Dana Point game," he said, smiling. "I have one in my wallet that shows his face better."

I studied the 8x10 telephoto shot in the frame. The boy was high-stepping, frozen in full stride, the ball tucked against his left side, his right arm outstretched despite thick, white tape binding his wrist and thumb. Impact marks streaked his silver helmet. Mud tattooed the team name, Mustangs, and the large number 37 printed across the chest of his shoulder-pad swollen jersey. Behind the helmet cage, the kid's eyes strained forward to the end zone, searching the defensive line for a chink to slip through or, failing luck, for a weak spot to ram through with heart and legs.

"Take this one," Manning said, removing the only photo in his wallet from its plastic window.

Ricky looked almost my height – six, six-one maybe – but forty pounds lighter, still a boy with a boy's waist. His chin was strong, his eyebrows dark and bushy, his eyes boyishly clear.

I glanced from the picture of the son to the father. Richard Manning had the same blue eyes, but – having seen more – his were etched with tired creases at the corners. He hid a weak chin beneath a full, brown beard, but defied a receding hairline by cropping short his gray-streaked, brown hair. He was small-boned, about 5-8, but mostly muscle. I figured he jogged, hoisted weights, rode a Life-cycle with two fingers pressed periodically against his neck to count the fleeting heartbeats. The doctor had to know, of course, that life was a fatal disease whose symptoms were falling hair, failing ears, fading eyes, flagging strength. He could treat the symptoms, but ultimately? ... Waiting was what you did. I guessed Richard Manning's age about five years shy of mine.

I peered once more at the kid's expression in the big game photo, then pushed it aside, and pocketed the other picture, the check and the list.

"Call as soon as you have anything, Mr. Pinel," Manning said. "Anything at all."

I left him sitting at his wide, empty desk cradling the picture of his boy. I wondered what he was thinking.

* * * * *

The Manning's lived 10 miles south of San Dismas in Vista Viejo, twice five miles of fertile ground billboarded as *The California Promise*. Desert ranchland and orange groves had been transformed into green-lawn housing tracts, sinuous tree-lined boulevards, bike trails, jogging paths, golf courses, tennis courts, a boat-dotted, man-made lake, and a pleasure-dome swimming-pool complex that spawned what's-his-name, the Olympic star. Now the surrounding brown hills were awash with greedy builders and eager buyers – more houses, more people, more cars, more money, politicians, ballot drives, campaign funds, kickbacks, dirty deals, litigation.

And broken promises.

I exited the 5 at El Toro and waited 90 seconds for the light at the foot of the ramp. I waited two minutes more a half-block farther at El Toro itself, cut under the Freeway, and waited another two minutes at the next light. The California Promise. You couldn't see L.A. from where I sat, just the stain in the northern sky.

I found Via Mocedad in a Thomas Guide, and parked my Chevy Blazer in front of the Manning place, a modest house for a doctor, middle-sized in a middle class, middle-aged neighborhood. The skeletal branches of a front yard pear tree still bore dissolving garlands of toilet paper – remnants of some victory celebration. Dry, red leaves dotted a brown, winter-dormant lawn.

Mrs. Manning opened the door, ushered me into the kitchen, and sat me at the breakfast bar separating the kitchen from the adjacent, book-lined family room. In one corner of the family room, presents mounded under a real Christmas tree. Mrs. Manning poured two cups of coffee from the drip brewer on the sink counter.

"Cream or sugar, Mr. Pinel?" she asked.

"Cream, please."

Probably just into her forties, Mrs. Manning was a good-looking woman who overdid her make-up, trying to break even with the clock, I suppose. The mascara made her brown eyes a little too large, a little mournful. Straight, brunette hair fell to the lace collar of her plaid, Laura Ashley dress. A tiny gold cross dangled from a delicate chain at her neck.

"Am I keeping you from something, Mrs. Manning?" I asked.

"Bible study group at two," she said, glancing at her wrist watch. "The church is a refuge for me. Particularly today. Are you saved, Mr. Pinel?"

"No," I said.

"A pity," she said, lowering her eyes.

I shrugged. "Tell me about Ricky. He's *your* son?"

"Why, of course. Why do you ask?"

"You're young to have an eighteen-year-old."

She smiled wistfully. "I suppose accomplished liars thrive in your profession, Mr. Pinel. I *was* young when Ricky was born."

"What's he like?"

"Well ... he can be exasperating sometimes. An only child, you know."

I sipped the coffee and grimaced.

"Oh, I'm sorry about the coffee," she said. "It's from this morning. Would you like fresh? It's no trouble."

"No, it's fine. Go on."

"Some lunch, perhaps? A sandwich?"

"No, thanks. I grabbed a hamburger on the way over. You say Ricky is exasperating?"

"*Can* be ... but nothing major. I have to nag him about the usual things. Clean your room, take out the garbage, mow the lawn, finish your homework. Like that old song, 'Yakkety-Yak?' Remember?"

"I lived it. Have his grades fallen lately? Trouble at school?"

"Just the opposite. When Ricky began high school, he took up with a group of – how can I say it – not *bad* kids, but going nowhere kids. Then he found football and things changed." She sipped from her cup. "Last year, he played junior varsity, but all spring and summer he lifted weights and lived on some muscle-building powder he discovered at the health food store. Believe me, it tasted worse than the coffee we're drinking. Anyway, this year he made varsity and school is fine, except for English. He and Dr. McDermott, don't see eye to eye."

The kitchen window overlooked a small, sunlit swimming pool and an ice-plant covered slope. At the foot of the slope grew an orange tree, its branches sagging with ripening fruit. A few wind-picked oranges, mostly green, littered the base of the tree. Midway up the hill, a forgotten plastic football lay entangled in the ground cover. .

"How about yesterday ... anything different?"

She gnawed her lip. "No ... No, not that I noticed. I was here all day. Ricky came home a *little* late. The team had worked out some trick play for the game. Richard was late, but that's normal. I ordered a pizza and wrapped a few presents while Ricky did schoolwork in his room."

"You don't work outside the home, Mrs. Manning?"

"How politically correct, Mr. Pinel. No, I'm just a housewife."

"Your husband mentioned starting a new practice. Was that a problem?"

"For Ricky? Teenagers are pretty self-centered, don't you think? Actually, Richard is working less that ever, it just seems harder to *him*. He spent ten years at the university ... joined the faculty right after his residency. He's a born teacher, Mr. Pinel, but a very poor salesman."

"What do you mean."

"UC San Dismas is a newer UC campus, smaller with a short-man complex, I'm afraid. The administration insists that Orange County needs a world-class research mill, no matter how much we lose to obtain it. Do you know how they measure world class research, Mr. Pinel?"

"Probably in dollars," I said.

"Exactly! Research grant dollars. Growth has brought big money to campus. Corporate offices. Endowed chairs. Professional fund-raisers. And hyenas drawn by the *stink*. Scientists who spend less time on truth than they do currying any horse-ass –" She put a hand to her lips and blushed. "... Excuse my anger, Mr. Pinel. My husband was denied tenure in September."

"I see. Financial problems?"

"You *don't* see. Richard makes twice as much in private practice as he did in academics. It's more that ... well, he's forty-five now. I suppose he thought he would always be a teacher."

"But you don't think any of this was troubling Ricky?'

"Honestly, I don't think so"

"Okay. How about last night? Phone calls? Visitors? Arguments?"

"Nothing. Richard came home about 9:30, warmed the pizza, and watched 'It's A Wonderful Life' with me. I love to cry over old Christmas movies this time of year." She paused. "You know ... Ricky joined us. *That* was different. Usually he treats us like lepers, but he sat with Richard through the whole movie. Richard talked about the game and Ricky described the new play. He seemed fine at the time, but now? *Something* was bothering him. He was still up when Richard and I went to bed. "

"You found the note this morning?"

She handed me a sheet of paper from the counter, a three-hole, loose-leaf sheet scribbled "Sorry, Dad. Love. Rick.

"Sorry? ... Was he feeling guilty about anything?"

She touched the tiny cross at her throat and shook her head.

"Any depression or suicide attempts?"

"My God, you don't think! ... No, Mr. Pinel. No. Ricky's a moody boy, a little on the melancholic side like his father, but never *depressed*. I think we would notice depression. Besides, since football, he's been different."

"That's good to know. Narrows things down." I gulped the last of the acrid coffee and clinked the cup on the saucer. May I see his room now?"

Mrs. Manning led me to a room just past her husband's book filled study.

"Was anything missing?" I asked.

"His money jar was empty. A hundred dollars or so, mostly birthday money from his Grandma last month. His car, of course. A new Ford Escort. Blue."

"Okay, let me poke around in here."

"You ... you want me to leave?"

"Thanks. Ten, fifteen minutes. If I find something important, I'll let you know. Anything unimportant is unimportant."

"Well ... I'll wait in the kitchen then," she said, stepping out.

The room was a narrow rectangle, close or cozy depending on the perspective of the occupant. The bed was small for Ricky's size. The springs squeaked and the mattress sagged with age. It looked uncomfortable to me, but then, it wasn't my bed. The kid slept on top of the bedspread beneath a rumpled, green comforter, probably to avoid making the bed each morning. Beneath the box springs on top of the bed-slats were a few skin mags. They weren't important and Mom probably knew anyway.

Football posters, a Mustangs team photo, and a Vista Viejo pennant covered the walls. Three shelves held Little League trophies, a Hot Wheels car, a blue and silver pom-pom, a wooden train – various valuable but untranslatable objects – rocks, ticket stubs, a Smurf key chain. On the top shelf squatted a short row of dusty books – The Black Stallion, a few Hardy Boys, a child's Bible – gifts, most likely, little-used gifts stashed out of reach like fondue pots.

The closet and drawers held mostly clothes. Under a drawer lining, however, I found a photo of a young girl in a cheerleader outfit. On the back was scribbled, "You said you wanted this one, Rick. Love, Cyndi." Despite an almost up-skirt angle and the 'I'm yours' look on the girl's face, the photo was PG at most. I imagined that he'd hidden it only because it was important to him and private. I put it back exactly as I'd found it.

The desk was a litter of papers, a brown apple core, two Classic Coke cans, a single Cheeto, a printer, a password-protected laptop I'd deal with later if I had to, and an English Lit anthology that sat propped like a pup tent. I flipped the book and recognized the selection.

'Smart lad, to slip betimes away. From fields where
glory does not stay. And early though the laurel grows.
It withers quicker than the rose.'

Wadded paper balls filled a wastebasket next to the desk. Unfolded, the sheets revealed an eighteen-year old boy's fruitless attempt to understand a disillusioned old man. *A.E. Housman's great poem 'To an Athlete Dying Young' is good because ... The significant poem 'To an Athlete Dying Young' by the great poet A.E. Housman, has much meaning ...* Nine others, none close to complete, were much the same. The rest of the desk held nothing of note, unless you counted the oval-framed snapshot of the boy's Dad.

Returning to the kitchen, I stuck my head in the doctor's study – three walls of books and a fourth wall of sealed, cardboard, file boxes. Four months had passed already. Soon the unopened boxes would find their way to the garage, later to the rafter storage space, much later to the dump. Three walls of books and a fourth wall of boxes, but, then, walls do not a prison make, I hear.

Mrs. Manning looked up expectantly from the breakfast counter. "Did you find anything?"

I sat down. "Nothing to suggest trouble. Did Ricky say anything about English?"

"Only what I mentioned. English has been Ricky's toughest class this year because of Dr. McDermott."

"It looks like he was fumbling an assignment."

"He rarely stews over schoolwork. Just that silly Championship."

"I gather you're not much of a football fan, Mrs. Manning?"

"I like what Ricky found in it."

"How about your husband?"

"Richard? A fan?" She chuckled. "Richard is notorious for never knowing the Super Bowl teams. Even *I* know the Super Bowl teams!"

"Then he wasn't interested in Ricky's –"

"*Except* for that. He attended every game, canceled patients if necessary, insisted I go, too. This season he pored over the Sports section and clipped stories about the team. It seemed to lift him from his funk about the University, but during the playoffs, he became morose again. What does that mean?"

"Maybe you should ask him."

"Mannings don't talk all that much," she said.

"How about a girl named Cyndi? Ring a bell?"

She shook her head. "No ... no one I recall."

She was right about the talking.

"One more thing. His laptop. Know the password?"

"I ... I should, shouldn't I?" she said.

"At his age? Probably not. I if get stuck, I'll have someone take a look."

"Certainly. Anything."

I shook her hand. "I can let myself out. Or are you leaving now?"

"I'll just tidy up a bit before I leave for Bible Study," she said. She stood to rinse her empty cup, but stared distractedly through the window, perhaps at the forsaken football among the ice plants.

Pausing at the front door, I took in the cathedral emptiness of the small house – father at work, son gone, mother waiting for the son's return. All was silent, save for the faint murmur of a sobbed prayer.

* * * * *

Viejo Vista High School was, indeed, new. The ground cover was still isolated green clumps on brown slopes, the shade trees mere saplings. I butted the usual wall of paranoia at the principal's office, convinced an assistant principal to call Dr. Manning, and finally got a list of Ricky's teachers' classrooms. The English teacher had a free period before his last class. The coach was on the playing field.

I found McDermott hunched over his desk, red-penciling themes. He was a stunted, frail man with thin arms, a corded neck, and bony, brown-spotted hands. His dry, ashen face looked as fragile as a pressed flower. His gray mustache was pinched, his gray crew cut sparse. Thick, glasses distorted black, cataract-surgery flaws in the fading green irises of his eyes. He squinted at me and puckered his face into a pout.

"Have you registered at the principal's office?" he snipped after I introduced myself.

"You bet. Give 'em a call. I was told I could speak with Ricky Manning's teachers. He's missing."

McDermott slashed across the paper he was correcting and printed in the margin FRAGMENT!!!

"Melodramatic, don't you think?" he muttered, pretending to read. "Probably playing footsie with that cheerleader of his."

McDermott wore no ring.

"Did Ricky act upset or frightened lately?"

"I have studious pupils who, unlike jocks, warrant my attention. When you see him, inform him that failure to complete an important assignment has turned his 'C-' into an 'F.' Perhaps losing athletic eligibility will help him focus on priorities."

"What's your beef, pal? The one kid or the whole world?"

"I am not your *pal*. My name is McDermott. *Doctor* McDermott."

"Really? Say, I've been having this pain in my shoulder, Doc. What do you think?"

He scowled. "Worthwhile endeavors languish while ignorant armies clash for some inane championship. I imagine you're *quite* the football fan, Mr. ... uh, whatever."

It was silly to let him get to me, but I did. I leaned across the desk and grabbed his tie.

"You're a bitter little bastard, aren't you?" I said.

"See here, you can't—"

"Sure I can. Because you won't do anything to stop me."

"I couldn't."

"You could, but you *won't*. The difference is more than semantic, *professor*."

I released his tie.

"You're wasting your time on that boy," he said.

"I haven't jumped to that conclusion yet. But I *do* hate wasting time, so teach me something, teach. You vs. the world, I get. But what is it with Ricky? He's good at something you're not? What?"

"He's *not* that good."

I let the *Aha!* sink in for a moment.

"So *that's* it," I said. "You'd tolerate a natural, wouldn't you? If playing were just a gift ... some inborn trait like the tangle of neurons in your head. But Ricky's thirty pounds light. He didn't make varsity until senior year. It takes *work* for him to play. And *guts*. Bigger, faster, stronger guys hurt him, embarrass him. A *doctor* hiding in a high school wouldn't appreciate that. Or *would* he? ... Go ahead and smirk. Symbolism is *your* game. You know what I'm saying."

"I have a class."

"Not yet, teach. First finish this one. *To an Athlete Dying Young* wasn't on the lesson plan, was it? You squeezed it in because the kids were fighting for the championship."

"Sic transit gloria mundi."

"You feed that weary, old man's lament to kids who need the promise of glory like ... like *food*! Like *vitamins*! You couldn't even allow them the *moment*. They're up against linemen guarding the goal, and you point out the leering death's-head in the end zone. Then what, *teacher?* You leave them to face it *alone*."

I sighed.

"But they're going to play tomorrow *anyway*, McDermott. That's the part that eats you. They're going to play anyway."

Somewhere a bell rang. A squad of tired, disinterested kids shuffled through the doorway and dissipated over the rows of desks. I leaned forward to whisper in McDermott's ear.

"I saved the best part for last. You and I will never meet again ... *unless* you take this out on Manning. Understand?"

He bobbed his head. I strode to the door, noting in his students' faces an ebbing light. I wished that I could save them, but everyone has to play the game and McDermott was just one team in a very long season.

* * * * *

Coach Barnett was running laps on the dry, brown practice field. The sun was bright, but low and winter cool – a good day for laps, as laps go. Not that the coach was running laps himself. He supervised a puffing freshman class from center track, periodically tooting a whistle that dangled from a lanyard around his neck. I could tell from a distance that he was long past running. He was shiny bald, with flabby jowls and a belly that sagged so far over his waistband he might need a sling if he did decide to take a lap. I figured him near retirement.

Astonishingly, he loped off suddenly toward the track. I jogged behind as he drew even with a pack of stragglers.

"Giddy-ap, there, *vaqueros*. Haven't even got a lather up!" The words prodded as a coach's words always do. He coaxed for a furlong, trotting on the grass alongside the track, then slowed to a walk and spiraled back toward centerfield. "Use your arms, Gentry! Good pace, Patterson, keep it up!"

"Coach Barnett?" I wheezed.

Turning, he chuckled. "Try outs were six months ago, Redshirt. Besides, you're downright out of shape." He blew a shrill blast on his whistle. "Get back in there, Sanchez! No strolling!" He looked at me.

"What is it with young'uns these days? It's more than lazy. It's no *heart*!" He shook his head. "So. What can I do you for?"

"Pete ... Pinel ... Private ... Inves ... tigator."

"Suck in some deep breaths."

"Good ... safety ... tip. Ricky Manning. He's missing."

"Don't I know it! Called his house after morning practice. Talked with his Ma, poor lady. Why in hell do kids break their Ma's heart like that? ... I'd sure hate for Ricky to miss the game."

"I hear it wouldn't change the odds much."

"Did you play anything?" he said sternly.

I looked at my hands. "I played."

"Good coach?"

"Yeah. Good."

"Then you know about *teams*."

"What if I played singles tennis?"

"Don't be a smart ass, sonny. On a team you might warm the bench all season. That's not your call. But if you *earned* a spot on the bench rather than pay to watch from the stands, you're *equal part*. Ricky earned his share. If he's missing, it hurts him and it hurts the team."

"You like him."

"I never saw a boy his weight hit the line so hard. All heart."

"Any idea where he is?"

"Cyndi Peck would know."

"She his girl?"

"More than that, I reckon. He gets that goofy look on his face when she's around."

"*That* look."

"Yeah, that one. I checked this morning. She's absent, too. No answer at her house."

"Happen to have an address?"

He riffled through a nest of folded papers from his shirt pocket. "Jotted it down with the phone number ... No ... no ... Here! This is it!"

He handed me the slip of paper. "When you find him, drag his ass to the game. Boy will hate himself if he misses it. Tell him he'll have to square it later for ditching practice, but tomorrow I want him suited up."

I promised to relay the message and sprinted off the field to prove something to someone. Driving a half-mile to what I remembered as an empty ridge, I found the right tract of red-tile roofed houses, eyeballed the Peck place, and meandered along the curlicue streets, looking for the license number on Dr. Manning's list. Spotting Ricky's Escort a block away, I returned to the Peck house, marched to the front door, and rang the bell.

From inside came muffled footsteps and scratching around the peephole.

"Who is it?" said a girl's voice.

"Police. Open up."

I flashed my wallet shield for the peephole. It often fooled kids.

"Uh … just a minute." The door opened a crack. "My parents are away skiing, sir," said a pretty blonde anxiously. "What is it?"

"Get Ricky Manning."

"Rick? What –?"

"I know he's here, Cyndi. If he's in trouble, maybe I can help. Regardless, his folks are hurting and need to know he's okay."

"Gee, officer, I haven't seen Rick since –"

"Forget it, Cyndi," interrupted a resigned voice behind her. "Let him in."

She looked over her shoulder, shrugged, and opened the door.

"I was heading home anyway, officer," Ricky muttered. "Let me get my things."

I followed the kids to the kitchen. An open, grease stained pizza box littered with pizza bones sat on the breakfast counter between two Coors cans. Something like music yowled from a radio. With blinds drawn and the sun setting, the room was dark. I switched on a light, turned off the radio and took a stool at the counter while Ricky grabbed a backpack and gathered belongings.

"I'm not really a cop, Ricky," I said. "Private Investigator. Name's Pete Pinel. Your parents hired me to find you."

"Didn't get very far, did I?" he said.

"The longest journeys are round trips."

"What are you, a Jedi?"

The girl touched his shoulder. They both sat.

"Sorry," he said. "I suppose you're trying to help."

"Are you in trouble?" I asked.

"Not like you mean. I just ... Oh, you wouldn't understand."

He stared silently at the floor. I gave him time, toying with my ring. Beneath the gold was a perfectly white band of skin as soft and unmarked as baby skin.

"It's the game," he said finally.

I got the impression that *this* Manning talked to someone when the girl squeezed his hand.

"I wasn't running away. I ... I'm no coward. I played my guts out all year. I'm not scared. We'll win that game, but ..."

"What?"

"Damn, I don't really *know*! It was McDermott, but then ... maybe it's just the way things are."

"The Housman poem?"

"You read it?"

"I know it."

"You *like* that stuff?" he said surprised. "Well, English isn't big with me, see? Especially when I'm psyching up for a game. But McAsshole-Dermott springs this dweeb poem to write on. I mean, it's just words, right? But I kept going over it and over it in my room and ..." He glanced at Cyndi and looked away. "I ... I got scared like I never been. I ... I started to cry!"

He struggled for words as if the feelings were too much for words, as if all he could grasp were images.

"Look, picture this. My mom was Miss California twenty years ago," he began. "True! She has this yellowed ribbon thing hanging in her closet. I've seen her put it on, and, man, you don't want to see her face then. And my Dad used to be some hot shot at the college. Some nights lately ... you don't want to see *his* face either." He shook his head hard as if he had stumbled into cobwebs "For me ... this year, the team, the championship. We *did* something. Something special, and I was part of it. People knew my name. In the hallway I'd hear strangers shout, 'Say Rick! Kick Woodbridge ass!' I was a star, man! There's no feeling like it."

I nodded.

"But look at me! 170 and no more. I mean, what's my Dad's size, right? All the weight-on powder in the world won't make me a college player. Tomorrow is it."

"For *football*, maybe."

"No! If you wanna understand, you gotta understand. Tomorrow is *it*. What's after? Community college and a nothing job somewhere – runners whom renown outran and the name died before the man. I can't get that out of my head."

The girl scooted closer and put her arm around his shoulder, but he didn't seem to notice. He was deep inside himself now, all alone, seeing shadows, listening to echoes.

"Runners whom renown outran ... There's no way out."

I felt like something was sitting on my chest. "You've got a whole life, kid," I said, knowing it sounded as empty to him as it did to me.

"Yeah? ... Well, what's life when it's just some long good-bye; when all of it is AFTER! I see it now, man. Everything ahead is just ... *after Friday*, and ... and I didn't want Friday to *end*!" His face was red from choking back tears. "I wanted it to go on, you know? The team, the games. I didn't want a *last* game, you know? And somehow it got all mixed up, like if I didn't play that game, it wasn't really over." His eyes pleaded. "... Oh it's crazy, I know that."

"Talk with your dad."

"A *shrink*, you mean?"

"A *dad*, I mean."

"Dad's done important stuff with his life. What's he know from football?"

"Give him a chance, Rick," Cyndi murmured.

Ricky grabbed a backpack and slung it over his shoulder. "Fine, let's go. Let's go play the big game and kick Woodbridge ass. What choice do I have?"

I stood. "Maybe you should see it differently," I said as we moved to the front door.

"See it how?"

"Well ... Why do you play?"

"I dunno ... To kick ass, I guess. It's fun."

"But sometimes *your* ass is kicked, right? And either way, *someone* loses. That's not fun. Why does anyone play?"

"Okay, sure ... winning's *better*, of course, but it's dope either way."

"But why?"

"Because ... because you're *playing*. You're doing something hard that you can't always do, but you're always trying. For me? Rest of my life? Who knows. But *playing*? ... Win or lose I know I'm giving the best in me."

"Play for mortal stakes."

He turned at the doorway.

"I don't know what that means."

"It's a poem."

He shook his head. "Figures."

"You know you're giving your best because ...? You just said it. Now *hear* it."

"Because ..." He combed a hand through his hair. "Oh ... I get you! Because I *don't* have to. I *do* have a choice."

I opened the door.

"And when it's fourth and goal, so close you could almost reach out and touch the end zone, and you hit the line with all you have, but they nail you with what *they* have ... what do you do?"

"Give 'em the ball and try to take it back!"

"And even if you do make it – over the top and into the end zone – what do you do?"

"Well, then you ..." A half-smile surfaced. "You give them the ball and try to take it back."

"Right. You kickoff ... Forever?"

"Until the clock runs out," he said somberly.

I stepped outside while Ricky bundled Cyndi in his letter jacket. It was dark already. A chilly, north wind whispered across the roof tiles. An empty moon rose above the school.

"Shorter tonight," I mumbled, glancing at my watch.

"What's that?" said the boy.

"Thinking aloud," I said. "Today's the first full day of winter. Last night was the longest night of the year. They get better for a while."

Ricky closed the door solidly and crossed his arms against his chest. "Oh, man, man, man," he said. "How do I stand it?"

The girl hugged him around his waist and nudged him forward. "C'mon Rick, let's go home."

I dropped the kids at Ricky's car, tailed them back to his house, and walked them to the door. Dr. Manning was home. The boy and his Dad embraced without words. Cyndi introduced herself. Mrs. Manning took the girl's hand and led her inside. I didn't go in.

My place wasn't far, but it was far enough – beyond the spreading pastel stain of houses in a niche the stain hadn't sullied yet. Half way up Saddleback, squeezed against the mountainside, was a cedar-shingled cabin – a single, narrow bedroom on a wide, tree-strewn yard.

The trees were tall, older than me, and, if I could help it, they would be there when I died. From my porch chair I could see the mountain, the trees, patches of sky, and not another house or person at all.

Inside I swept a half-dozen Sapporo cans from my desk into a trash bin. The empty, silver cans reminded me of spent .38 casings. I took my pistol from the desk, and stuffed it back into its holster.

Birthdays.

Can't live with 'em; can't live without 'em.

I typed a simple report for my files, slipped an old Brubeck album on the turntable, and fetched a cold Sapporo from the fridge. I flopped on the couch and switched out the light.

Next evening, way up in the stands, I watched the game. I saw the Doctor and Mrs. Manning down front, rooting and waving Vista Viejo pennants.

Rick played some.

Cyndi cheered him on.

The Mustangs won.

And then, about a week after Christmas, I received an invitation to the football awards banquet in January. I went because I felt like shaking Rick's hand when he received his championship ring. After the ceremonies and the speeches, they played videotape highlights of the season. Some of the team, mostly juniors, crowded together in front of the projection TV, and they boasted about next year, and they shouted, and they laughed a little too loudly.

Sitting a row of tables behind, the Doctor and his boy silently watched the season passing. Cindi held Rick's hand while Mrs. Manning squeezed her husband's knee.

Leaving early, I bumped into Coach Barnett sneaking a cigarette outside.

"Say, Redshirt. You've lost a few pounds," he said. "Bulked up a mite, too. New Year's resolution?"

"I may have another season left in me."

"Keep it up. You never know." Shaking my hand, he noticed my ring. "What year?"

"Sixty-eight."

He blew a cloud of smoke. "Sixty-eight, let's see, Division I?"

I nodded.

"Costa Mesa. I know all the Division champs, all the way back."

"Good memory for an old man."

"Not *too* old, sonny. I still got a game or two left myself." He sized me up. "Linebacker?"

"Full-back, second string."

"First string, second string … What's the dif' now. Time of your life, right?"

I twisted the ring on my finger and watched the ruby catch the light, flare and fade.

"Right," I said. "Time of my life."

Rhapsody

Sasha called. Empathy was Greek to her and, sure enough, she said nothing about my play folding. She called because she had finished her shoot and Hagop from Detroit, the buyer or whatever, was what Sasha dubbed an *artiste collector;* one of those Leyden-jar people who store the jolt they get rubbing shoulders with painters, musicians, writers ... that ilk. Sasha was casting me as a struggling writer. And Richie B. – an old live-in with whom she could occasionally still manage civil words – was playing at Guignol's. Shouting over the club noise, Sasha begged me to meet her there. Two *artistes* wouldn't generate much of a charge, but, probably, Hagop wasn't much a whatever.

Having sacrificed several hours to an empty sheet of paper, I said yes. I needed noise. Light. Something to fill my ears, my eyes. A loud place, loud people. A cabaret. A party. Even Sasha's party. As it was, I was already two martinis down a path that led to the corner bar and some noisy whore, whatever din I could find.

Outside – awash in honks, headlights, neon, squeals, shouts, slams, bangs – I whistled a cab, tried to pile in on the roll, and – half-drunk – faltered. I tumbled onto a sticky seat and grunted Guignol's at the dread-locked cabby. Jerked uptown, I wallowed in Bob Marley and traffic sounds while liquid colors cascaded down my closed eyelids. Light and sound folded into a strange kind of white noise that evoked some Discovery Channel squib about queer people in the southwest.

Hummers? ...

That didn't sound right.

Whatever.

People who hear a hum off the desert. Others don't, they do. Can't shake it, unless they move away.

Noise.

Constant noise.

Deposited at the club, I elbowed my way into anarchy so loud I winced. The room was a miasma of pheromones, sweat, smoke, attar of weed, beer, juniper berries, Mennen Skin Bracer, Chanel No. 5.

"William! William, here. Over here!"

Sasha waved, jangling her bracelets. I plowed toward her table.

Most people thought they recognized Sasha, not merely because her face appeared in magazines, but because her hungry, Cleopatra eyes *clamored* for recognition. She had sharp, white teeth, a wide mouth, lush dark lips, and an African-Semitic complexion as perfectly smooth and lustrous as the cool surface of a brown pearl.

Across from her – meticulously bored – posed Bristol, mannequin by profession and propensity. Bristol's vacant gaze converged halfway in the distance, an expression she adopted even in bed. A satin, cowl-neck chemise draped her slight shoulders. Swirling moiré patterns shimmered where erect nipples and tiny quivering breasts disturbed the hang of the fabric.

Bristol was an iron maiden whose consecrating embrace I occasionally pursued as an obbligato to my Danse Macabre. Tonight, I surmised, she was my reward for being fixed and formulated in Hagop's *artiste* collection. She would acquiesce to a night of cold, drunken sex from which I would awaken with a headache and bad breath.

Sasha, on the other hand, would wake alone. She, too, occasionally slept with Bristol and readily might have joined us, but only for sport and never mixed with business. As for Hagop, Sasha was a panderer, not a whore. She would trade sex only if necessary, and then maneuver toward something fastidious like a blowjob in the cab.

I squeezed into a chair and immediately grabbed Bristol's half-empty glass. Something red.

"Can't walk on one leg," I said and gulped. I grimaced. "Christ, what is this stuff?"

"*My* drink," Bristol replied.

"I'll get you another."

"Do," she said, staring at nothing.

A puffy, middle-aged man, palm wet from holding his glass, reached over the table to press my fingers. He mouthed something I couldn't hear. I leaned closer.

"Arzmanian!" he shouted. "Hagop Arzmanian! Sasha tells me you have a play off-Broadway."

"Sasha is generous. I – Wait a sec."

I grabbed the arm of a passing waitress. She cupped a hand to her ear.

"Another of everything," I said, making a circling motion. "And a martini for me. Dry, double, and quick."

She disappeared.

"I *had* a play," I shouted back at Hagop. I disliked shouting, but took comfort that no one would hear. "It's less misleading to say it was in New York."

Hagop cocked his head. "What did you say?"

Noise.

"I *had* a play in the city! It closed yesterday."

Hagop elbowed Sasha. "Exchange seats with me," he said. "I want to hear what Mr. Alton has to say."

Sasha wriggled over his lap, trading places. Bristol stole a cigarette from Sasha's purse and lit it with a thin gold lighter lying on the table. Hagop's, I suppose.

"So ... the play is kaput. Bad reviews?"

"It wasn't big enough for reviews. Some notices. Not all bad. Some good."

My martini appeared. Tall, triangular, cold, and crystal clear. Hagop sipped something red. Bristol smoked. Sasha cast her hungry eyes around the room.

"I love creative people!" Hagop shouted, his shoulder touching mine. "That's why I come myself to New York for these shoots. It's all here, isn't it?"

"Hagop supervised the shoot himself," Sasha said. "Quite the eye for appearance!"

"Oh, I help, I help. And seeing the photographs, I must agree that ... well, you must know, Mr. Alton. That feeling?"

I clinked his glass.

"To the feeling." I said.

I shifted my leg under the table to rest against Bristol's thigh. I felt the satin of her dress in the way the material slid over the nylon of her pantyhose. I imagined the soft wispy sound of satin against nylon – another kind of white noise, a subtle version of the noise in the room. Bristol did not move.

"Where do you get your ideas, Bill?"

"Who knows," I said. "Ideas just—"

He looked away and gestured at the waitress. A finger circling.

"What?" he said, turning back.

"It's a mystery," I said.

"Well, tell me this. Do you ever sit down and say I'll write a play about, say ... I don't know, say *the Internet*? Just yesterday I was thinking, I bet there's a market for Internet plays these days. You know, like with all those AIDS plays a few years back."

Even close up, his mouth spraying against my ear, his words were drowned. I found myself bellowing replies as if Hagop were a foreigner.

"I don't care much about the Internet."

"But, surely, you consider the market."

Another martini appeared. The tiny table was littered with glasses. Empty, full, half-full, half-empty.

I swallowed the old and began the new.

"Hagop, my friend, I would write about the Internet if someone would pay me to do it, but they won't until I write it. And since I don't write well about things I don't care about, it won't be any good and no one will buy it, so I go ahead and write what I care about. It's a strange system."

Hagop nodded knowingly.

"Strange, but it works, no?"

"No." I said. "It doesn't work at all. I'd much rather someone pay me to write a play about the Internet."

My leg still rested against Bristol's. The contact had become warm. I remembered her gamy smell, the olive-like feel of her hard nipple in my lips, the noises she made. Bristol was exactly what I needed tonight.

"So you're strictly an instinct man, is that it, Bill? Well, that's how I picked Sasha. She's doing our next spread, too. The cover! Right Sasha?"

She nuzzled his cheek.

"Anything for you, dear Hagop, you know that."

"… Full frontal nudity …" uttered Bristol to no one, as if the words were channeled. She often spoke with a fragmented, oracular ambiguity.

Sasha's eyes flashed like light off a blade.

"For Art's sake, perhaps, darling Bristol. *Taste* above all."

Bristol declined to engage. Her gaze drifted back to some spot midway to the horizon. What did she see there? Perhaps she saw nothing. I shivered and swallowed half my drink.

Lights dimmed. Noise abated.

"Richie will join us after this set," said Sasha.

"Sasha believes …" Hagop began, still shouting. He caught himself and lowered his voice. "Sasha thinks he might do a jingle for us."

Before I could ask if he needed words for his jingle, the band appeared. Richie B., the headliner, plopped onto the piano bench. Paul

McClellan – easily as good as Richie, a name in his own right – diddled with his sax. The original members of Richie's group had gone separate ways. The new drummer was a fill-in I didn't know, as was the bass player, a shiny-bald, black man with thick, purplish lips and a diamond stud in his left ear.

A few coughs. Clinking ice. The band talked, found sheets, adjusted knobs. I couldn't hear what they said as they prepared for the set, but the moving mouths fascinated me. Smiles, nods, gestures – pregnant symbols all meaningless without words.

They waited, fingers poised.

Whisper quiet.

Richie nodded a countdown and exploded in a foot-stomping, block-chord progression. The others joined in. Time suspended, the band glided from raggy-waltz through swing-blues to boogie-woogie. Relishing my drunkenness, I swayed and pat beat.

Sasha jabbered with Hagop about the April catalog. Bristol sucked on a cigarette and blew the smoke back out almost disgustedly. My eyes swept the other tables – people watching, listening, half-listening, tapping the rhythm, talking, nodding; people in and out of the moment, in their own moments – but the noise, the *anarchy*, had been quashed by the rule of music.

Halfway through the set, I focused on the bass man. As a fill-in, he would have seen little rehearsal, relying instead on his ability to glean intent from a gesture, direction from a nod. His fingers flew like a typist's, linking the sax and the piano, his passacaglias and chaconnes a tail on the kite of the melody.

He pulsed with the beat. Rhythmically, his head snapped backward, his chin jutted forward. Confident of the music, he closed his eyes and savored it. Other times, he watched Richie or the sax man and followed like a dance partner, creating intricate counter-steps to their lead.

Richie finished the set with his signature "Pick-Six" – you've heard it a hundred times – but the piano riff suddenly billowed like a cloud changing shape. The bass man's thick lips opened in surprise, then excitement, then appreciation, then something like ecstasy – understanding, maybe; communion, maybe – as he solved Richie's musical equation, predicting as a whole, the middle and end from the beginning. He laughed aloud and began to bounce with his own elaboration of the new and never heard "Pick-Six."

I was bobbing in my seat, making faces, tapping the rhythm, awash in a hot wave from somewhere behind my heart and below my stomach, when the bass man saw. He flashed a white-toothed thank-you for my gift of having heard and *that* moment, those chords, that surge of notes were for *me*.

And in that brief tide of reciprocity, my old play's demise dissolved like a sand castle. Because a *new* play had germinated inside me, a play complete in all but words, words that, in time, would coalesce around the chafing image of a side man communing with his lead and his audience.

Set over, I stood and clapped, near bursting with a pressure to converse, to talk about my idea. No, not the idea – too fragile – but just to talk. To say words, hear words, create a nurturing amnion of words for the idea.

Sasha was deep into dollars and headcount with Hagop. Bristol appeared deaf. I stole a deep drag from her cigarette, smoldering in the ashtray.

"I thought you quit," Bristol said.

"I did."

"Don't hotbox it," she said. "Take one from Sasha."

I lifted the pack from Sasha's purse, tapped out a cigarette, and left the pack on the table. I lit the cigarette with Hagop's gold lighter.

The idea glowed in my head like the ruby tip of the cigarette. Bristol's eyes were cold and blue like shallow water.

"Do you want to fuck tonight?" she said.

"I have to see Gordon first thing," I said, exhaling. "About contracts."

"Your play flopped, I hear," she said, sucking on her own cigarette.

"You heard right, Bristol."

"How sad," she said, examining her nail polish. She stubbed out her cigarette and said nothing more.

Sasha uncoupled from Hagop and shouldered her way to the stage. The drummer had retired to the men's room. The bass player was finagling a drink from the bartender. Waving his hands, Richie huddled with the sax man.

Sasha interrupted. Richie snapped. Sasha retaliated with thundering words and flashing eyes.

Just like old times.

She stormed back to the table.

"Is he coming?" Hagop asked, an edge to his voice.

"Later," Sasha said.

"You said you knew him," Hagop said.

"That's why he won't come," Bristol cooed with a rare smile.

"Bristol, darling," said Sasha. "Leave Oscar Wilde to our playwright companion."

I grabbed a half-filled glass – not a red one – from the raft of glasses on the table and gulped it down. Interest flagging, Hagop pushed back his chair and surveyed the room, for *what* I didn't know. On his way back to the stage, the bass man squeezed past our table.

"Ahmal!" Sasha blurted, hooking his large hand. "Marvelous set! Marvelous! Let me introduce you to someone. Hagop Arzmanian this is Ahmal Yusef. Hagop is with Tattler Fashions out of Detroit."

Sasha guided the bass man's hand into Hagop's. Hagop pumped the hand up and down as if trying to raise water.

"You a designer, Hagop?"

"Actually, Ahmal, I'm a cog in the marketing machine. But I *adore* creative people … Say! I bet you know Richie pretty well. Do you think he might—"

"Fill-in gig," said Ahmal, drawing back his hand. "Barely met the man."

Bristol snickered, a brittle sound like cracking ice. "Sasha, you're ignoring poor William."

Sasha's irritation flared like a blemish beneath make-up.

"Ahmal, meet William Alton. He thinks of himself as a playwright, although, actually, William is a teacher, aren't you William? Those who can …"

Ahmal offered his hand across the table.

"You two queers should get along famously," Sasha chirped, adding at my raised eyebrows, "Oh, shame, William! Everyone knows what I mean. Queer for your *art*. You know. *Artistes*."

Maybe she said it because he was queer.

Maybe she thought I was queer.

Maybe to her, all *artistes were* queer.

Bristol giggled.

"Sasha is *not* queer," she said. "Gender is merely a variation in sex toys, like a new vibrator. If anything, Sasha is electro-sexual."

"Ignore the creature, Ahmal," Sasha said. "Bristol is a woman of no importance."

I laughed, enjoying the Wilde allusion. Sasha was bright and had a sassy way with words, even when few understood them. She was a consummate bitch – tenacious, narcissistic, sarcastic. I guess that's why I liked her.

Hagop squirmed.

"What's all this talk of … well, you know. That's not a very popular word these days. I wouldn't want people to think—"

"They won't, Hagop," I said.

Ahmal raised his drink, something clear and sparkling and bubbly with a green wedge of lime and a red and white striped swizzle stick. "It's been a kick. Enjoy the show." Starting to leave, he turned back. "Alton? ... *William* Alton. You wrote *Says the Preacher*, didn't you?"

"That I did."

"I dig your work. Got a new one in Soho, right? *Vanity Fair*? Something like that."

"Vanity *Fear*. Folded yesterday."

He nodded as if he were feeling the beat of a blues riff. "Next year Jerusalem, man," he said.

Ahmal shouldered his way back to the stage. Hagop was restless. Sasha – probably hoping to salvage *something* – suggested they try a different club ... a long cab ride uptown. I stood to say goodbye and sat back down with Bristol.

"What was that with the black?" she said.

"Communion."

"Let's go." she said.

I want to hear the last set."

"Rather than fuck?"

"Not tonight."

She stood, collecting Sasha's forgotten cigarettes.

"Too *glum*, William?"

The music began.

"No ... actually, Bristol, I'm not glum at all anymore."

WayFinder

He had lost his way.

Remaining on the right road had seemed hopeless at the time; finding a shortcut prudent. But now?

Second thoughts.

Gaping at signs and storefronts, he garnered honks and middle fingers from angry drivers, but no clues. Everything felt *strangely* strange. There was a name for that feeling ... what? He knew where he was (he hadn't gone to the moon!), but everything looked alien and darkly threatening.

Jamais vu! That was it. The *opposite* of déjà vu ... Nothing was familiar.

Street names, for example.

Limit Way?

Had he passed a Limit?

Memory Lane? Surely he would have remembered.

And gentlemen's clubs on either side of the road? Flashing purple neon and giant billboards plastered with swollen breasts, stung lips, zombie-eyes. How could he have forgotten those?

He glanced at his watch and cursed.

Shortcuts. You meet your fate on the road you choose to avoid it, don't you? If he missed his flight, he'd be stranded overnight in this dead-end *dead end* and Susan would sulk ... *Again*. He often wished she would just accuse him of cheating, something he could at least deny, but no. She took the travel itself as infidelity.

Such a *steamy* affair! Restless nights in one night cheap hotels and the muttering retreats of lobby bars. Any lust he felt was merely lust to *survive*, although *will* to survive was more accurate.

He *had* to make a living. And for an out of work programmer, selling software was a living. A *decent* living. Survival *plus*. Should he simply bail out? Without a parachute? Was that what Susan expected? What she *wanted*?

So close to landing that promotion, and all he got was flak. Granted, it was more travel, but *everything* has a down side. It was more money, he thought. A lot more money. A *good* living.

He sighed.

Right now, he just wanted to get back, he *had* to get back. He looked for a sign – something, *anything*, to point the way. The only signs he saw, however, were purple neons above neon-bordered doors and the billboards – hard breasts, lacquered lips, bandit eyes. He felt a sudden déjà vu at the smoky-eyed stares, an eerie familiarity, as if he had known the eyes already.

Glancing unconsciously at his face in the rear-view mirror, he snatched up the rental car map and flailed to unfold it over the steering wheel. The car lurched onto the shoulder and fishtailed back. Flinging aside the map, he squeezed a trapped breath through pursed lips.

A GPS came with the car, but only as a tease … no charge *until* he switched it on. His company preferred him lost, however. If he pressed the button, the charge would appear automatically on his corporate credit card as a *prohibited travel expense*. He cringed contemplating the inevitable, soul-flattening conga-line of boss after boss eager to prove gravitas by dancing on the pinhead of a twenty-dollar indiscretion.

No way! He'd ask directions along here. Duck through a purple-bordered, looking-glass door. See his reflected face neon-washed with the hue of a telltale dye pack. Endure the black-eyed stares and bruised-lipped greetings he imagined rife with contemptuous familiarity.

Comrade! Brother!

He punched the ON button of the GPS.

Hi! Welcome to WayFinder.

The female voice was surprisingly friendly. Having worked with speech synthesizers, he knew that simulated emotion, while engaging, posed a problem. A voice *too* appealing risked suspension of disbelief, a misperception of feelings that muddied content. He would have made the voice more aloof, a tone he thought he might hear in a gentleman's club pushing drinks, a voice whose feigned interest greased the wheels of commerce, but – clearly programmed – left scarce room for misunderstanding.

Which way can I help you find?

"Back. Back before it's too late," he replied, as if she could hear, beguiled for a moment by her timbre of concern. He tapped *RETURN* on the console. The screen flickered and displayed a street map. A 180-degree arrow appeared.

Make a legal U-turn as soon as it is safe.

Dammit!

Going the wrong way. *Diametrically* the wrong way. But what could he expect of a long trip wrong from the start – a work of days, days of hands, glad hands ... buyers whose feigned interest approximated his own. He reminded himself (he needed consolation) that he was no huckster. The software he pitched, while glitchy and not without bugs, was cheap and met the average needs of average users. Should he feel dishonor? Of course not. So why did he? Why the struggle to keep his head above an overwhelming sense of betrayal? Of whom?

Recalculating.

Dammit! Boxed-in on the far right, he had missed a turnaround. He veered left.

Attention must be paid!

264 | Joseph Hullett

He jinked right. A motorcycle, splitting lanes, swerved and shot past. He eyed his rear-view mirrors and waited for a break.

Perhaps he'd betrayed *himself,* he thought. He knew he could design *better* software ... he *had* before he took this salesman turn. He'd built a computer when he was twelve. He was coding in BASIC and FORTRAN in high school and versed in graphics and game logic before college. He had a *master's degree,* for goodness sake! Software design was his *calling.*

A calling sent to voice mail.

For what? ... For a *decent living.* Sales of average software that met the average needs of average users.

On average.

I never thought I'd end up here, he mused.

You are approaching an opportunity.

Okay, I see it. There! He squeezed left, but spied a sign: Emergency Vehicles Only.

Make an illegal U-turn.

Aiding and abetting? Now *that's* a new wrinkle, WayFinder.

But keep an eye out. This stretch has put the sheriff's kids through college!

He wheeled onto the gravel crossover, but had to straddle the median, trapped by whizzing traffic. If the law happened by, so much for the last plane out.

Seize your second chance.

A gap! Gunning the engine, he swung into a line of cars. When no blue lights appeared, he whistled softly and reminded himself that reliance on luck was a piss-poor strategy. He aimed to remember that next time.

Looking good! Bear right ahead.

If looking good meant finally finding his way after choosing the wrong direction on entirely the wrong road, well ... maybe. But the map still showed the airport 20 miles east. Oh, how he *hated* the thought of another complimentary *breakfast* in a lobby *"Gobble-de-Nook,"* another bathroom *"sterilized for your protection,"* another shower on tiptoes, another night alone on some stained, *"Snuggo-Pedic Posturecizer."* He craved a hot bath. He yearned for his own bed. He longed for Susan.

Prepare to merge.

Zipping over the entrance ramp, he saw that the freeway ahead was almost empty. Looking better, he thought. *Much* better. The fixed blue arrow on the map display seemed to fold space beneath it and draw the hopelessly distant airport ever closer along a straightaway path.

Getting home to Susan tonight had become vital ... surprisingly so, since he rarely confessed to himself that he missed her. Missing her frightened him, especially when she so achingly missed him, when the yearning in her voice steeped even a patchy cell phone connection. He had programmed himself not to feel how much they *both* had missed. It was an anesthesia that made possible the amputation of a decent living.

Exit here and proceed to rental return.

He signaled and sped around the loop.

Your destination is ahead.

Jouncing over one-way traffic spikes, he zipped between orange cones to a row of parking slots marked RETURN. Jotting the odometer and fuel gauge readings on his contract folder, he scrambled from the car and dragged out his suitcase and computer bag. Leaning over the steering wheel, he switched off the ignition and pocketed the key. Eager to get home to Susan, eager to decide which way they should go, he hurried into the terminal, grateful that he still had time.

"Thanks, WayFinder!" he said to himself.

My pleasure, Joe, said the voice in the car. *You have arrived.*

And All Ye Need

Hugging a filing carton, Cates elbowed open the door of a small scientific laboratory and barged across the threshold like an eager bridegroom.

"I made it!" he crowed, waltzing his carton around a marble-top workbench. "The *National Academy!*"

He lowered the carton lovingly onto a battered, wooden desk, then reeled from desk to sink to workbench, drumming a ruffle, spritzing water, goosing the gas taps.

"BI..IG mistake, Blumford!" he shouted, shaking a fist at the ceiling. "Lured to your web, am I? Right where you want me, am I? Ha! First I'll show *you*, and then–" He began to shadow box. "Duck Darwin! Look alive Louis Pasteur 'cause John Cates is in the ring. *Doctor* John Cates." He grabbed a chalk stub to scrawl it across a blackboard. "Doctor John Cates 'P' 'H' dot capital 'D'!"

"Wow! My wagon is hitched to a rocket!" said a voice.

Cates cringed. In the doorway stood a young woman flashing a mirror-bright smile.

"Oh cripes! My, uh … first real lab and … well, I–"

"So have fun!" said the woman. "My first apartment, I broke a bed slat bouncing!" She plopped her backpack on the desk and extended her hand. "They told me you had arrived. I'm your research assistant, Callie Ernst."

The girl was decidedly endomorphic, packing most of the *endo* in her hips and chest. She wore jeans dangerously threadbare in the seat and a strained, black tee shirt embellished with a likeness of Einstein. Long, golden hair spilled down her shirtfront.

"*You're* Ms. Ernst?" Cates blurted. "Well, of course, you're Ms. Ernst. That's something you'd know, isn't it? Stupid question. *Stupid*! I'm John Cates."

"'P' 'H' dot capital 'D'"

Cates hastily erased the blackboard with his sleeve.

"Please, Doctor Cates ... I *like* chutzpah. The noble soul respects itself."

"Oh *double* cripes," he groaned. "Nietzsche! What are you Ms. Ernst? Sophomore? Freshman?"

"Don't mock me!" she shot back. "One in a thousand undergrads lands an assistant spot at the Academy. I haven't worked as *long* as you to get here, but I bet I've worked as *hard*. I'll work just as hard to stay. And I'm a JUNIOR."

"Talk about chutzpah," said Cates with a chuckle. "Okay, okay, look. In this league, no one's more *junior* than I am. All the Laskers and Nobels upstairs will be giving me noogies in the locker room."

"Say! Maybe it's a lucky match," Callie said, returning his smile. "Your first lab. My first time as an assistant. Maybe–"

"Newbies always draw newbies," Cates interjected. "Either that or..."

"Or what?"

"Y.. you're, uh ... comely, Ms. Ernst."

"As in comely is only skin deep?"

"Don't get those hackles up! What I'm saying is that whom the gods would destroy they first make muddled. I already have enemies here. Enemies who might try to complicate things." Cates prodded his thick glasses back up the bridge of his nose. "An attractive assistant can be, well … a *complication*. Rest assured, I eschew entanglements with beautiful women and–"

Cates halted, suddenly mesmerized by the picture of Einstein on Callie's shirt.

"What?" she said, examining herself.

"Einstein."

"And?"

"Well … your *hair*."

"Something's wrong?"

"No, no, it's adequate hair," Cates reassured, "Quite healthy, but … the way it drapes, uh …" He made awkward circling motions over his chest. "Einstein looks like Fabio and, well … goggle-eyed!"

"Oh, this is a *compliment*!" Callie laughed.

"Listen, Ms. Ernst. Breasts and brains are both lipid-based organs which, I imagine, compete for nutrients. A good assistant has to be able to find her behind with two hands."

She jammed her hands into the back pockets of her skin-tight jeans.

"Are you always so stuck on anatomy, Doctor Cates? Or is it me?"

Cates sighed. "I'm making a bad job of this, aren't I? Look, I'm not a *lech* or anything, I'm just … backward. I've never had anyone work for me before, and, well … I'm not so good with people. Not much practice."

"How come?"

Cates looked away. "What a tedious story that would be. Suffice that sometimes the harrowing of foster parents can cultivate a wallflower."

"I'm sorry," the girl said gently.

"Don't be. Besides it's…" He turned back. "Well, it's the Academy."

"Flop sweat?"

"I think so."

"Me, too! We're in the same boat."

"You know, Ms. Ernst, despite that chutzpah a minute ago, our boat is, actually, a little leaky."

"I've heard the rumors. You and Blumford."

"Cripes! There I was, still a grad student, but making a name for myself among the alpha-2 kinase crowd, when my work *bloomed*!"

"The trigger sequence," she said.

Words gushed from him like an unexpected spurt from a fountain.

"And it's *everything*! Know the genetic trigger mechanism and everything falls into place. Take Belzer's blind fruit fly. Born alone. In the dark. Isolated until a female is slipped into his black little universe and unawares –"

Cates stuck out his right arm and began to flutter his hand.

"Behaviors. Responses ... A *purpose* present in his genes from the beginning made manifest by a trigger. He *knows*! He vibrates a wing. Not the left, the right! Exactly the proper frequency. Exactly the correct angle. Suddenly he knows *why* he is, *what* he's doing, his universe made clear at last."

"That's sweet," said Callie.

Cates blushed. "Well, I'm romanticizing it a *lot*, but the point is that Blumford and the rest were looking for peptoids! Ha! We don't need no stinkin' peptoids! Telomeric nucleotides! That's the beauty! Eighteen nucleotide pairs linked to–"

As he spoke, another part of him – a part that never spoke – watched her listen.

"This is all Greek to you, isn't it?" he said abruptly. "I'm ashamed of myself."

"No! You'll teach me the science later, but the excitement I can share today."

Puzzled, Cates drew closer to examine her face.

"What now?" she said.

"Your eyes. There's something in your eyes. Like ... like little stars."

She blinked several times.

"No, still there. Must be the light ... Anyway, *Genetics* published my paper as a *lead article*. And what does Blumford do? He writes a ridiculous letter to the editor. A *letter*, mind you, not a paper. Claimed he had 'hinted' at nucleotides first. Probably hinted at relativity, too." Cates pounded a fist into his palm. "That administrator doesn't know a test tube from a teacup! Cripes, any darn fool can say any darn thing in a letter. They only published it because he's such a high muckamuck here."

"He *lied?*"

"You're new to this, Ms. Ernst, but believe me, research is *hardball*. Pros can spend years on a study? Why? … Truth? No! To get grants to do more studies that win more grants! Money buys the name. A name attracts more money. They'll step all over you for either. Remember that. Hardball!"

"Well … you're *here*, right? You got the position? That must mean something."

"It does. Blumford could've easily blackballed my application, but he didn't."

"So maybe he's a good man after all."

"The goodness of men is not something I would count on, Ms. Ernst. The job is a setup, see? Blumford made sure I was offered six months *only*. No tenure. Publish or perish. Just time enough to fail. Fail at the finish and people forgive you, but fail at the start and it's 'thanks for playing.' I'll end up teaching junior college."

"Then why take the chance?"

"Because I *did* discover the trigger sequence. It's MINE! At a place like the Academy, I can finish the work and show the world."

Unconsciously his arm draped the filing carton on the desk.

"You cuddle that box like a child," Callie said.

Cates patted the box and smiled. "It's my data. Funny, isn't it? … How attached you get to an old box full of numbers and graphs and equations." He looked up. "Six months is an awfully short time, Ms. Ernst. If I fail, *you* fail. You might want to unhitch that wagon."

She stepped backward and eyed Cates with a curious expression, a look he imagined a sculptor might wear striving to discern the figure contained within a stone.

"Can we do it?" she said.

"Yep."

"Then let's do it!"

"That's a big bet on someone you don't know."

"My Dad used to say 'enough is sufficient.' Maybe I know enough."

"People are rarely who they say or what they seem. You *can't* know enough."

"Well, I think you're noble."

"Oh, cripes! ... Be realistic. Blumford will make it tough. Take this office junk." He plopped onto a wobbly, rolling chair. "A broken chair, a rusted filing cabinet. And how about this beat-up desk. Probably used at Pearl Harbor. Tell me administration couldn't scrounge a better desk from storage. Blumford's work." He tugged at the center desk drawer. "C'mon! C'mon ... Open Sesame!"

The drawer jerked free.

"Now *here's* a real find," Cates said, holding up a long, paperclip chain.

Callie pawed through a side drawer.

"Chains and chewed pencils," she said. "Someone was a *nervous* sort."

Cates groped in the bottom drawer and withdrew three yellowed forms and a crumpled sheet of paper he pried from a drawer glide.

"More chain maker trash. Blank Federal Requisition Forms ..." He tossed them on the desk. "And a draft memo from ... CRIPES!"

Callie peered over his shoulder.

"Not *Foster*!"

"Foster! See the scratch-outs? This old desk belonged to Justin W. Foster!"

"Doctor Foster *was* the Academy! His books, his articles ... and that TV show 'Searching for Truth.'"

"Eons and eons!" drawled Cates, mimicking Foster's signature accent.

"If anyone deserved the Prize, *he* did. So why would he ... " Her voice trailed off.

"Kill himself? ... Try to figure people. You've seen his lab on TV, right? Everything imaginable! And yet, apparently, this yard sale reject was his desk."

"Well ... like you said, people get attached to things."

"Sure. Go figure."

"... You know ... if the forms belonged to Foster, they *might* be important."

They each grabbed a form.

"'*Requisition of Unneeded Equipment, Paraphernalia, Supplies, and Stores*,'" read Callie.

"Something about requesting things from a pool of materials," Cates added, scanning the gobbledygook. "If it's in the pool, it's yours. When you don't need it, you turn it back in."

"Re-cycling! Ask for something."

"Federal researchers could fill Yankee Stadium. Fat chance this pool has anything I need."

"It can't hurt to try."

"Look here.*1944!* Some forgotten wartime measure."

"Forgotten is why *most* government programs exist. You want to finish the trigger sequence, don't you? So *what if? ... Just supposing.* What do you need?"

"What *don't* I need?" sighed Cates. "How about a Biggman 1200c Recombinant DNA Synthesizer."

"Ask for it."

"That's a cool million, Ms. Ernst, *without* the extended warranty. With a Biggman I'd have a whole new lab in a month."

Callie touched Cates' filing carton.

"And you'd find the truth."

"I'd certainly be someone to reckon with. I'd have grants coming in the mail like magazine sweepstakes."

Callie extended a form.

"You may already be a winner!"

"Oh, all right, all right. People like you keep the lottery afloat."

He clicked a pen from his pocket protector and completed the form, printing in the 'NEEDS' box 'One (1) Biggman 1200c recombinant DNA synthesizer.'

"Happy now?" he said, scribbling his signature. "See if there's anything else."

Callie opened the file drawer.

"The poor thing!" she exclaimed, removing a red, clay pot holding a mottled cactus. "Left in the dark!"

"It's a goner. Throw it away."

"I will not!" she snapped, carrying the pot to the sink. "I'll nurse it. I have a green thumb, you know."

"You'll need a magic wand," said Cates.

"See these dark green spots here and here? And this little bud?"

Cates joined her at the sink.

"Don't be fooled. This little guy looks beat, but, in truth, he's not."

"If you say so."

"I do."

She dribbled a careful stream of cool water over the forlorn plant and nestled the pot on the window sill in sunlight.

"So what should we call it," she said.

"*Call* it?"

"Our mascot. It needs a name."

"Call it Dead Plant," said Cates.

"Mendel had his sweet peas."

"Call it Dead Sweet Pea."

"It's a *cactus*, Doctor Cates. C'mon! Name a thing and it's yours."

"I don't know. You name it."

She rotated the pot a turn or two and announced, "Veritas!"

"Harvard may sue."

"Let 'em. If Truth is why we're here, Veritas is perfect."

"You win, you win!" Cates said, throwing up his hands. "Veritas can die with dignity at Cates' Botanical Hospice. In the meantime, I'll dig out some of my papers so you can—"

Callie glanced at her watch.

"Yikes! Have to run. Baby-sitter has a late class."

"You ... have a *baby*?"

"I have *the* baby" Callie beamed. "Almost a year old. Here, look."

She tugged a delicate chain around her throat and pulled a tiny heart-shaped locket through the neck of her tee shirt. She opened the locket and leaned forward so Cates could take it in his hand.

"Kids are sure easier to figure than people," Cates said, holding the locket a little too long, savoring the warmth imparted to the gold by Callie's skin. Abruptly he let go. "So you're married."

"No."

"Then how ...? Well, uh, I mean – Oh, Cripes! I've blundered into some swamp of intimacy!"

"It's okay, Doctor Cates. It's *okay*!"

She carefully closed the protective heart and tucked it back inside her shirt.

"Mike was a senior. A running back. He promised me the world, but ... maybe you're right about relying on goodness. He was drafted by the Giants and, well ... he ran."

"I, uh ... I'm sorry ..." Cates stammered.

"Don't be," she said brightly. "He kept his promise. Tricia *is* the world! I really have to scoot, but first things first."

Callie swept up the requisition form, detached the preprinted envelope, and scribbled a return address. Kissing the form for luck, she dropped it in the slot and crossed her fingers.

"By..ee!" she said.

Alone again, Cates sat for a moment. Puzzled, he looked around and stood to click on the lights.

"Must be getting dark," he muttered.

* * * * *

"Hi..ee!" Callie chirped, breezing in the following afternoon. "Hey! Your stuff came from the University."

The lab was dotted with a smattering of equipment – a poky old Macintosh, a balance, chemical bottles.

"I'm glad you came back, Ms. Ernst," Cates said, looking up from a catalog. I thought I might have scared you away yesterday."

"Who was scaring whom, Doctor Cates?" Callie chuckled. "So what's that you're ogling?"

"A couple of real beauties!" he said.

"Marilyn vos Savant in a wet lab coat?"

"A scintillation counter and a spectrophotometer." He held up a scientific equipment catalog covered with red-circles. "Oooo! What I'd do with those."

Turning the page, he lassoed more dreams with his red marker.

"Like a kid at Christmas," Callie said.

"Only you don't always get what you want, do you?" Cates sighed, tucking the catalog in a desk drawer.

Callie took a vial from her pocket and unscrewed the eyedropper lid. "What's that?"

"First aid for Veritas," she said, dripping emerald liquid around the base of the plant. "Everything it needs."

Cates stood, picked up a stack of reprints, and carried them to the workbench. "Here's some of my recent work to get you up to speed. Did you bring your class schedule?"

"Yes, but don't worry. I won't be a stickler for time."

"That's good, because we don't have much. So I want you to be honest with me. Are you even *interested* in genetics?"

"I *love* genetics," Callie said, joining him at the workbench. "And history and physics and art and chemistry and music. That's my problem."

"I don't see a problem."

"How do I know what's important?"

Cates dusted off feelings he remembered from grade school. The feelings seemed hopelessly out of date, like an old hat from the attic, but they still fit. Seized by an idea, he dashed to the shelf and grabbed two beakers.

"First lesson," he said. "Turn around. No peeking."

"Don't you shout BOO or anything!"

"Trust me."

Cates splashed clear liquid from a bottle into a beaker, squeezed a dropperful of a second clear liquid into the empty beaker, then filled the empty beaker with water.

"Now look," he said. "What do you see? Two beakers of water, right?"

He upended one beaker into the other. The crystal clear liquid turned deep purple.

"Water to wine!" Callie said. "I know that trick. It was in my first chemistry set."

"Mine, too," said Cates. "And it taught me all I needed to know. Something can *look* like water but not *be* water. By changing circumstances with experiments, we discover the truth." He held up the beaker of purple liquid. "Water hiding baking soda becomes purple when ..." He shook the empty beaker. "... Water hiding phenolphthalein is added. What *looked* true, wasn't. And now we *know*. From the day I did this experiment, important to *me* meant finding out the hidden truth of things."

"Like the trigger sequence."

"Sure. But that Gilbert chemistry set had no *genetics* in it. Genetics came later, just as whatever finally grabs you will come later. My point is, if you know what's *really* important – *Truth* – *give* the rest time. Priority will come with perspective ... Say! Let's have some fresh air," Cates blurted, glancing at the window. "Cripes, I feel ... I don't know, I feel cooped up."

He jostled the sash.

"Stuck?" Callie said,

"Probably never been opened," he grunted.

"You on one side, me on the other," offered Callie.

Shouldering the window open inch by inch, Cates found himself dwelling on the golden heart just beneath Callie's solid, black tee shirt.

"I sent Einstein to the eye doctor," she said with a grin.

"I..I don't know what you mean," Cates stammered, craning through the window as if air were what he needed.

"Don't fall, professor," Callie giggled.

A telephone rang. Cates ducked back inside to answer.

"John Cates," he said.

He listened silently. His eyes went wide. Hanging up, he rushed back to the window.

"What is it?" asked Callie.

"That!"

Commotion surrounded a delivery truck unloading a large crate.

"Is it ...? Oh, Doctor Cates! What you *need*?"

"A Biggman 1200c," he whispered reverently.

"It worked! It worked!"

The telephone rang again. Cates scrambled to answer.

"John Cates ... Oh, *really*? ... Yes, of course, of course, Doctor Blumford. Memory does play tricks ... Sure. We'll do that."

Slamming down the phone, he grabbed Callie by the shoulders.

"Blumford! Says he was mistaken about the trigger sequence. Wants to have lunch. Says he has some ideas we might collaborate on. Biggman sharing ideas, no doubt."

The telephone rang again.

"John Cates ... Why, that's exciting, sir ... Yes! Yes, of course, I'm honored, but I think I'll be too busy with my own recombinant work to co-author any ...*Principle investigator*! ... I'll get back to you."

"Who was that?" said Callie.

"THAT was the chairman of the Genetics department. The Chairman! He wants to work with me. Me! My work; *he* collaborates. I told you! They're swarming like panhandlers around a cash machine."

Yanking open the desk drawer, Cates removed the two remaining requisition forms and stared in amazement. The telephone rang again.

"Cates here," he answered brashly. "Well, I'm rather busy with the Biggman, of course, but ... oh, what the heck! A few minutes won't hurt, will it? See you in ten."

Cradling the phone, Cates danced about, waving the forms.

"Some people are coming down, Ms. Ernst. And I mean *some people*! *Top floor people*. Do you know what this means? I'm important! That machine makes me an important man!"

Cates patted his cowlick and straightened the pens in his shirt pocket. Remembering the forms, he returned them to the desk, covering them with a stack of journals.

"What are you doing?"

Cates removed a key from his pocket and locked the drawer.

"Playing the game, Ms. Ernst. And those forms are our curveball." He placed a finger to his lips. "Let's not mention them just yet."

* * * * *

Later that evening, purring softly, the Biggman sat ensconced on the marble-top workbench. Mustard seed indicators glowed red and blue.

"Sure you won't have some Chablis?" said Cates, splashing more white wine into a beaker. "Six bucks!"

"Water is fine," Callie said, swirling her own half-full beaker. "Tricia's sitter can only wait an hour."

"Thanks for coming back after class. New town, I don't know anyone to celebrate with and ..." Cates took a gulp of wine. "Heck, who am I kidding? I don't know many people *anywhere* to celebrate with."

"You had swarms of friends earlier."

"You don't celebrate with a swarm, you survive it! I was able to answer my question, though, without giving anything away. No one knows about the forms."

"How can they *not* know?"

"Like you said ... some forgotten program ignored in the bureaucracy like ... like my trigger sequence in a DNA chain. The pool must be managed apart from anything else." He retrieved a yellow paper from the desk. "And look! This was taped to the back of the Biggman."

She scanned the sheet. "It was Foster's?"

"He got it from the pool. When he died, back it went."

Callie raised her beaker. "Then here's good luck blown by ill winds, Doctor Cates."

Cates poured himself more wine.

"I'm not really used to this *'Doctor'* thing yet, you know? A friend would call me John."

"Of course she would, *Doctor* Cates,"

Cates flushed.

"Just kidding, John. *Kidding*! Getting even for your stubborn insistence on *Ms. Ernst*."

"First names aren't easy for me," Cates confessed. "But I'll try." He raised his beaker. "To Callie."

"And to getting what you need!"

Cates brushed his fingertips over the keyboard of his old computer. "But did I? I mean … what good is a Biggman, if I can't analyze the data? Might as well use an abacus! I should have made a list … *That's* what I need. A list! Pros and cons."

Callie took Cates' beaker and sat it on the shelf next to the wine bottle along with her own beaker of water.

"Relax, John," she said, massaging his neck.

"Relax my behind!"

"Finally we get around to yours!"

"This isn't funny, Ms. Ernst!"

Callie squeezed his shoulders.

"*Callie* remember? I won't feel comfortable making bad jokes unless it's Callie."

"I should've thought this through. I should've–"

"Here's a thought! Let's think at my place. Continue the celebration. We'll order a pizza and you can tell Tricia all about the trigger sequence."

"I … I don't think that's smart."

"She won't blab, John. She can't talk yet."

He pulled away. "Look, I … I don't think rules allow any on-the-job monkeyshines. It's probably illegal! And—"

Callie blocked his escape.

"You're afraid of me," she said.

"I can't make a mistake, Callie."

"What are you afraid of?"

"I still have forms. Everything I need is mine if I play this right."

"What are you *really* afraid of?"

Cates wriggled past and scurried around the workbench.

"People, Callie. *People*! Matter is predictable. Chemicals are pure. People are–" He covered his face. "You never *know*! They're never what they seem."

"I am, John."

"Am I?"

"Yes."

"You don't know that. People never *really* know each other. Too many variables. Too much data. I'm a scientist, Callie. And with people I'm … I'm in the dark."

Callie retrieved her backpack. Unable to hold her, unable to let her go, Cates followed to the door.

"I can't let myself be distracted, Callie. I have to decide what I need. But I … I don't know how to do that without a … a *supercomputer*."

"Maybe you start with a more *basic* question," she said, pausing in the doorway.

"What's that?"

She smiled. "Do I need *more*? Or do I need *enough*."

Cates stared at the door closing behind her. Alone again, he blurted, "Hogwash! I'm a scientist." Stamping back to the desk, he unlocked the bottom drawer, removed a requisition form, and began to print.

"Needs …" he muttered. "One (1) Cray mainframe supercomputer."

* * * * *

Two days later, Cates sat nervously across an expansive desk from Doctor Mepps, Chairman of the Grant Committee. Mepps was a monolithic man with a stentorian voice who, like everything else in the top-floor office, seemed larger than needed and conspicuously intimidating.

"Blumford was an imbecile," Mepps said finally.

"I wouldn't be *that* harsh," Cates said, eager to talk about his work. "I mean, *everyone* was thinking peptoids. But that's the beauty! Nucleotides! Eighteen pairs linked to—"

"THE GRANT COMMITTEE is not concerned with NUCLEOTIDES!" Mepps boomed. "The Grant Committee is concerned with SUCCESS."

He lowered his voice to a rumble.

"Blumford led us to believe ... well, let's just say he failed to suggest how *successful* you could be with resources."

Cates fidgeted silently.

"Your new space will be adequate for the Cray?"

"The hardware will take a while to arrive, of course, but the specs came this morning and the engineers are pretty sure. They've already started knocking down the connecting walls."

"Two labs are sufficient? We can always get more."

"No, no, it should be fine. And on the top floor, too! But ..." Cates squirmed. "Blumford was ... crying."

"Guilt is unbecoming of success, Doctor Cates. We found a cozy little basement nook for Blumford. The other fellow? ... *C'est la guerre.*"

"F..fired?"

"A polymer chemist. Knocked down less than two mil in funding last year. Polymer studies are dogs. Ha! Polymers."

"Actually, there's an interesting polymerase reaction in the trigger sequence that ... well, uh..."

Cates withered under Mepps' hot glare. Mepps opened a desktop humidor and removed two fat cigars. He extended one to Cates and stroked his own cigar like a violin bow beneath his nose.

"Did you know that with Foster kaput, you have the only Cray Mainframe outside the Atomic Energy bunch?" Mepps ran his lips over the cigar to moisten the leaf wrapper. "We've been dying to taste that weapons tit."

Never having smoked, Cates fumbled with his own cigar, settling on a fingertip grip. Mepps laughed aloud.

"You look like a cinema Nazi."

Cates tried thumb and forefinger in a loop.

"Newsreel footage of Al Capone."

He changed to a full-fisted hold.

"It's not a hammer, Doctor Cates," Mepps said tolerantly. "Here. Allow me."

Mepps prepared the ends of both cigars with a pocket guillotine device. Jamming one cigar between a 'V' of Cates fingers, he struck a wooden match, lit and savored his own cigar and offered Cates the flame.

"You'll get used to it, Doctor Cates," Mepps said with a wink. "The budgets for your new projects will accommodate a few civilized extras."

Cates returned the wink broadly, puffed on his cigar, and choked.

"What .. new .. projects?" he coughed.

"Oh, this and that. This and that. Stratospheric things, rest assured. A name, man. You'll be a name like Foster."

Cates frowned at his cigar and tried to fan the smoke away from his eyes.

"I never met him, of course, but ... his TV shows, interviews, his books ... I feel like I grew up with him. What was he really like, anyway?"

"Foster? Why, that old goat taught me everything I needed to know. He started here during the war. A *botanist*, for heaven's sake."

"Botany? But his work was in—"

"He got wise, Doctor Cates. As will you."

"... All a scientist could need ..." Cates mused. "Or *want*, for that matter, including the Prize. Why would he kill himself?"

Mepps shrugged.

"Anyone's guess. All I know is that he stood up in a Grant Committee meeting, croaked *'The horror,'* and took a running dive through that glass."

Mepps pointed with his cigar at a plywood covered window frame. He paused for a moment as if replaying the scene. A faint smile tugged the corners of his mouth.

"But let's talk about *your* future here, Doctor Cates. *Quite* a future. Providing ..."

"Providing *what?*" Cates said finally.

"That your phenomenal success with resources ... continues?"

The dangling question mark felt like a poised sickle. Cates jumped to his feet.

"Excuse me one moment, Doctor Mepps. A little detail downstairs. The move and all. Details, details."

Darting from the office, he scurried through the maze of hallways and stairwells to his old lab and burst through the door. Callie stood at the window, dripping plant food on a resuscitated Veritas.

"You scared me!" she gasped.

Cates barged past, fumbling with his keys.

"What do you need, John? Almost everything is upstairs already."

Cates thrust the cigar at Callie. She pinched it between two fingers and held it at arm's length. He unlocked the bottom desk drawer and clawed out the last requisition form.

"I know what I need now, Callie," he said, filling in blanks. "What I needed all along."

"Fifty more forms?" she said, reading over his shoulder.

Cates scrawled a signature, added 'OVERNIGHT EXPRESS!!!!' and tucked the form in the attached envelope.

"I'll see you first thing tomorrow and we'll move the desk and data ourselves," he said, dropping the envelope in the outgoing mail slot.

"John? Your cigar!" Callie called.

"I don't need it," he shouted as the door closed behind him.

Upstairs, Cates plopped back into Mepps' cushy chair.

"Sorry," he panted.

"The devil *is* in the details," Mepps soothed. "Now, about your staff. I've assigned you several of my most ambitious new Ph.D.'s. This, uh ... what's-her-name was—"

"Callie?"

"Whatever. Another Blumford brainstorm like that ludicrous office equipment. He had personnel assign you their greenest candidate."

"But she's terrific! And she's–"

"Completely unqualified for your work. Be a realist, Doctor Cates. You are rising. She is ballast." Mepps rolled his cigar between his fingers, spinning tendrils of smoke. "She is also, perhaps, a distraction?"

Cates blushed.

"Come, come, man! We've put you on the first team. Isn't that what we all work toward? This girl can stay with the lab, with whoever gets the lab next. No harm, no foul. Believe me, Doctor Cates, we know what you need."

Mepps leaned back in his chair and blew a perfect smoke ring that sailed toward Cates like a lasso.

* * * * *

Next morning, trudging into his old lab for the last time, Cates avoided Callie's eyes.

"What's wrong?" she said.

"Circumstances have changed, Callie."

"How?"

"Doctor Mepps says there's no money in the trigger sequence. He has his sights set on *big* projects. Foster's unfinished work, special favors for the senior staff. Maybe even a taste of the weapons ... er, uh... some defense grants."

Callie glanced involuntarily at Cates' box of data. Following her gaze, Cates saw that Veritas had bloomed, a brilliant red blossom that seemed to waste its sweetness in the deserted lab.

"You *are* a magician, Callie!" Cates exclaimed, moving to the window sill. He studied the cactus cautiously, wary of its needles. "Cripes, I think I've grown attached to this silly thing. Are you thirsty, pal?"

He looked around for a cup or a glass, but the shelves were bare save for the Chablis bottle from their celebration and two half-full beakers. Cates picked up one beaker and sniffed, but his sense of smell had never been keen. Was it water? Or wine that looked like water?

"The proof of the pudding..." he muttered, touching the tip of his finger to the liquid, then to his tongue.

Water.

He dribbled the water over Veritas.

"So ... we won't be working on the trigger sequence?" Callie said.

"You don't always get what you want, do you? We won't be working together at all. Mepps was emphatic. You're to stay here with the lab." He shrugged. "You know how it is."

"Sure, I know," Callie said. "I just thought it might be ... different."

"Hardball, Callie. I warned you, remember?"

A thunk sounded in the incoming mailbox. Cates sprang for the box, snatched out a thick express mail envelope, ripped the seal, and withdrew a stack of fifty requisition forms.

"Got 'em!" he exclaimed. "Just what you need, Callie."

She looked up.

"Me?"

"Abso-darned-lutely! These little babies will mean the world to you."

"But..."

Cates tossed the forms onto the desk and pressed the drawer key into Callie's palm.

"I tried my best to get you upstairs anyway, assigned to some big shot so you can make a name for yourself, but Mepps wasn't listening. He kept screeching about losing the Biggman and the Cray. Cripes, does that man have a voice!"

"Wait a minute! Y..you *quit*?"

"Of course, I quit," Cates said with the air of a prosperous man purchasing a simple necessity. "Anyway, here's what you do. Hide the forms. I mean *hide*! Even from your new boss, okay? No *goodness-of-men* guff. Every so often, one piece at a time, request something I circled in that catalog. Mepps will have you upstairs before you know it. By graduation, you'll have Foster's old lab and Mepps' job!"

"You really quit?"

"Man, that Mepps! What does he think I'm made of anyway? I must look like some *gigolo*."

Cates prodded his coke-bottle glasses back up his nose. Callie patted down his cowlick and straightened the pens in the pocket protector of his short-sleeved shirt.

"Hey, reminds me," said Cates, pulling a pink-framed mirror from the pocket. "I got this for Tricia. It's safe, I asked the man at the store. All plastic, see? And babies love mirrors. You clip it on the crib and when she wakes up, she sees a face and she won't be lonely." He stared at his own face in the mirror. "It's, uh ... not good, being lonely."

"Where will you go, John?"

"The town has several colleges. Maybe one of them is still interested in truth ... Think it exists?"

"Yes," Callie said, her eyes welling. "Yes, I *know* it does."

"Say, Callie ... maybe, well, uh, maybe you wouldn't mind if I, uh ... call sometime or something? Maybe?"

"Call? Of course you'll call. That's what a helpmeet's for. I'm going with you."

Callie placed her hands on Cates' shoulders. Startled, he backed away, but she mirrored his movements, trapping him against the workbench.

He closed his eyes and trembled in a self-imposed darkness. All the illogical, cruel and contradictory things that people say and do … what sense could he make of it? How could he ever know the truth of *people*? *What* they are? What they are *really*?

"The proof of the pudding…" Callie whispered.

And suddenly something inside Cates opened like a blossom. Eyes shut, he seized Callie and kissed her – long, deep – surrendering to the blind kiss like a parched man in an arid land surrendering to the unmistakable embrace of an oasis pool.

"Water or wine?" laughed Callie.

"Callie Ernst!" proclaimed Cates. "And she is beautiful! And she is true!"

"John Cates, *P H dot capital D*. And *he* is beautiful. And *he* is true," Callie responded. "Don't be afraid."

Cates waltzed her around the workbench.

"I'm not! For the first time I'm really, really *not*," he sang – cooled, quenched, baptized at last in the knowledge – the *sufficient* knowledge – that Callie was everything she seemed.

"Then let's go," she said.

Cates grabbed up his box of data and dropped the requisitions in a shredding bin.

"Don't forget that silly plant," he said. "Who knows, we may need to–"

Callie shushed him with a fingertip to his lips.

"Don't worry," she said, cradling Veritas on one hip. "We'll have all we need."

www.ingramcontent.com/pod-product-compliance
Lightning Source LLC
Chambersburg PA
CBHW060523260626
47161CB00003B/737